The Mollybush Nude

BY

Jim Read

Published by Unsolicited Press
First Edition Paperback.

Printed in the United States of America.

Attention schools and businesses: for discounted copies on large orders, please contact the publisher directly.

ISBN: 978-1-947021-54-9

For My Parents
James and Margaret Read

Contents

God hides the mysteries he offers us
so that he might teach us to search
for them in love.

Narsai of Edessa

You can't stop ART.

Gully Jimson

Chapter 1

From CBC Sports online, Winter 2015: Whatever Happened to: Bill Burnon

William Henry Burnon was born in the village of Mollybush, in the province of Ontario, on October 16th, 1952. He was a goaltender noted for an unorthodox style of play, something he attributed to his height (he claimed to have shot up quickly and once remarked that he was 6'4" before he was a teenager). He played minor hockey in the Mollybush Marauders system that, in those days, was supported by the Detroit Red Wings. He played junior hockey with the Toronto Marlboroughs. The Toronto Maple Leafs owned his NHL rights.

In 1975 his rights were traded to the California Golden Seals, subsequently the Cleveland Barons. Bill spent two years in the AHL before getting a chance with the big club in the winter of 1977, subbing for an injury. He played fourteen games for the Barons. His career was cut short in Denver against the Rockies when his knee was torn up during a goalmouth scramble. He would never play another hockey game at any level.

Bill went on to become a painter of landscape scenes, particularly around the lakes Temagami, Temiskaming, and Mollybush. He exhibited under the name Henry Burnon. His first professional show was at the Anna Carey gallery in 1982. By all accounts, that show was a success and launched a career that continues to this day. Currently he divides his time between the Village of Parkdale in Toronto and a small island named Bad Bob, on Lake Mollybush, about 600 kilometres north of Toronto.

Notable quote I: when asked by a Canadian reporter whether hockey was different in Cleveland, Bill replied, *'No, it sounds like hockey, smells like hockey, sure as hell hurts like hockey. It's the same wherever you go.'*

Notable quote II: The artist Henry Burnon rarely spoke to the media, however during his Mollybush Landscapes opening he gave a cryptic response to the magazine Canadian Art when questioned on his segue from professional hockey: *'I once said to my old compadre in arms Marion Barkley when she was going through a rough stretch with her restaurant business, sweetheart, you made the choice yourself, you live well or you don't with that choice.'*

From the 1ˢᵗ entry of Marion Barkley's personal diary: THE BOOK ON BILL, (formerly THE BOOK OF BILL) written in the spring of 1985, a few days after the opening

of Marion's, a nineteen fifties style diner in the Village of Mollybush.

The big day. The biggest day of my life, second only to the day I met Bill Burnon and my life changed in a way that I am now, as a grown adult, only beginning to comprehend. Yes, sirree, that Bill was a life changer, he pulled me out of a hat, slapped me down on the table, (actually, it was sand) and said, welcome to the big wide world, kid. He called me kid. I was a kid. I thought I wasn't and maybe that was my first mistake. I wasn't even as old as Juliet Capulet, but I was just as horny.

Now Marion's is up and running and I am run off my feet. I don't have a penny to my name so if Big Man's Breakfast, Power Poutine, Sweaty Split Pea and Pig's Feet Soup, Mighty Mac and Cheese, The Great Northern Fat Burger, Sweet and Suicide Chicken, Maple Sugar Pork Back Ribs, Mice Cream and Peanut Splatter Cookies don't fly then sayonara, I'll be teaching snot nosed kids with Klingon assholes the alphabet until I get up the courage to throw myself off a bridge.

Bill said, 'I wouldn't miss the opening of Marion's for all the world,' and to my eternal embarrassment I stood in the parking lot after the last customer left and after Hilda and I had washed the last dish and mopped the floor, after we had downed a bottle of Baby Duck in celebration, after Marion's had sold out everything, breakfast, lunch, and dinner and I stood there, dead on my feet, looking towards the ramp off the Eleven Highway, hoping against hope that Bill had been in a life threatening accident, and for all my relief and exhilaration at the successful kick-off it all felt like nothing at all, a dud because Bill said he wouldn't miss it for the all the world and then he did.

Some of the recipes that might make it into the new menu, Fuck You Bill Burnon Arsenic Soup, Bill Burnon is an Asshole Hash with Crushed Glass, Fuck Off and Die Bill Burnon Pancakes with Drain-O Syrup.

'For all the world,' you said, and Bill I will remember that you missed the second most important day of my life until the day you die.

Chapter 2

He was distracted from Anna Carey's gossip by the petite waitress who reminded him vividly of Marion Barkley when she was around fourteen, that essential summer out on Bad Bob Island, on Lake Mollybush; Marion was radiant as a polished gem, a lithe diamond with black bangs, dripping wet, coming out of the water like a nymph dripping sharp charms of light, that time of the big bang that set their universe in motion and that had continued to expand over nearly half a century.

"Henry, pay attention."

Bill shifted his gaze and pieces of his dilated vision clung to his hair like spider webbing wafting on the vapours of steamed milk. He palmed the bright webs and shipped them into his pocket, a practice from his childhood, when he would gather the silver webs that floated in the watery air as he walked in the bush or when he would lie on his back looking up at the sky and pull down handfuls of stars. He focused on the silver hoop bangles that matched Anna's long platinum hair and hung under her lobes like two tiny jousting rings.

"Sorry."

He wasn't, but that's what you said to be polite and anyway it was nice to chat with Anna and catch up on the *Art pour l'art* bullshit. But now Anna Carey, art dealer and one-time lover, just that once, a momentary indiscretion, never repeated, had her game face on.

Bill, now shrived of his joyous vision, gouge that he was, rudely put his elbows on the table and shifted his view from her long ears to observe the plate of demolished oysters between himself and Anna.

"Sorry," he said, concentrating on the plate.

"Burnon, look at me."

Bill looked into her narrow, pale grey eyes. Yes ma'am. It was business-Anna now. He prepared himself to be admonished. Time for the bad news that he was expected to swallow and regurgitate tidily in a corner of his life, preferably in an out-of-the-way place, next to the razor blades, the valium, the quart of rum, the single barrel twelve-gauge, and other romantic paraphernalia of the old-fashioned *Art pour l'art* or any kind of Art narcissism and get on with something new or die.

If it was to be the final option, the more flamboyant the better, a Modigliani coughing blood onto the cobble of a back street in Montparnasse, Mishima, with his entrails spilling onto the floor. Or Hemingway's brains splattered across the foyer. If not that then the messier, patient rending of flesh by the sharp brush strokes of madness.

"Sales were a little off," she said, gently, lowering her nails.

Bill raised his empty pint to the waitress who reminded him of Marion and who, it appeared, was ignoring him.

"Third year in a row, Henry," she said, her tone softening.

She meant sales were down, commission was down, thus a reputation, and reputations dwindled. Suddenly he had arrived at that place where all the alphas go to final humiliation. Not death necessarily. The new wolves over your shoulder, more alpha types, enneagram profiles off the chart, males and females, metaphoric slavering, teeth gleaming titanium white in the frost of dark moonlight, closing fast.

Then they were nipping at your heels. Oh my, and then they've torn off your testicles and all you can do is stand there and chirp secular hymns to a glorious and exaggerated past, the blood from your balls making a nice Clement Greenburg-inspired colour field display on the snow. Fuck Art.

She pointed a long and slender bright red fingernail right between the eyes and cocked her thumb and said, "Have you ever thought of a nude?"

Kapow. Metaphorical brain splatter, right side brain cells screaming *no, no, no* as they wimpled madly and then winked out of existence. What a mess. Send over for the left side brain, please, to clean this up, sirens blaring, pedestrians vomiting in no parking zones. Bill paused, his pint firmly under the control of the left side of his brain and suspended over the demolished plate of oysters. He blinked, not sure he had heard correctly.

Anna prompted him, "A nude, Henry, something different, a new challenge."

"No." Bill drained the pint and wiped his mouth with the back of his hand. "I might paint clouds this year."

He looked past Anna Carey.

"She's ignoring us."

Anna looked over her shoulder.

"It's the end of her shift. She's cashing out."

Anna turned her attention back to Bill.

"Do you think that, perhaps, you've come full circle?"

Anna leaned forward, her delicate chin hovering over the empty drowned shells of Raspberry Points, silent as a field of ears. He felt the urge to lean forward and kiss her; lovely Anna, a wanton looker at seventy.

What he really wanted was another pint of beer and another plate of buck a shuck Raspberry Points and maybe not have to face the discordant music and to travel back in time with that doppelganger of a waitress; dangle their feet into the lake, a quadruped of innocence separated by desire, in the days when you could live in both, like parallel worlds, joined by the mystical cadence of a Pure Prairie League song, Amy what you. . .

What he meant was that time of innocence when you could live in harmony, swim in the deep and peaceful waters of the song until you woke up and had to face the music, the treacherous pebble of land fall.

"Your first show, your first real show as a serious artist, was Brown's Creek, and it made your career. Now it's Brown's Creek again and it raises certain questions."

"Back in a sec."

Bill went along the bar towards the doppelganger waitress and he could not help recall, briefly, because it had been brief, though nonetheless life changing, with consequences he could not then imagine. That day, out on Bad Bob Island, after the funeral of his Grandfather, just him and Marion, seventeen and possibly fourteen respectively, late in the hot day and the lake warm enough for a swim.

They had skinny-dipped on the secluded west side of the island, the western hills in the distance, the sun drawing a crimson blanket over their wet bodies. Afterwards, lying on a sun-warmed pan of granite, he began caressing her and then she was drawing him onto her. He felt something ignite deep within her and the heat began to spread, and it was as if his skin was suddenly alive with caterpillars and they were pouring into his brain.

Bill dropped off his glass in front of the waitress.

"You remind me of my youth."

"That's nice. I'm cashing out. Jeffry will bring you your pint and oysters if you'd like another plate."

Fair enough, stupid thing for an old man to say to one so young and so lovely. Bill slid into the bench seat across from Anna, who was dragging her wallet out of the enormous shoulder bag she carried, her cane getting in the way.

"My treat," Anna said.

Bill held up his right hand, the I-do-solemnly-swear gesture.

"There's one more thing," he said.

Anna put her wallet away and settled her hands on the table in front of her, a gesture Bill recognized, a show of indulgence, not to be indulged more than thirty seconds or the claws came back out.

"These Brown's Creek paintings are different. It's thirty years later. The creek goes dry in the summer. The lake has shrunk, and it doesn't freeze over until mid-January. The pickerel aren't there the way they used to be, not the moose or deer. I used to see black bear in the spring. I haven't seen a marsh hawk in three years."

Anna dipped a finger into the pile of oyster shells as if she were stirring a pot. She smiled at him and he knew to be wary of that smile; a grinning eel.

"You have painted a nude."

Bill knew right away what she meant; that one lovely summer of the big bang, skinny dipping.

"As I remember, tacked above your work table." Anna hesitated, as if recalling a painful memory. "It's quite lovely. There's a simple charm there."

"Marion Barkley."

"Yes, that horrible woman who crashed your first Brown's Creek."

Bill held up his hand. Yield.

"I invited her," he said, his tone hardening, though not enough to provoke.

"You still see her, do you?"

"She owns the diner in the village. Pretty hard not to."

"Why are you being so defensive? She might still be attractive. Is she?"

"Yes."

"Well, start with her or a younger woman, if you can find one who can sit still for half an hour."

Now Anna Carey was starting to bother him.

"I drew that Marion a long time ago, hardly qualifies. I was still a kid. I doodled and one day I doodled Marion. I thought I was going to be hockey player. If it's of any value, it's by accident."

Doodled her all right.

"Is she your muse, this Marion Barkley? Is that why you've never married? Artists shouldn't marry their muses, Henry, you know that.

"Come again?" Bill said, moving past merely annoyed to completely irritated because Anna had shifted the conversation from the mundane and practical to the intimate, as in, the department of none of your fucking business.

"Just asking. Never mind. It doesn't matter."

"You and I both know that the only muse is hard work."

"It's an enduring myth, though."

Thank you, Anna Carey, you were never anyone's muse.

"There's something else. I'm having this damn hip repaired and once that's over with Patrick and I are planning to travel. India, that sort of thing. We going to try and spend our money before we die. Lucy will take over running the gallery."

Bill took a long swallow. She was abandoning him. He had to admit he was surprised it had lasted this long. Bill shrugged. Her granddaughter, Lucy, was real piece of work, a snob.

"Good for Lucy. She'll do a wonderful job. We'll stay in touch, then, me and you."

Anna wiped a small tear from the corner of her eye with her baby finger.

"And in summation Bill," she said, gathering up her panama hat, her vast purse, and her cane, "you're a real piece of shit for ditching me all those years ago."

Bill nodded his head at Anna Carey, who laughed and waved her cane, just kidding, but he ignored Anna and the comment as he was watching Marion's doppelganger sling a purse over her shoulder, wave to Jeffry and exit out the front door with a cell phone held in front of her like a tassel on the end of a bell. There was a literary reference there, but he couldn't remember what it was. The real Marion, whose living room was lined with books, would know.

Chapter 3

A pizza crust about the size of a Chinese porcelain spoon fell out of the sky and landed on the pavement in front of him. He kicked it aside. Back in the day, when he worked out of a damp basement where cockroaches skated in his greasy fry pan and silverfish surfed the baseboards, there was often something falling to earth.

Sometimes it was a broken sign masquerading as a kite, or a piece of moulding, or tar shingle, rolls of toilet paper with tails bucking in the free fall, and all sorts of other things from open windows. Once a flower pot, once a Barbie doll that had landed in the street and was immediately crushed by a rear packer garbage truck.

Cutlery flew about, and more; there were electrocuted squirrels, drunken racoons falling out of the elm trees and split open on the road like watermelon, a bald skinned chick gargling on a worm. Nowadays, with the gentrification of the old village, the sky itself was rebuilt, stronger, better and was no longer much of a health hazard.

Bill stopped and watched the seagull land on the broad butt of the cow moose and settle its wings. Seagulls were sardonic, even as they mobbed a crust of pizza, disdainful of humanity's arrogance and duplicity. Seagulls were cynics, like himself. He looked around, expecting to see more gulls, but there was just the one, eyeing him, one cynic to another, from its fiberglass perch. It seemed to be saying to Bill, *man, you are so washed up*.

The moose was placid and had her nose pointed towards the traffic and a big chain around her ankle. She had been covered with little squares of coloured glass that sparkled under the streetlight. A vandal or souvenir hunter had torn off both her ears, in anger or in anarchy or in sympathy with both, the nightly river of despair that flowed in all directions, as the gentry slept.

The seagull lifted itself into the dark sky and with powerful strokes flew to the moon that sat on the canopy of the century and a half old scotch elm that rose high above the roofs of the Victorian brownstone houses.

Bill stood square to the moose, hands in his pockets. In one of his Brown's Creek paintings, the first go round, an early board, third or fourth he couldn't remember, he had painted a cow moose and her calf at the mouth of the creek. Later he had painted them over because he didn't think he'd gotten them right.

"If I can't paint a moose, what makes Anna Carey think I can paint a human being," he said to the fiberglass moose.

"Mooo."

"Well, I can see you're an optimist. I supposed you'd have to be in your current situation."

He hunched his shoulders inside his leather jacket.

"Cheer up, Bill," he mumbled to himself and passed by the sad monstrosity.

He had helped Anna Carey to the door, the Anna of kindness and generosity, mother-Anna, protesting, wanting to stay for another pint and plate of oysters after all, until he almost had to drag her along between the tables. In the end she had apologized and sobbed a little on his shoulder, contrite at the end. 'I feel as if I'm deserting you,' she had said.

He flagged her down a cab. He hadn't needed the apology. They both knew she was right, spend the money before you die.

"I'll be fine," he said and helped get her feet in the door of the taxi.

"Nudes, Bill," she said and kissed him on the mouth.

The Parkdale Chop House was a grungy dive west of the Dufferin bridge, an anomaly borrowing on time against rising property values along the gentrified strip of upscale bars and restaurants. It was a small, dark bar and sometimes eatery, depending on the sticker; currently yellow, meaning a conditional pass from the city. No visible rats or cockroaches, minimal standards of cleanliness in the kitchen. Better than average chance of avoiding salmonella, were you brave or foolish enough to order the nachos.

The wind tipped the cigarette can outside of The Chop, as the clientele affectionately called the venue. The lid clattered and spilled onto the sidewalk and skittered between the legs of the regulars having their smokes out on the sidewalk. Bill leaned over and blew a big wad of snot out of his nose, following the wind the way his Gramps had taught him so that it didn't land on his boots.

A hoarse voice caused Bill to look up from his shadow.

"Are you sending over? Evening yer honour, you sending over?"

The man braced open the door of The Chop and Bill found himself looking into dark eyes. He was a skinny guy with a mutton chop moustache, long dirty hair and a blue tattoo of a dragon on his throat. He was wearing a torn leather jacket and scuffed work boots with no laces. His blue jeans were busted out at the knees and shredded at the cuffs.

"Your honour, I hope you're sending over," the guy with the mutton chops said, showing his gums and giving Bill a military salute with his left hand while holding out the right hand in expectation of a donation.

Normally Bill would have ignored the man, dropped some coin, careful not to touch the filthy hand, the dirty fingernails, angling away from the body stench, reminding himself that the guy probably grew up in a domestic war zone. However, after the headache and despair inducing tête-à-tête with Anna Carey earlier in the day just the sight of the man got his back up.

"Sending over for what?"

"Whatever you can spare."

The mutton chops guy gave him a toothless grin.

Bill poked him in the chest with a finger. "You sending over?"

The guy twisted his toothless mouth like a wet cloth. "You bet I'm sending over, every chance I get."

The smokers club at the curb had stopped talking and turned to watch the little scene play out. The guy backed off the door. Bill held it with the toe of his boot.

"Make sure you're sending over," he said. "I find out you're not, I'll tell The Big Man."

The smoker's club at the curb was laughing at the guy with the mutton chops as Bill let go of the door and went inside.

That night there was a light turnout, probably because the welfare cheques weren't out. Bill took a seat at a sticky table, flecked with bits of taco shell, near the window, away from the speaker that bleated country and western standards.

The waitress was new from the last time he was in. This version of the waitress had a pretty face with a full pouty mouth and lipstick to match her hair. Bill guessed she was in her forties. She had a lurid, neon pink wig in a bob style and false eye lashes. Her presence at The Chop, along with a sagging figure and the heavy makeup, suggested to Bill that whatever fantasy entertained her in youth hadn't exactly panned out.

"Have you ever done any modelling?" he said as she wiped down the table with a dirty cloth.

She blinked her black butterfly eyes once; on the far side of the world mountains tumbled into the sea.

"Food menu?" she said.

"I'm a real artist and I might be looking for a model."

The waitress deadpanned him again.

"Gosh, a real artist, let me ask my boyfriend, he's over at the bar: the skinhead with the swastika tattooed on his forehead, just out of jail for setting fire to his dog."

"No menu," Bill said, suppressing a smile. "Pitcher of the house draught."

"Got it."

Bill realized what was strange about the waitress. She was wearing a pair of blue neoprene gloves and it occurred to him that she had a rash or some communicable disease; a fungal infection of some sort, or eczema, dermatitis, impetigo, not that he'd recognize any of them, or warts, he'd recognize warts, maybe scabies.

Whatever, it was a good match for his current bout of despair. He recognized the symptoms, knew the cause and knew that it was a matter of riding it out, 'live well there,

Marion,' he had said. 'Nudes,' Anna had said and kissed him on the mouth; her lips had tasted of peppermint lip balm.

The waitress moved into Bill's general scope of view scooping empty beer bottles and pitchers off the tables and taking new orders.

"Refill?"

She reached for his empty pitcher and he got a look down the front of her V-neck tee shirt at a little fish cresting the wave of a large breast.

"Is that a porpoise or a dolphin?" Bill said.

The waitress stared at him for a beat, one blink, two beats, another blink of her winged eyes and a populous island in the archipelago was swallowed by sea, and then turned away.

Bill stared at his empty glass.

"No, I don't suppose it does matter a whole lot," he said, and a mirror of despair spread out on table and he saw himself as he was at that moment in time; a wretched thing. Paint that, he thought.

"Stop it," he said to himself and to all his selves down through the years, all washed up, dry and hard as drift wood, yearning for the fire. Why not? Piss Marion off for sure. He believed that.

He polished the table with a bare hand, the table wet from the moisture that had dripped off the pitcher of beer. The mirror rippled and settled with a tiny burble, and bubbles of glassy air rose to the surface and broke open, sprinkling his face with watery dust. He saw clouds. The clouds broke open and the sun shone into his face and he felt its powdery wetness drying on his face.

Beneath the sun a small boat skipped across the water piloted by a girl with long black hair. She waved at him and Bill found himself standing on the dock at the base of his little island. The girl was doing donuts and then, crashing into the wake from the boat, she was spilled into the lake. He polished the table again hoping for a closer look at the girl in the boat only to find the vision had broken apart and he was staring into the dull chipped wood of a bar table.

"That's Marion," he said aloud and spun his empty pint. He slapped his hand on the table, and then had to wipe his face with the back of his hand from the splash back.

"Paint clouds, Bill," he said to himself as he reached into his pocket and took out a toonie and dropped it into his beer glass. Clink. His mood all summed up.

On the sidewalk the guy with the mutton chops and dragon tattoo was leaning up against a locust tree.

"Hey mister, yer honour, you sending over?"

Bill came abreast of the guy and mutton chops sprang off the tree and came at him. He had the lid from the cigarette can in his hand and aimed it at Bill's head. It was clumsy move and Bill saw it all the way. He ducked, the man lost his balance, and Bill cuffed him on the back of his head as mutton chops went down.

Bill reached down and helped the man up. The guy was a little wobbly and Bill had to hold onto him to prevent him from falling over.

"How you doing?"

"I'm alright."

Bill took out his wallet and pasted a twenty into the man's dirty hand.

"Pitcher on me. No hard feelings."

The man pushed away from him. He crumpled the bill in a fist and stumbled off towards the door of The Chop.

The wind had stopped blowing things around. There were a few cars rolling through the darkness. The buildings were darkened and even the streetlights seemed dimmed. Bill turned up his collar and shoved his hand into the pockets of his jacket and headed for home.

"Henry."

Bill turned around. The waitress with the dolphin or porpoise on her breast waved at him.

"It's Henry Burnon, right?"

"Bill, to my friends."

She had a Canada Goose parka draped over her shoulders. Her pink neon wig seemed pinker in the wash of the streetlight and when she stepped forward the bob wig seemed to glow of its own accord, as if syphoning electricity from her brain. Bill looked into the woman's face and it seemed less mournful, not so lined with fatigue, open to some possibility outside of the burden of a fragile existence.

"I'm on a break. My skinhead, dog-burning boyfriend said he knew you. Said it was okay."

There was a little spark in her eyes, not so dead, a seed of loveliness in the faint fractal blue of her irises.

"Were you serious about the modelling thing? I did some modeling."

She held out her hands. The blue neoprene gloves were off.

"I was a hand model. If you wanted a hand shot, that was me."

Bill looked at her hands. They were lovely; long, slender, elegant.

"I could kiss those hands. What's your name?"

"As a hand model I was Chloe, but my real name is Alice."

"Nice to meet you, Alice."

She tugged on the shoulders of the Goose.

"I'm sorry if I was a little cold back there. You get all kinds in The Chop."

"Including me."

Alice shrank a little inside her Goose.

"Bill if you want a model I might apply. I could use some extra cash. My granddaughter needs braces."

Bill took her lovely slender elegant hands in his and regarded them for a moment. They were cold and the nails were beautifully formed elongated ovals, painted pink to match her hair. He had never seen hands as beautiful as this.

"You like my hands."

He looked her in the eye.

"It would be nude modelling."

He let her hands drop.

"I'm okay with that."

They shared each other's eyes and what she saw in his he could not guess, but in hers he saw the dark light of fear and sorrow. He wondered how she looked upon her granddaughter and, if in looking, the darkness lifted and something like love shone out of her eyes.

"What's your granddaughter's name?"

"Diana. After the princess. I look after her for my daughter, who is not currently around."

Bill looked at her hands again. They were beautiful.

"Not tonight, Alice."

Bill looked up. Her eyes were dead, the spark might only have been a glint from the streetlight, but the hands were beautiful.

"Keep me in mind, then."

"I will, thank you. And goodnight."

Bill paused and looked into her dead eyes again and wondered how a woman with such beautiful hands could end up in a place like The Chop. He didn't know the answer and, if there was one answer, it was probably one of several.

Chapter 4

Marion Barkley went across the ramp to the municipal wharf and past the condemned hotel, a squat five storey brick bunker that Marion thought was ugly as sin, bland as a meat loaf in search of redemption. It occurred to her that if the hotel was condemned somebody should be tearing it down and carting away the rubble, but so far that hadn't happened.

The rumour in the village for the last couple of years was that it was 'imminent'. It occurred to her that nobody in the village would use such a word as imminent and so the rumour had come from somewhere on high; a lowly provincial bureaucrat had mentioned it in passing, across a counter, perhaps on a stop-over during a sledding trip. Marion had even gone so far as to check in the Merriam-Webster online just so there was no mistake. Confirmed; the word 'imminent' means fairly damn soon.

She was in a hurry and so she nearly sprained her wrist when she went to push through the door of the hardware store and found that it was locked. It was the middle of the afternoon, for heaven's sake. She stuck her nose up to the window. The lights were on. She knuckle-rapped on the window and waited. Libby Khrys appeared from behind a row of shelving. She yawned and stretched.

"Well, for heaven's sake."

Marion rapped on the window again. Libby just stared at her. Marion tapped at her wrist in what should have been a pretty clear message that she was in a hurry and so please would you open the damn store so she could buy a washer and fix the leaky faucet in her kitchen and still have time to relax for half an hour and read her Irène Némrovsky, before she got back to the diner to get ready for the dinner rush on the off chance there was one to be had.

Libby responded by holding up three fingers of her right hand, followed by two fists and a flash of ten fingers followed by four fingers of her right hand. Marion looked at her wrist. I am going insane, she thought.

"You can't even tell time, you silly woman," she said to the window as her wrist read somewhere about three twenty-one.

Marion, ever impatient, ever in a hurry to be somewhere, whether it was one end of the counter or the other or across the lake or driving on the highway twenty kilometres over the speed limit north or south at the flip of a coin when she was bored into some sort of action, however wasteful or meaningless, waved at the woman to come and unlock the door and was relieved to see that Libby seemed to understand the gesture.

"Hello Marion," Libby said, and yawned as she pushed the door open, "sorry, I was having a quiet time and anyway, I don't think I should be serving you."

Marion stepped through the door.

"Where's Joe?"

"He's somewhere that's for sure and I said, I shouldn't be serving you."

"That's a good one. Every time you set foot in my place I was down a salt-shaker. Now, I'm in a hurry."

"It was just the once and it was an accident and I don't think I should be banned from Marion's."

"Really. Just the once? Now, look I need a washer for my tap and some of that spray-on gunk for another leak," Marion said brushing past her.

"A washer and spray-on gunk, hmm."

Marion could not help but notice that the shelves looked a little bare.

"That's more Joe's department," Libby said and yawned again, "but I'm guessing you want plumbing."

"Just point me in the general direction, and don't trouble yourself on my account," Marion said and headed down the main aisle followed by Libby.

"Left, and at the end of the aisle, right."

Marion turned down the next aisle and it appeared that the plumbing section had been plumbed. She stopped, not plumbed, which among other things meant to understand something, as in 'I'm unlikely to ever plumb the depths of Bill Burnon's mind since it is shallow as tinfoil.'

Not bad, she'd have to remember that for The Book On Bill formerly known as The Book Of Bill, or 'shallow as a drainage ditch in July' or 'with about as much depth as an empty swimming pool.' Maybe not an empty swimming pool as it had depth, though it was the kind of depth that could cause you serious harm if you weren't careful, which maybe wasn't a bad general description of the man himself. Was she obsessed by Bill Burnon? Did he intrude on her thoughts without permission? Did he, whenever he felt like it, insert himself into her daily routine? No. Was he part of her slow downward spiral into insanity? Just for the last fifty odd years.

"Not a whole lot," Libby said, and Marion was startled from her musing on the nature of Bill and then it came to her, the plumbing department had been drained.

"Where is everything?"

"We have exterior paint in white on sale," Libby said.

"That is ridiculous," Marion said, annoyed at having wasted her time.

"No, it's not," Libby said and stepped back as Marion pushed past her with a perfunctory 'Thank you.'

Marion hurried back across the ramp and passed behind the diner and went in through the mudroom to the kitchen of her bungalow.

She confirmed that the tap was still dripping and wondered whether she should turn off the water in case by some bizarre act of fate her drain became accidently stopped up and the sink flooded while she was attending to the non-existent dinner rush-hour.

Marion got down on her knees and turned off the hot and cold feeds. She felt her knees ache as she stood up and remembered how last summer Bill's strong hands had rubbed peppermint cream into her sore feet after a long day in the diner and wondered if there was a special cream for sore knees.

Marion flicked the nasally challenged faucet until she was satisfied that it was drained of all moisture. She had a thought. If she was running on Libby Khrys time she'd have a good five more minutes per day of time here on earth, while the clock on her kitchen wall, if it was running on time could have her in the ground, days maybe weeks before . . .

Marion said an impromptu prayer; "God, almighty, please don't let me be losing it just when I've come into the prime of my life, ripe as a peach, firm as a lemon rind and with a mind sharp as a barely used razor's edge. Not that Bill Burnon would notice, or he would notice, but he'd be parsimonious, as in, good morning Marion, you're looking lovely, as usual."

She opened her refrigerator and took out her package of Putters, just half full, good for the rest of the week and just as she was going through to the veranda there was a knock on the mudroom door.

"Morning, Rick," she said, "come on through," and put her smokes aside.

Rick Adler sold eggs and free-range chickens up and down the Eleven Highway. He was about her age, or a little younger, a thin, handsome man with the bluest eyes Marion had ever seen. Two years past he had gone on 'vacation' to Thailand and come back in the fall with a bride half his age. That first winter no one had seen her other than to catch a glimpse of a small figure behind a curtain. The gossip at Valentina's Unisex was that she never ventured outside the house and slept on the living room floor next to the fireplace and ate rice with her fingers.

The following summer she was still not to be seen and there was some speculation that an accident had befallen 'Amy', for that was the name Rick used when talking about her on those occasions when a customer inquired after the Missus.

Marion would have none of that. The woman had seen what a Canadian winter had to offer and she had fled back to Thailand, end of story, depleting Rick's bank account in the process. Marion had known Rick and his late wife Molly for decades. They had bought the old LeBlanc farm about the same time she had opened Marion's and she had been buying eggs and chickens and the occasional duck from them for just as long.

After Molly's death Marion thought that Rick might want to take up with her as they always had a nice rapport and a low wattage physical attraction to each other. It had caused her some distress at first because of Bill Burnon, but as his official mourning period ended, she was prepared to 'let the chips fall where they may.' And then he had gone off to Thailand.

"Good morning, Marion," Rick said, shaking off his Wellingtons.

"Coffee?"

"No thank you, I have a busy day."

"Alright then, relax a minute."

Rick sat at the kitchen table while Marion went through to her office and came back with her chequebook. There was an invoice on the table. Marion scanned it and wrote out the cheque. She also noticed that Rick was fidgeting in his seat; he was most often a sea of calm, with a smile on his face, even in a north wind and a blizzard howling across the sky, stamping his feet as he came into Marion's. Marion passed him the cheque across the table.

"Everything okay?"

"I've heard from Amy. I guess she's quit me for good."

"I'm sorry."

"Nothing in common, I guess. She hated winter."

He sounded immensely sad. Marion wondered why he was confiding in her unless he felt that he could, that she would treat his sadness respectfully.

"I know what a lot of people think, that she was practically a whore, and I bought her in some bar," he said, angry now, a fist on the table.

"No."

"She was educated and came here on a visa. We weren't actually married. It was all a trial."

Rick stood up abruptly.

"I'm sorry to have troubled you, Marion. I just wanted someone to know the truth."

Marion rose and knew, or thought, felt, whatever it was, surely if she took his hand just then, in that moment he would be hers for life, this kind and heartbroken man.

"You were always a friend to Molly and me and we were always grateful for that friendship. Bill Burnon is a lucky man to have you."

At the mention of Bill Burnon's name Marion flinched and she was unable to move, to do anything more than bend her head slightly.

"Thank you again Marion, you have yourself a good day," he said and went through to the mudroom and she could only stand there, stiff as a board and watch as he dipped his feet into his rubbers and went out the door.

Only as the door closed was she able to move and she picked up her Putters and went through the living room to sit on her porch and look at across the lake and, unavoidably, at Bad Bob island, just a narrow smear in the distance unless she put on her glasses—where it became a more defined sliver, where Bill Burnon had his smelly, dust laden lair.

And where, back in the day when she was made of elastic knees and could jump about like a gazelle, he had cruelly refused her every advance, though to be fair as all is fair in love, she was total jail bait.

Then, just when she thought he was never going to bite and she would be better off throwing herself under a bus, he jumped her, or she made one last attempt to jump him and he caved, skinny dipping on a hot July day. That would have been his first year of junior hockey and him back north for the funeral of his Grandfather and they'd gone out to the island for the day and then, after the great event, the weather had closed in and she had dared him to draw her, *au naturel.* God, she was something else back then.

"Bastard," she said aloud, as she lit up and joyfully inhaled a pillow of smoke and just as she was reaching for Suite Française she noticed that Bill Burnon's little green hulled Doral was tied up to the concrete municipal wharf.

"He's on his way, then," she said aloud and relaxed now that, with the imminent arrival of Bill Burnon, her leaky faucet problem was all but solved.

She flicked her butt onto the gravel scree under the veranda and slipped her cell phone out of her back pocket and punched in Valentina's Unisex Hair Salon.

"Can you fit me in?" when Val picked up on the second chirp.

"Let me see, did I notice Rory at the marina pulling Bill Burnon's Belle-verte out of the barn this morning?"

"News to me," Marion said and cringed.

Fuck, was she so transparent. Well, yes.

That evening Marion wrote in THE BOOK ON BILL (formerly known as THE BOOK OF BILL), a manuscript in various notebooks that, over the years, had grown to several volumes and thousands of pages:

I almost put the moves on Rick Adler this afternoon. I say almost, but thinking about it just now, it wasn't even close, but in the moment I had the feeling that if I had initiated some sort of physical contact he'd probably be snoring away next to me happy as butter on toast. I suppose I am exaggerating my allure, though probably not.

I didn't because at the last moment when I was ready to allure him into a new life of unlimited happiness, I couldn't, because that would be breaking faith wouldn't it. All my life I have been faithful to one man, except for once and that doesn't count, and this fidelity has been the foundation of my self-respect, an ideal of behaviour, in a world that, if you take the time to look and think about it, has no ideals, is duplicitous, bigoted, and brutish in the extreme.

Nevertheless it is Bill Burnon we are talking about here and so despite all my virtue, he is no Rick Alder, who has a gentle greatness about him, and who is a kind and generous heart, and so I have bound my own great heart, my real or imagined goodness, to a real dissolute bastard and so it's one part virtue and one part absurd.

The new novel is awesome. I am lapping her up. Unfortunately, my latest helping was interrupted by the appearance of the Belle-verte on the municipal dock. It was useless. Why is it that these books that are so true and heartbreaking, seem to pale with the imminent appearance of that man? I suppose there is a big difference between reading about love and suffering and having to actually suffer love. Welcome back, or should I say home, Bill Burnon.

Bill once said to me, this is years ago, when we were just falling into the trap that we had unwittingly set for ourselves, I mean this crazy fidelity to each other that we practice, that I do practice and I believe he does too, though I wonder, I really wonder, anyway wise Bill said that the world was ruled by The One-eyed God.

This would have been shortly after he made the switch to being a landscape painter and totally wowed me when he showed me one of his Brown's Creek paintings. I was blown away by its lush beauty and I wanted to own it as much as I wanted to hop back into the sack with its creator.

I got one of my wishes anyway. I wish I'd had the four or five grand, then I could say I had a Bill Burnon who was actually worth something all these years later. Ha. Back to the One-eyed God.

Bill was actually talking not about the universe but his pathetic little worldview. I should have listened. There's something to be said for the narrow view, not that I am saying it.

He's up early this year. I've had Valentina dye my hair and I got myself a manicure and a pedicure although I don't think the colour is quite blood red enough. I can only hope that when I throw myself at him yet again it is from a great height and I miss and fall on my head and kill myself. I can't tell you how wearying this has become, another year, my last but I say that every time, over and out, Bill.

I can't get enough of Bill Burnon and then there's too much of him and then I can't get rid of him fast enough and then I want him back and eventually I go numb and number until, usually in March, the numbness/dumbness starts to crack and it oozes a little and then it starts to itch in that part of my miserable soul that I'm unable to reach. Hiya Bill and I roll over every time, my pitiful four-legged soul, paws in the air, butt wriggling on the floor, desperate for a scratch. Meow.

Chapter 5

Libby locked the door after Mad Marion left and went down the aisle and sat on the cot tucked under the stairwell to the second-floor storage area. She crossed her long legs and concentrated on not being angry. She picked up her new charm, her charm of everything, a little teddy bear key chain from Brenda's Crafts and Hobbies.

Brenda was watching her like a hawk. Everybody watched her like a hawk, but then an OPP cruiser hit the siren and lights right on Brenda's doorstep and Libby just could not resist the cute little teddy. She had been so good. Years since she had done anything, except for the salt shakers from Marion's and who got upset about a salt shaker? It was just luck she had the chance. She paid for the blotting paper for her flower press and Brenda didn't suspect a thing.

Libby lay on her side with the little teddy, whose name she decided was Buddy, little Buddy, tiny enough to fit into the palm of her hand and reminded herself that Bill Burnon would soon be up and he'd be along to inspect the four by eight three quarter inch finished one side plywood boards that he used to make his paintings.

Last year she saw him taking pictures over at Brown's Creek and she wondered what it was going to be this year.

She thought of the violets she had discovered on one of her hikes into the bush and wondered if he'd be interested. Thinking about Bill Burnon enabled her to calm down, a little anyway, after her encounter with the Madwoman of Mollybush.

Everyone in the village knew that Marion and Bill had been lovers forever. The relationship puzzled everyone. Really, though, how could she say that? She didn't know if everyone was puzzled because she didn't know everyone except to see. For the most part she really didn't know anybody except Valentina, who cut her hair and was the closest person to a friend. Libby happened to overhear her say to another customer, that, in reference to Marion and Bill, quote, 'that is one puzzling relationship,' unquote.

Well, on a scale of one to ten, Mad Marion was her least favourite customer, a total zero, and Bill was a ten plus. She was always a little nervous when he came into the store and always hoped that she was there instead of her old stick of a husband.

Bill was very polite. He was never in a hurry and he seemed interested in her. Talk about puzzling. What could possibly be interesting about her? The only possibly interesting thing she could think of was she liked to hike in the bush. But that was the feeling she got for Bill Burnon.

She might even tell him about the violets if he came in and said something like, 'Hey Libby, how are you?' or, 'Good morning Libby, how's the world treating you?' and she might say, 'well, Bill, the world has just treated me to some lovely violets. Would you like to see them?' Bill would say, 'I sure would. I might paint violets this year.' Something like that, that's how it would go because as soon as Bill Burnon said hello, she lost her nervousness and, to be perfectly honest, tingled a little in his presence. What a nice man.

Libby heard the back door open and hugged her shoulders. She settled on her cot and drew up her long legs underneath her. She heard her husband stumble and curse. The recent cursing had surprised her as, in all her years of marriage, Joe Khrys had always been a man not given to expressiveness of any sort, even on those rare Sundays when pastor Kirby let him loose on the congregation.

Libby's husband, in her opinion, could make the hellfire of eternal damnation sound like listening to the drone of an air conditioner. But then it was hard times for Joe, and by association, her, though she'd begun, after all these years, to weave the strands of loss, want (the other kind) and boredom into a grand cocoon. A nearly done cocoon with summer coming on and maybe or maybe not a little of Bill Burnon to flannel dry her emerging wings.

She heard the shuffle of her husband coming along the aisle. Joe the scarecrow. Mean Joe, with his clothes hanging off his bony frame. Long faced Joe. He was dragging his feet and she pictured him with a rope slung over his back and he was pulling a huge Santa Claus sled, but instead of brightly wrapped presents the sled was heaped high with boxes of disappointments and, as everyone knows, a disappointment is a heavy and sometimes impossible weight to carry.

"Pass on by," she said, in a whisper and crossed herself reflexively, a sure sign of heresy according to Pastor Kirby, who as a good Pentecostal pastor shunned any sort of display that might be interpreted as Papist heresy, but Libby had always made the sign of the cross when no one was looking, even as a little girl, twitching her index finger at the dinner table, while her devout parents were bent over an interminable prayer of thanksgiving, one tiny act of rebellion in a lifetime, that is except for teddy bear Buddy and a few others.

She looked up to see her husband scowling up at her.

"Now you're talking to yourself," he said.

"I was saying a prayer," she said.

Joe Khrys sneered at her.

"You'll need more than a prayer."

Libby let it pass. She wasn't about to go all theological with her husband, who could quote scripture the way some people chatter on about the weather.

"Did you pay for that?" Joe said pointing at Buddy the little teddy bear.

"I did when I bought my blotting paper at Brenda's."

"Give it to me."

Joe reached out his hand. Libby slapped at his hand and pushed herself up against the wall. Joe stared at her and his face was twisted up in anger.

"I have laundry," he said.

"Well, Joe, you also have a washer and a dryer and if you don't have any detergent or Bounce you can stop at the Food City on your way home."

Joe Khrys wiped his nose with the back of his hand. He scowled at her.

"Shame on you," he said.

"You can't get away with that anymore. There's no shame on me and there never was."

Joe squatted down so that he was eye to eye with her.

"Shame on you," he said.

"I'm not doing your laundry," Libby said and gathered up a pillow to hug along with Buddy.

"Shame on you," he said and raised his hand and faked a swipe at her.

Libby flinched.

"You hit me I'll tell Pastor Kirby."

Joe Khrys's scowl relaxed into a sneer.

"He wouldn't recognize you, and even if he did he'd say 'shame on you'."

Libby squeezed the pillow and Buddy. It seemed that her husband's handling of their current circumstances had gone a little off the rails.

"I've never known you as a violent man," she said.

Joe Khrys barked out a laugh.

"Say I go over to Brenda's and ask her about that key chain bear."

"You go right ahead."

"Where's the receipt?"

"It's in the trash. Go look if you like."

"A non-violent man would surely have clean clothes in the morning, wouldn't he?"

Libby squeezed back some tears.

"Alright Joe, I'll go up there and do laundry for you."

"You could also run the vacuum cleaner."

Libby shook her head.

"No."

"There's something else."

"Or run the dishwasher," she said.

Joe Khrys stared at her. He was making her nervous. The raised hand was new to Joe and it was possible he had truly lost his way. He stood up and gave the leg of the cot a kick with the toe of his boot.

"I've just seen Bill Burnon's Doral at the wharf. That means he's on his way up, later today or tomorrow. He'll want his boards."

"He's not going to take them because you turned off the heat in the barn."

"I did what I had to do and with little help from you."

He wiped his nose again.

"I was more help that you ever deserved."

"You're a stupid woman, that's all."

"I am not, and those boards are warped, and you know that. Bill Burnon won't take them."

Joe Khrys stood up.

"You sell him those boards."

"And how am I supposed to do that?"

Her husband stared at her and she knew what he was thinking, and she cringed, but he didn't say anything.

"You are a vile and unwholesome creature," he said.

"And where are you when I'm lying to the man's face, or whatever it is you mean?"

Joe made a quick grab for the teddy bear and caught Libby by surprise. He grabbed it from her and pushed it into his jacket pocket.

"You give that back."

Her husband didn't answer but turned on her and shuffled down back and out the door. Libby listened until she heard the door close and at that moment her grand cocoon had turned to dust. She lay on the cot and thought about what her husband had implied.

It was Joe that was the vile and unwholesome creature, and maybe it was time she took the next step, whatever that was, and maybe that was something Bill could help her with. She sure hoped so because she couldn't think of anyone else, and why not? Bill, can I ask your advice, I need to spread my wings and fly, do you have any suggestions?

Chapter 6

He came over the steep hill in his antique baby blue Ford 100 Belle-bleue, who he had bought years before, at the beginning of his artistic career from Old Zach Vincent in Ville Marie. He bought the little Doral runabout, Belle-verte at the same time and M. Vincent had advised him not to change their names as it would be bad luck. And so he had not and so far he'd stayed out of the ditch and out of the drink.

Bill, out of habit, shifted the three on a tree into neutral to save on the gas and coasted down between jagged blasted out ridges of pink dappled granite cropped by the wash of the truck's high beam headlights. There was luminous white deer moss and a wall of black spruce mixed in with some spindly poplar and woven into the darkness like the fine workings of a murky quilt.

He saw the headlights and the dark shape of a southbound pulp truck and lowered his beams. He tightened his hands on the wheel. The pulp truck rushed by and his windshield was pasted with flying shards of spruce bark.

"Thank you and welcome / *merci et bienvenue* / to the north."

Above the luminous wash of his headlights he saw a good luck shooting star over the bright shell of the Jiffy Gas and just under the star the blinking lights of an airplane headed over the North Pole. There was sugary sky and he imagined a drunken angel had gotten into God's larder and was seeding the dark and bitter sky with sweetness.

A white tail deer leapt into the beam of his headlights. He broke hard and geared down. The deer kicked up its rear end and scampered up the granite and was gone. The rear end of the pickup fishtailed and for a second it looked like the gravel on the edge of the road might drag the pickup into the ditch. Then the brakes gave up and there wasn't anything he could do except hold on and do a little steering.

He coasted and worked the emergency brake a little until he slowed and made the turn off the Eleven no problem and then coasted down the ramp that became Main Street. Bill worked the emergency brake and got the truck stopped. He rolled down his window.

"Here I am. Fucking hell."

Looking northeast above Main Street there was the spire of the Anglican Church rising above the vague outlines of a wood frame and two-storey brick houses etched into the darkness. The green spire of oxidized copper shone in the moonlight. Here and there were little squares of light so that the village, flattened by the darkness, seemed to hang from the moon like a delicate glass wind chime on an invisible thread.

A truck sped past him and glided through the stop sign at Main and Mollybush and then broke hard to a stop and then, tires screeching, backed into the intersection and went up Mollybush Avenue. The driver must have been prescient because no sooner was he out of sight that an OPP cruiser appeared at the end of Main Street at Taylor Avenue.

Other than that, the village was asleep, tucked into a comfy night, a little on the cool side, a moist breeze off the lake that he felt on his arm and cheek. Bill put the truck in gear and nosed it forward past the condemned Mollybush Hotel. He coasted Belle-bleue into the parking lot of the marina and shut her off. She ticked and shook for a few seconds and then went quiet.

"Alright, old girl." He patted the dash. "Time for a tune-up and some new brake lines."

Bill stepped onto the limestone scree of the marina parking lot. Across the ramp the faded Mollybush Hotel sign, split nearly in half, lay against the wall under a large window arch that was boarded up and splattered with boxy graffiti.

The hotel was a sorry sight now, but in its day it had vied with the Anglican Church for the soul of the village and, though the Church lived still, it was mostly empty come Sunday, and though the hotel did not live, it was full of outlandish ghosts and legends from a time when wild mammon reigned in the resplendent rooms and then, in its final days, from that time when poverty had set in like frost through a crack in a brick wall, there were the enduring ghosts and remembered luminaries such as Ben and Sparky Burnon, his parents.

Marion's bungalow was unlit and though he knew she was an early riser he wondered if she wasn't watching him from the darkness of the veranda and if so would she not make herself available, if only for a hi-ya-how-are-ya, from the top step?

There was, Bill knew, a protocol that guided her behaviour. Sudden expressions of warm welcome, something that might project anything other than coolness, were not part of the ritual; any part of the languid stroll down the stiff line, until, the superficialities exhausted, they arrived at the end of the world where mad dragons swam and hearts cast themselves into the forgetfulness of their treasured desires.

Bill had a brief vision as he reached into the bed of the truck for his canvas duffel bag. Marion emerged from the darkness of the veranda, wearing the one of the three colourful Marjolaine silk lace robes he had bought from Harrods's online catalogue the previous spring. Her white thighs shone in the lunatic light of the moon.

The vision morphed into another and Marion was on her back draped across the warm hood of his truck, vapour steaming from under the Marjolaine. The sweat on her

thighs was shimmering like the underbelly of a pickerel
flashing as it rose through the dark water to strike at the
moon.

The vision morphed again and Marion, wanton as a
nymph on caffeine, leapt into his arms and, throwing her
firm thighs around his waist, crushed his lips with lips red as
pomegranate juice and a tongue tasting of Spearmint gum.

The visions expired, poof, not even a trace of smoke,
nothing real there, nothing to burst into flame. Bill looked
for a sign of movement on the veranda and nothing. He
resigned himself to a later encounter. Well, experientially, he
knew that was for the best, you never knew what to expect
with Marion except the ubiquitous dishrag. He lifted his
duffel bag and backpack out of the truck box and without
looking back went down to the dock to make the straight
shot out to the island.

There was a woman sitting on the far edge of the
concrete wharf, shoulders facing the low moon and with her
head looking up to the stars. She turned as Bill came along
and he saw that it was Libby Khrys, who he had encountered
a few times over the years when he went into the hardware
store, owned for several years now by her husband after the
death of the elder Joe.

"Hello, Libby."

She stood up, shy as a mouse, as he remembered.

"Hiya Bill."

She pulled up the collar of her jacket and put her hands in her pocket. It seemed strange that she should be out so late, or at least out late on her own. There was some gossip about her that he had heard over the years, but he couldn't remember what it was.

Late thirties maybe with a Tinkerbell ponytail, though Anna Carey platinum rather than Disney blonde and she reminded him not of the cartoon but rather of the Botticelli, or was it the Parmigianino, both at the Uffizi and that he had viewed during a vacation with Marion that, afterwards, he referred to as 'The Italian Fiasco.'

"How's Joe?"

"He's good, I guess."

The gossip might have been something to do with the marriage. Joe, older than her, fifteen years possibly, a part time pastor in the local Pentecostal Church, was as dry as a broken stick. No kids. Who had he heard it from: Marion probably, when he was only half listening? Shoplifting?

"Nice evening."

"I was counting stars."

Bill felt his moon lighten. Counting stars took him back.

"How many you got?"

"I was up to a hundred and nine when you turned onto the ramp in your truck."

That was it. Libby Khrys was a little odd, which, in the local lingo, might mean anything from she played bridge to she ate insects for breakfast. The shoplifting things as well.

"You ever count stars?

In fact, he did.

"I used to, but mostly in handfuls, the way you take hold of a blanket. I haven't counted any for a long time. I used to lay on my back on a flat piece of granite while it was still warm from the sun."

Bill looked up at the sky and stretched out his right arm and gathered in a handful of stars.

"Tonight, I'd say you could easily get a hundred or more handfuls of stars."

Libby turned towards the lake and stretched out her right arm and took a handful of stars.

"About twenty in a handful," she said.

"About that."

"And those are just the stars we can see," she said, turning back to Bill.

"My grandmother used to tell me that the stars would turn out at the Mollybush Hotel."

"That old place?" she said.

"Back in the roaring twenties. The Old Lion had invested in Hollywood movies, B movies mostly according to my grandmother. He'd bring some of the stars up here for a getaway, mostly men and their mistresses and a few women and their gigolos."

"I didn't know that. Who?"

"Mostly actors and actresses I'd never heard of, but she did say that she saw Gary Cooper and Clara Bow, who were lovers at the time, get into the gondola to watch the fireworks set off from the roof of the hotel, but she might have been mistaken. It was a beer hall with dancing in my parents' day. As I remember it, seen through a child's eyes, it was a magical place."

"Tell me."

Bill was tired, ready for a nightcap and to fall asleep to the creaking of trees and a chilly breeze off the lake, but he found that, as someone who did not converse easily, he liked talking to this woman who counted stars.

"I was only ever in there once. It was closed down afterwards and when it reopened as a rock and roll nightclub, I was south playing hockey."

Libby zipped up her jacket and pointed north along the shoreline.

"Did they call it the Strand, then?"

"They did."

Libby tapped him on the forearm.

"I remember once, I was just a kid, it was winter and Sunday morning after church we came past the hotel and there was a huge pool of yellow spread out from the door and

onto the ice of the lake and I heard at school the next day
that the pipes froze in the woman's washroom and so the
women used the men's washroom and the men went
outside."

"Beautiful image."

"Sorry, I didn't mean to interrupt."

The woman who counted stars also had a sense of
humour. Lovely, then. Bill started towards the hotel. It
seemed natural that he would seek that physical closeness as
he drew near the building in the intimacy of a fond memory
that was so troubled by sorrow.

Libby followed. As they came nearer to the hotel he
found himself on the memory road. The sky lightened and
cars began to appear, and he heard music from a car radio
parked at the curb. There were pedestrians on the sidewalk.
A guy on a dirt bike, wearing a black and red Marauders
jacket, did a wheelie in the intersection.

"One day my grandparents sent me to fetch my parents
who were late for . . . I can't remember what. I came along
Main Street past the Women and Escorts neon sign that the
women ignored, turned the corner and went through the big
oak door, and into the foyer of the Mollybush Hotel with its
big desk that had been refashioned into a canteen that sold
fish and chips. The foyer smelt of deep fried fish and oil.

"Beyond the foyer, the old ballroom had been
refashioned into a beer and dance hall. The room was dark as

the curtains had been drawn down the windows that opened onto the strand and the lake. There was a jukebox playing a slow country tune I didn't recognize.

"I stepped up to the door and saw my mother and father at a table, near the middle of the room, under the large fan that rotated slowly above their heads. The table was crowded with glasses of beer and ashtrays brimming with folded-over butts.

"My father sat with his back straight and his big arms folded across his chest. He was talking to someone that I couldn't make out, a woman maybe. Sparky Burnon, my mother, was seated across the table. Maybe it was a trick of the light, but it seemed that her blonde hair was on fire and the glow from her hair illuminated the faces of the men around her."

They had reached the middle of the ramp and stood before the old hotel and Bill felt Libby take his arm as he stepped forward. Not that shy, then, he thought.

"Watch." He looked down and the pavement at his feet was torn up and there was a small ditch that had been made by rainwater run off from the street.

"Break your leg," Libby said, and Bill stepped back a pace. He waved at the hotel and then pocketed his hand.

"The men made me angry, the way they were looking at my mother, but then it seemed to me that my mother's eyes were always returning to my father and it seemed that my father outshone the other men. I had the feeling that my father radiated something that made other men defer to him and want to be near him, women as well. I thought he was like a stove in a frozen winter, silent and dark and with hidden fire."

"There were rivers of smoke, clinking beer glasses; the hum of conversation rose and fell like a chant. There was sharp sputtering laughter, slow trembling music, the smell of sawdust, sweat, women's perfume, the sweet, sticky warmth all woven together in a dull tapestry except where my father and my mother had their table. Sorry."

"What?" Libby said.

"I dunno. Too much talk I guess."

"It's wonderful."

"It's all the old stuff I carry around and near this place they all seem to come together, and I don't know. I call it the memory road. It's narrow with deep ditches."

"Bill, what happened next," Libby said and gave him a nudge with her shoulder.

Bill let out a long deep sigh.

"I watched as he stood and, as he stood, my mother looked up at him and smiled. Big Ben Burnon inclined his head towards the dance floor. My mother stubbed out her cigarette and stood, slinging her purse over her shoulder and without so much a nod to her assembled admirers took her husband's arm. They began to dance through the tables, and the tables and the people seated at them seemed to light up as they passed.

"I was transfixed; my mother seemed to move in perfect rhythm and unison with my father and, as they moved around the dance floor, they cast a brief light on the other patrons. People smiled or laughed and pointed out the shining couple and then, as Ben and Sparky Burnon spun away, were suddenly cut off from the light and their facial expressions and gestures were frozen and then consigned to the darkness that trailed the radiant dancers. They glided away, the light passed, and I, too, was consigned to darkness."

Bill paused as the street dimmed and the street music and noise dwindled. Telling the memory had lightened him, but the end of it told, he was bone tired again, heavy as a stone.

"Come on, then," he said and started back towards the municipal wharf. Libby let go of his arm.

"Were you able to fetch your mother and father?" Libby said.

"They waltzed right out the door and my father grabbed onto me and slung me over his shoulder and carried me right out into the street. I'll never forget that."

Bill couldn't help but yawn and covered it with the back of his hand.

"Sorry."

"You don't think it's stealing, do you, if you keep some of the stars?"

"Stars are like memories. If you can catch them, they're yours to keep."

"Right," she said, laughing.

Bill covered another yawn.

"Sorry. I am bagged. Almost home," he said and inclined his head towards the island.

"Good, I can cast you off."

Bill wasn't sure she should be out so late and all alone, thinking of the guy in the car roaming about.

"I thought I'd walk you home."

"No, I'm fine, I'm going to sit out for a while. Yesterday I saw Jack Frost, but the maples have just leafed out so I'm pretty sure everything is as it should be. I have some things to think about. I was thinking I might go into business for myself."

"Good for you."

"You think so?"

"I sure do."

"Well, thank you, Bill. I appreciate it. That's a big help."

They came up to the boat. Libby squeezed his arm.

"Sorry."

"No. Geez," and Bill thought whoa, there, hmmm. Not that it wasn't nice. Quite nice, just unexpected.

"And thank you for sharing your story."

"Sad, though, in the end," he said and stepped down onto Belle-verte. He pulled on the recoil chord and the engine burped and turned over and caught and then ran smooth with a low syrupy growl.

Libby untied his lines and pushed the Doral away from the marina wharf. Bill gave her a little salute and it amused him to see her straighten up and salute him back. It wasn't exactly Marion splayed across the hood of his truck, but it was all right, more so because it was unexpected and because of the pleasant surreality of the conversation. Libby Khrys, then. Quite nice.

The air smelt of composted shit, maybe from a septic tank that had ruptured. There was a layer of mist in the air, like grease on a mirror, along the edge of the lake. Towards Brown's Creek, on his left, the mist was thicker, obscuring the reed thicket that choked the mouth of the stream.

Bill took Belle-verte slowly through the marina buoys until she was pointed due west towards the island and then let out the throttle when she had made open water, let her have her freedom, manumitted her to vast sky and shimmering lake. The prow came up and then flattened out as she hydroplaned on top of the glittering path.

The little boat split the moonlight carpet that was spread out before him all the way to the island, unnamed on the maps, but everyone called it Bad Bob, after Robert Smiley. A sorry tale however you told it.

Smiley owned the island in the early part of the twentieth century. He took up with Lionel Hammond's youngest daughter, Millicent, and subsequently murdered her and disposed of her at the bottom of the deep ravine that traversed the lake.

His own end came when he was killed in a shootout in the foyer of the Mollybush Hotel by henchmen in the pay of The Old Lion. That was one version. Bad Bob was twenty acres of spruce, mixed hardwood and granite in the northwest corner of the lake. It was about a half mile off the northern shore of the lake and about a mile out from the western shore.

The island was pasted onto the distance, a vague shape, barely visible. There was a full moon, high in the sky and balanced on the head of a dark angel, with outstretched arms juggling black holes in the fabric of existence while astride a plank of wood, itself balanced on a horizontal bollard made out of ice from a dark comet. It was a heavy, close moon that shone white as a shimmering bridal train on the dark waters, a moonlight path that lit his way home.

Bill cut back on the throttle. He was surprised and pleased to see that the small floating dock had been dragged down and guessed that Rory, who owned the marina along with his wife Donna, had done him a favour. He angled the Doral and then swung the wheel around so that the boat drifted sideways into the dock bumping softly as the backwash from the propeller rolled into shore. He tied off the boat. Up above he could make out the rectangular shape of the cabin roof over the screen of bush cedar.

"Safe and sound. No deadheads. Arrive alive, always calls for a drink."

Bill stood on the dock, closed his eyes and breathed deeply. He felt relieved to be in this place, and despite the dark emotions and turbulent nothingness of his creative circumstances, he was there, on that gently swelling dock, for the moment, happy as a bell that has just been rung and hears itself reverberating into the future.

Bill slung his backpack over his shoulder and picked up his duffel bag and went up the steep stairs. He opened up the cabin and stepped in. He lit the kerosene lamp that he'd left on the kitchen table the previous fall. The cabin smelt musty and there were dust motes swirling in the yellow light of the lamp.

Bill poured himself a rum and warm coke from his backpack and went out to sit on the porch in his Gramps' old wicker chair.

There was a big old furry night sky. It was a wide black sky that God had sewn up with a whole lot of shiny buttons. It was the kind of soft, bright sky that you wanted to pull over you like a blanket. Bill reached for a handful of the sky and pulled it down and spread it on his lap.

He looked out across the lake along the glittering moon path towards Mollybush and thought, right there, that's the memory road. Bill pulled up the collar on his jacket and looked up at the starry sky. The mournful loons cried out: *ooo . . . ooo . . . ooo . . .*

"Maybe I'll paint clouds this summer," Bill said, as he got up and went inside. He came out with an old sketchpad. He sipped his drink and flipped through the three remaining pages by the light of the moon.

There were three Marions from the original twenty or so he had done over the course of an afternoon. One he had pinned to the wall above his work table in the city and Marion herself had one for a total of five that survived the burn box.

The three in the sketchpad caught her likeness, and he could see it, the Louise Brooks look, the bangs, but her hair longer at the side, but thick and black, Melanesian black, Sidhe and Banshee black, and with a mad Irish heart to match.

Though she had been born in Haileybury he could see the line of blood drawn back through the generations to the famine, the calculated Spenserian genocide that drove her ancestors to board the coffin ships..

The drawings were clumsy. The proportions were off, not much but enough. Nevertheless, they were fluid and that he liked because he liked fluidity in everything; fluidity being the distillation of complexity into simple truth. Fluidity and colour and an inner radiance shining through. That was his Art, whatever the fuck it sounded like.

He had glimpsed it on rare occasions, often in the Eden of their youth and rarely in the past few years, so it would be difficult, capturing her, the hardest obstacle to a decent result: the quicksilver of her soul. Not impossible, but difficult, as over the years, Marion for all her lithe petite-ness had accumulated so many layers of distrust and cynicism she clanked around like a monumental knight in armour whose only light is reflected light, though he had to admit, if he was being fair and honest, sometimes, in that respect, from a certain angle, she was beautiful to behold.

Not that it mattered. It was the clouds. Or nothing. The 'or nothing' thought came right out of nowhere. Part of the credo is that the act of creating Art is, in and of itself, a revolutionary act in that it is witness to the primacy of individual freedom and, as we all know, nothing fucks up a despot more than a bunch of free individuals running around doing who the fuck knows what; swearing at the drop of a hat, smoking dope, fucking everything in sight, all sorts of shit. So what if all the artists just stopped? Bill didn't have an answer. He was in the mood for a little nostalgia in the hope that it might cheer up the gloomy mind set that had nagged at him since he had laid down the last brush stroke to the last board of Brown's Creek ii.

Bill went inside again, less tired but also less relieved, and came out with a faded orange Hilroy notebook with The Book Of Bill written in tall block letters and underneath that, January, 1971. He flipped the notebook open to a page that he had marked with yellow Post-it note and read:

Bill has his dream. He wants to play hockey for a living and who could blame him when you have the kind of God-given talent that he has and why wouldn't you use that until it's all used up. I never understood what it is to have a real dream because my dream was always Bill Burnon. How can anyone be so stupid to have a dream that depends on another person?

Bill Burnon is the light of my life. Is that corny or what? He has a dark side, but don't we all. I only have to believe that light is more powerful than darkness and when it truly shines into or out of the darkness, the darkness cannot win.

Bill turned to another page, also marked with a Post-it note:

I have to stop writing this stuff. It's becoming an obsession. It's morbid. It's the product of an unbalanced mind. I should be writing nice little nasty observations about FC and the other girls who are so stuck-up and act so superior to everyone else because they may or may not be on the pill. I should be sniping at so and so who got pregnant and who now lives in a basement apartment with no television and a baby who screams all day long and a husband who comes home drunk every night after work and falls asleep on the couch, normal stuff. Instead I am writing about Bill Burnon who had me and discarded me without so much as a look back. He was gone like a receding tide leaving me stranded on the beach, my toes wiggling in the sand waiting for the tide to return. I think the term is love-sick and it is the most pathetic condition you can imagine.

There was one more favourite he often read before he went to bed:

It has been hard snowing all day. It was snowing so hard that when FC called me a tomboy, I simply had to walk a few feet in any direction to be rid of that stupid cow. Before that I bumped into CS who said, 'oh is it true you had head lice this summer and had to shave off your head.' I couldn't walk away from that one because I was in school and you could just see everybody moving to the side when I walked by. I mean people are gullible, which means they'll believe just about anything, particularly if it's horrible and they can use it to belittle you, which is why I went over to DB and happened to mention that I heard the most incredibly shocking story from an unnamed source and fortunately DB hadn't heard about the head lice rumour so she just was just about peeing herself when I told her that somebody had seen CS beating off a certain defenseman for the Marauders in his car last Saturday night after the dance at the Mollybush Hotel.

My guess is that in about two days CS's phone is going to be ringing off the hook. Anyway, just for the record, I did have head lice but I never had to shave my head, and for the record, it was my cousin Tammy's fault when she came to stay last summer and we had to sleep together, the first night anyway, until my mom discovered Tammy had head lice because her parents were alcoholics, according to my mom.

So the really big news to start off the day is that FC showed up at school wearing Bill's Mollybush Marauder's hockey jacket. I could not believe my eyes. Then everything just got worse from then on and including the above verbal shellacking, I also skinned my knee when I disappeared into the snow, stepped off the sidewalk, and was nearly run over by a Skidoo, and then I get home and there is Mom sitting at the kitchen table with 'The Momster' look on her face.

"What?"

"Don't what me young lady."

The 'Momster' crossed her arms across her chest. I went to the refrigerator and you know I didn't need whatever it was my mother thought I needed and so I drank the milk straight from the bottle and wiped my lips with the back of my hand.

Guaranteed to wind her up to the next level; the 'Mumkenstein'.

"If you are trying to provoke me you are doing a good job," she said.

"I need new leotards."

I pointed to my knee and showed her the broken-out heels.

"Mrs. Kaminski, who is a neighbour of the Connolly's, tells me you are spending a lot of time after school with your father's star goaltender."

"That old bag needs to mind her own business, doesn't she?"

I gave her my Marion-the-spawn-of-Satan look.

"You're supposed to be at the library studying."

"Sometimes I'm at the library and sometimes I'm not."

"And when you're not at the library, you're doing what?"

"Nothing," I said and attacked the cookie jar. Along with everything else I was starving because it was baloney sandwiches again and I hate baloney, which the 'Momster' knows, and I gave them to EL, who lives in Pigtown.

"There is no such thing as nothing, particularly when it involves a boy and a girl and particularly when that boy is older than the girl."

"Just what do you think we're up to?"

"You are going to need a new backside when your father gets home. I am your last hope."

"What's Daddy's problem?"

My Dad is a teddy bear, unless he'd had a few beers and his beloved Habs were gone in the tank. Then his cranky side shows, but only until the 'Momster' threatens to cut off his access to the cookie jar. As if I don't know what that means.

"Are you having intimacies of a sexual nature with Bill Burnon?"

I just managed not to choke on the peanut butter cookie I was eating. The 'Mumkenstein' huffed.

"Did you hear what I just said?"

I suddenly felt a little light-headed. I guess after all I'd been through that day. I managed to finish my cookie and I sat down at the table across from my mother and folded my hands on the table. I gave her my Marion-with-a-halo look. The poor Mumkenstein looked like she was on the verge of tears

"Not yet," I said.

'The Mumkenstein gasped out loud and slapped the table with the flat of her hand.

"Wash your mouth out with soap."

"The 'Mumkenstein'," Bill said out loud. He loved that, and the 'Momster,' and it was that summer that he and Marion got down to more, after the incendiary collision on the beach with another, and another great collision of bodies, the earth shook, and history was made. FC had to be Faith

Cheevers, but he had never been able to figure out CS. Bill yawned and stretched and thought he'd have another drink but he was comfortable in the chair. Though there was a chill in the air, he was warm enough with the starry sky pulled over his knees and with the fond memory of a fourteen-ish-year-old Marion with a halo above her head and, naked as Eve in the garden of Eden with an apple in her hand. He fell towards sleep and, even as he did so he thought; O tall and stupid man . . .

Chapter 7

Marion tossed a wad of spearmint gum onto the scree under her veranda and set her glass of rum and coke on the railing at her elbow. She fluffed up her brand-new coiffure with a little of the black tint to hide the gray that had crept in. She pulled her comfy cushioned wicker chair closer to the railing and tugged at the red Marjolaine silk robe, so it was snug around her shoulders.

She was wearing the red version because red was her colour. Bill had bought her three robes. She wore the blue day-to-day in the evening and morning. She wore the red on special occasions, and she had saved the black in case Bill met an untimely death and she thought of it as her mourning robe. Ha, ha.

She pulled out the tissue between her toes and admired her newly painted blood red toenails that matched her trimmed, newly painted blood red fingernails and the blood red lipstick she had put on and that had pretty much not survived a bevy of ounce-and-a-half drinks and put the barrel of John Connelly's (Bill Burnon's grandfather) old single shot .22 calibre rifle between the big toe and the index toe of her right foot.

She sighted down the barrel. She sighted on the woman sitting at the end of the concrete wharf. She was looking up at the sky. Silly woman. What was up there except stars? Marion shifted her foot and took a bead on the red rear running light of Bill Burnon's Doral, Belle-verte. She reckoned that if she elevated the barrel slightly and took into consideration a light breeze off the hills to her right she could park a little piece of lead right between his ears. Marion took aim. Welcome home Bill.

Ka-Pow.

From: THE BOOK ON BILL:

Of course, he didn't knock on my door. Not that I expected him to do so, me being so readily available, low hanging fruit, short order fast food snacking on a seasonal basis. He was tired, I'm sure, I am one of the walking wounded. It's not the smokes or the booze. As this tome knows I don't really smoke or drink all that much until around March and then it's the fucking liberation of Cuba all over again. The sight of that man makes me want to inhale tar. My plea to you The One-eyed God: impale me one last time or one last several times until I am helpless, and then one for the road to hell, and make sure it's through the heart.

ps: The Marjolaines go for about four hundred pounds sterling a pop from Harrods plus shipping. The first time Bill brought me a gift it was a creepy jar of maple syrup that he probably found in a ditch or, if he didn't, it might have cost him a dollar. If I do the math based on the incremental real cost of keeping a free mistress I guess I'm ahead of the game. I say 'I guess' because I haven't done the fucking math.

pps: He's bought me a watch this year. I know that because last year it was just after labour day and he had cleared out his boards and shipped them south and we had argued about something, or it was one long argument from about the end of July which is when we usually begin to get on each other's nerves and it's always something but I can never remember what, so he was sulking out on his precious carbuncle of an island.

For some reason or no not-reason but a morbid need to flog myself with emotional nettles, I went out there with a pork tourtière and a bottle of wine, no hard feelings, see you in the spring unless you develop an incurable fast-acting disease, anyway we ate the tourtière and drank the wine and then helped ourselves to each other and I was putting my watch back on, my twenty dollar Walmart watch and it had stopped and I wanted to know the time, because you know there is a world beyond that pile of rubble and I had an appointment for something or other, or at least that's what I told Bill because he would want me to stay and sleep in his smelly bed with his smelly sleeping bag, with the smell of the outhouse wafting in the window.

Bill of course doesn't have anything so advanced as a watch and his cellphone had lost its charge and so he looked out the window and said, after three in the afternoon. So it's a watch then, something dainty and expensive, he seems to have set the bar around four grand, low considering my considerable charms, but then I've wasted a life on this man and he, in that murky bog that he has for a mind is aware of that which, of course, is part of what makes his mind a bog murky and dark and smelly like his sleeping bag, and so one day when he's sitting in his usual place at the counter like some rotting old monarch dripping in algae I'm going make sure I am wearing the watch while I am up to my elbows mixing ground pork and ground beef for patties. Is that shallow and petty and childish? Yes. My guess is it's a watch.

Chapter 8

It was a day in which the air was constructed of woven threads of pastel yellows. The surface of the lake was flat and flowing with shallow streams of variable blues and greens and, in a few sun-seared places, white and pale yellow.

Bill made a straight, smooth shot to the village, roiling the lake streams in his wake, the froth spilling to each side like snow curling up from the wedge of a charging plough.

He tied the Belle-verte to the municipal concrete wharf. Over by the marina the white hulls of upturned lasers shone in the sun. Beyond the little sailboats, Rory himself was craning a powerboat from its winter cradle.

Bill went up the ramp and then had to go back and retrieve the small red leather box from under the dash of Belle-verte. He put it in the pocket of his windbreaker and went back up the ramp.

He stood near the intersection of Mollybush Avenue and Main Street. Across from the abandoned and decrepit old dowager hotel and den of iniquity, the white paint was peeling on the cinder block wall of the Food City. The curbs along Main Street were crumbling and the street itself was pitted with shallow potholes.

He reckoned the tiny council that ran the place didn't have much to work with. Still it was just a tad on the depressing side every time he came up and noticed a little further slide into what he figured was the civic version of senility.

Joe Khrys was coming across the intersection and the thought crossed Bill's mind that Libby might be left unattended at the hardware store where he bought his boards out of the lumber barn in back and he was curious about how many stars she had counted and who else besides Jack Frost she had encountered; Old Man Winter, for sure.

He was curious why he had confided in her, spoken so easily to a near stranger of the memory that was always the precursor to the pilgrimages to follow: the old mine, the old Anglican cemetery.

If he was going to paint a nude and he sure wasn't planning to and if Marion wouldn't do it—that was a long shot and currently untested ground, better left alone—Libby Khrys would make a nice model, but still (thinking of Alice, the down and out waitress at The Chop and her beautiful hands), it would be a stretch for him and best put aside.

He was thinking, with Libby, there was a low to mid wattage sensuality present and probably unaccounted for. He liked the way she carried herself, erect and yet with a nice little sway to her hips that probably didn't go unnoticed in the chaste aisles of the Pentecostal Church where her husband was the third string preacher. She counted stars or stole them and did not put them back, and if she did not, where did she keep them?

Bill held the door for Joe Khrys.

"Morning Joe."

Joe Khrys gave Bill a curt nod

"You're up then," he said

"I guess I am. How's the Missus?"

"She's fine."

"My regards if you see her. I'll come over for my boards later."

Joe Khrys didn't answer. Instead he gave Bill another curt nod and stepped past him and went through the door.

"You old stick," Bill said to the door as it clapped shut.

There was an aquamarine tinge to the muggy air and even the light seemed moist and lay as a film on the surfaces; sweaty glass windows, vinyl seats warm and damp, linoleum pale green like a stony lake bottom, white Arborite countertop, steaming food and coffee, and the various slippery metal edges.

There was the comforting aroma of bacon and toast. Plates clattered, cutlery clanged, dishwasher whined dully. There were voices like a beehive buzz, pierced, here and there, with a cackle or a guffaw. Yup, this was the place, good to be back.

Marion's was about half full, the first rush of the morning over. Not bad, but in the old days the place would have been full. He recognized four blue-haired members of the Anglican Ladies Auxiliary sitting in one of the booths at the back beyond the counter. He gave the diner congregation in general wave and said good morning out loud and received a few waves and a few grunts in return.

Bill angled himself towards the counter and took his usual seat in the middle. Marion brought Bill his coffee.

"You're up, Bill," she said, politely.

"Morning, Marion, you're as lovely as ever."

"That's nice of you to say. Can I get you anything else?"

"Just the coffee, thank you, Marion."

Very polite, cool, and a promising ever-so-slight sliver of a smile. Marion went along the counter to fetch his coffee. Blue jeans and a tight white tee-shirt, Marion's uniform since they were teenagers and they showed off her ever fresh, ever-young figure.

He leaned forward and peaked over the counter. She was wearing a pair of slip-ons that nicely showed off her slender ankles. Lovely. Bright red toenails. Promising for sure. Marion came back along the counter with his coffee and set it down in front of him.

"If you blow on that coffee you are in big trouble," she said and flicked her dishrag playfully.

Years ago, after an unexpected visit to Bad Bob by Anna Carey, she had put his coffee in the microwave and nuked it on high. Luck was with him that day and somebody had sat down next to him. By the time Bill got around to sipping the coffee it had cooled enough that he suffered just a second degree burn on his top lip.

Marion set herself up at the farthest end of the counter and leaned on her elbows and began flipping through her order pad. She caught him staring.

"Yes, Bill?"

Bill sipped his coffee, intent on ignoring the question as Marion knew perfectly well what he was looking at and to fabricate an answer would be redundant. She'd had her hair recently coloured and her nails done and she was wearing lipstick, eye shadow, and so on. He knew from experience that this was not normal. She tended to ignore cosmetics.

Marion stayed hunched over her order pad. This annoyed Bill who was feeling underwhelmed by the reception he was receiving. He was just about to make a sarcastic comment about her sudden preference for cosmetics when the door was flung open and some of the local 'boyce' stumbled in.

The last one in stomped his feet like a sumo wrestler, though he was skinny as an uncooked noodle and barely five-feet and then in an old-time-infielders move, tucked up his testicles before he sat down.

"Why does he always do that?" Marion said, stopping off on her way down the counter.

"He was a good ballplayer, if I recollect."

"That still doesn't explain why he does it."

"Sporting tradition."

"Big Man's, there Hilda," they called out one after another, in the general direction of the grill.

Marion served them coffees and came back down the counter and stopped in front of Bill.

"You are more transparent than glass."

She gave him one of her Marion-with-Fangs looks that he liked in a creepy way, the version of Marion from a book she had foisted him, Marion as a plucky vampire who chases him through the generations and the centuries, searching him out in cradles, monasteries, palaces, various arenas, hospitals, high rise buildings, semi-detached houses, parked cars.

"Marion, out of curiosity, a question?"

"Right, in a minute."

Marion went down the counter to the cash register as the booth near the door was clearing out. Bill wondered if he should bother with the question. This summer he was going to paint the clouds.

"A question from the great Bill Burnon," she said, on her way back. She took up her previous position at the counter's furthest extremity. Irritating.

"I'm thinking taking a new direction in my painting, a fresh start painting nudes, what do you think of that?"

Marion looked at him with a blank face. She blinked once and then again.

"You're going to paint nude women."

"That's the idea."

"Why?"

"Do I need a reason to paint whatever I want?"

Marion stared at him. She flicked her dishrag.

"Around me you do."

"Well, I'm going to need a model."

"That's not an answer."

"It is. My apologies if it's not the one you were looking for."

"Stop quoting pop song lyrics at me."

"I don't think I was there, sunshine of my love."

"Stop it, you know it annoys me."

"It only annoys you because you can never remember the song."

"No, it annoys me because it's stupid."

Marion flicked her dishrag at him.

"I was wondering if you knew anyone who might be interested in posing for me. It's a paying job."

"Pose nude?"

"You posed nude for me once."

"That was a hundred years ago, and I was just an impressionable kid who was taken advantage of. You shush about that."

"That's alright, sweetheart, not to worry. I'm a big fan of Renoir porkers."

Marion flicked her dishrag and went down the counter and into the kitchen. He was pretty sure Marion was standing on the edge, happy to see him, reluctant to let him know just how happy, that is unless she'd missed him so much and done the unthinkable. To be honest it wasn't so unthinkable unless he didn't think about it and he was inclined not to, though sometimes, like dog turd on the sidewalk, you step into it and then it follows you home.

Marion came along with the toast and set them in front of the 'boyce'. She went along the counter with her dishrag.

"Don't you start anything with my year-round regular paying customers, if you would be so kind."

"Unfortunately, I have an issue with authority."

"You start anything, and you will have an issue with pain."

Bill detected a note of humour in Marion's response. Repartee? Strange. Was she unwell?

"I thought I'd run down to New Liskeard and the Mennonite Butcher. You up for a couple of rib-eyes on the bee? If you're available."

"My dance card is pretty full, Bill. I have bacon to parboil and I have hamburger patties to make and I have to wash my hair and do laundry."

Again, Marion attempting humour.

"Everything okay, health wise?"

She flicked her dishrag at him. Marion paused, dishrag limp in her hands.

"You can do my errands. I'll give you a list."

"Say we take a run out to Bad Bob after you close. Sit out under the stars."

"We'll see."

Marion flicked her dishrag at him and went down the counter.

That was totally underwhelming. Run her errands? Bill was annoyed. Marion was being unnecessarily cool towards him, even obstructionist. The 'boyce' were loud, arguing about something that had the effect of magnifying his irritation with Marion. He leaned over and poked the nearest one in the arm and said, "A French fry walks into a bar."

"Huh?" the guy said, and three pairs of eyes turned to regard the man who had interrupted their robust discussion.

Bill turned in his seat to face them.

"A French fry walks into a bar and says to the bartender, I'd like a pint of beer. The bartender looks at the French fry and says, I'm sorry, we don't serve food."

The 'boyce' looked at each other. The guy closest to Bill said, "That ain't even close to being funny."

Bill leaned towards the guy.

"Maybe you have an underdeveloped sense of humour," he said.

"You're Burnon," the guy said.

That comment brought Marion right down on them.

"You boys cut that out."

She flicked her dishrag at Bill.

"Hey fellas," Bill said, taking a hold of Marion's dishrag, "I was just telling Marion here I'm starting off in a new direction with my art. I'm going to paint nudes from now on. Any of you boys interested?

The three men stared at him blankly.

"Come again," the guy closest to him said.

"Nude modelling there, young fella. I was wondering if you're interested. I paint you in the nude and for a large fee I can give you the dick you've always dreamed of."

"Go fuck yourself," the guy closest to him growled.

Bill was about to reply when he felt Marion's hand on his shoulder.

"Say we play a little catch up there, Bill."

She reached across the counter and squeezed his shoulder hard enough to make him wince.

Chapter 9

Marion ushered him out the back door and pushed him up against the big green propane tank that looked like a mini submersible.

"Don't move. You are under arrest, Mister Hefner."

She left him and hurried across the gravel scree and went in the mudroom at the back of her bungalow that was painted white with navy blue trim for the windows. Bill would have preferred something bright, a yellow with purple trim, but Marion said she liked the blue because it reminded her of a doll she once had as a child. Fair enough. There were worse reasons for liking a colour, beige for instance, or what he called refrigerator green, both, as far as he was concerned, symptoms of a deeper and more troubling neurosis.

He settled himself comfortably on the wooden cradle that surrounded the propane tank. He turned his face to the sun, his long-time comrade and man-at-arms who never failed him on those black mornings when his instincts had been bushwhacked by the heavy boots of banality and his shaky, intuitive genius had gone to ground under the plush petticoats of repetition. Old cohort, hoary co-conspirator, confidante and pal. Good morning sun shining on me.

Marion came out with a lit cigarette. She paused for a deep inhale.

"Alright, I am calmed down," she said.

"You quit."

"One of these days you are going to go too far with one of those boys and I would appreciate if it didn't happen in my diner."

"One of these days an MOT asphalt crew is going to come looking for your lungs."

"Thank you for the warning Mr. Count of Montecristo."

Smoking an expensive Cuban cigar on a warm night with the loons crying and the moon perched like a great white owl on the western tree line was health neutral, but he let that one go.

"How was your winter," he said, and right away the muscles in his neck tensed.

"As in what?"

"It's a simple question."

"I kept busy."

"I'm glad to hear it."

"We don't open for dinner anymore and close at noon on Saturdays and Sundays now that sledding season is over."

"I'm sorry to hear it."

"I went to Mexico for a week, as per usual."

"Mexico, very nice."

"Right, every year, you know that."

"And how was Mexico this year," Bill said, realizing that he had clenched his fists.

"I drank some piña coladas with little umbrellas for stir sticks. This year they were green. I went to a pyramid where in ancient times they cut out the live hearts of virgin girls. I read a Nora Roberts book, a Fidelma of Cashel, Margaret Atwood's latest, a biography of Lawrence of Arabia. I got a sunburn. Every year I get a sunburn."

"I'm sorry to hear that."

"I know that feeling."

More sarcasm. Bill was solicitous.

"You had some aloe for your sunburn?"

"I did."

"That's good. And you went for how long," he said, unaware that she had already told him. He was beginning to sweat and his mouth had gone dry, there was a look of mockery in her eyes.

"A week."

"Just a week."

"Saturday to Saturday."

"Six nights," he said.

Marion flicked her cigarette onto the scree.

"Are you done interrogating me? I go to the Yucatan every year. Every year it's the same. You'd know that if you came along."

He'd been to Mexico once. It was hot. He got the shits. He came home with a bloody asshole. Bill settled himself down and decided to let go of the Mexico thing, though it would probably bother him, like an itch in the middle of his back. Sometimes he didn't believe she even went, though you could bet by the end of summer the travel brochures would start appearing on her kitchen table with a post-it note open to some buff dude in a speedo stuffed with a sock.

"I might one of these days," he said lamely.

"I'm not holding my breath. All right, you can go. Keys to the truck are under the seat. Give me a minute and I'll get you that list. Meet you out front."

Bill was a little surprised.

"That's it. You don't want to hear about my winter?"

"Not now, but I'll do you mac and cheese if you're nice to me for a change and you can tell me all your adventures . . ."

"I am always nice to you."

Marion stood on her tiptoes and put her lips up to Bill's mouth and gave him a little kiss and slipped her tongue between his teeth.

"You are not."

When she let her self down, she picked his pocket and had the red leather Cartier box in her hand.

"When you get back from your errands there's a few other things I need you to do for me."

"Like what?"

"You can drive me out to Pigtown. I have a food hamper and one of the girls is pregnant."

"Can do."

"I need you to do some Bill stuff and not that Bill-stuff, other stuff."

"Yes ma'am."

Marion tossed the box in the air and caught it. She cast a smile on Bill as she went up the steps and into the diner. Good then, better than good, and he had a memory; Marion had set the hook and the pickerel, its tail thrashing the surface of the lake as it rose in agony against a yellow sky. It was that kind of smile.

Bill went over and stepped on the cigarette butt with the toe of his boot. Focus on the Bill stuff, Bill. Bill stuff that was not-that-Bill-stuff usually involved errands and chauffeuring and the crawl space under her bungalow or the septic tank or something that was wet or mucky or greasy or smelly or all of the above. He saw Joe Khrys crossing the street with a Styrofoam cup in his hand and reckoned he'd better go and see about his boards.

Chapter 10

Libby Khrys came out of her husband's hardware store with a two-tier trolley of area mats of differing colours. They were tagged with a sign: 50% OFF WHILE THEY LAST. Libby had on a paint stained red smock over a pair of blue jeans. She had her platinum hair tied back in a ponytail, exposing her long neck.

"Morning there, Libby, how many stars did you count?"

"Morning there, Bill. I forgot where I got to after you left so I had to start over again and then there was a siren up on the highway and then I watched the lights of a plane for awhile and then I guess I got sleepy. I forgot to ask, how was your trip?"

"I fell asleep after Huntsville and didn't wake up until Latchford, so I don't remember that part. Then, just before the turn off, I almost hit a deer and then the brake lines went, otherwise uneventful."

Libby smiled and bobbed her head; shy, reserved, but hadn't she taken his arm and sashayed a little with him just the night before? Hmmm.

"I thought I'd pick out some boards."

"Hold on, Bill," Libby said and held up her hands, palms outward, "Joe was just here, and he said we're not selling you boards this year because you're using them for pornography."

Bill was shocked.

"What's pornographic about clouds?"

Libby tucked her hands into the pocket of her smock and wouldn't look him in the eye.

"I don't know. That's what he just said. He's down back, you can go ask him."

"Pornography?"

"That's what he said."

"Where's the man?"

Libby inclined her head towards the barn in back. They went inside and first off, the shelves, usually crammed with merchandise, were a little on the bare side.

"Business slow there, Lib?"

"Well with the Rona just down the road we don't stand much of a chance, do we? Joe laid off our help after Christmas, except for me, and that's only because I pretty much work for free."

"I'm sorry to hear it."

Bill went down the aisle and out the back door into the yard. There was a large aluminum climate-controlled barn where the lumber was kept. Libby kept up with him.

"We had to turn off the heat. I'm pretty sure the damp's got into the boards and they'll be warped, but maybe if you're doing pornography that might be a good thing."

"It's not pornography."

"Well, Bill, I'm not throwing any stones," she said.

He was so used to the Marion's dour, cynical take on the world and to be honest, his own tendency to the sardonic that it took him a couple of breaths to realize that Libby was teasing him, and it was further surprising because he had unfairly formed a complete opinion of a woman he hardly knew.

They went across the yard and into the barn. Bill liked the sanded interior plywood sheets, three quarters of an inch thick. They were kept on the north side of the barn next to the unsanded sheets.

"Where's Joe?"

"I dunno, Bill, it's hard to tell just where he is sometimes."

Bill pointed to the boards.

"They're okay. I guess the damp didn't get in."

"You sure?"

"Well I've been buying my plywood from your husband and before that his father since probably the first time I came up here and took a liking to local birch veneer plywood. You were just a kid then. I don't expect you'd remember. Where is he anyway? They look alright. Anyway, Joe must have overheard me say I was looking for a nude model. I was just saying it to wind up some of Marion's regular dudes because they were being loud and annoying."

"A nude model, gee."

"Let's have a look at these boards?"

"I don't see anything pornographic in clouds, or nudes really, when you think about it, but if the boards are damp?"

He thought for a moment she was going to laugh, but she just nodded her head a little and looked down at her nicely polished Blundstones. Bill went over to the shelf with the plywood boards. They could have been worse, but really they were only good for rough carpentry.

"Sorry Libby, I can't use these."

"I didn't think so."

"Tell you a joke?"

Libby gave him a playful slap on the arm.

"A fish walks into a bar . . ."

"Nope, French fry."

"Bill, honestly, is that your only joke?"

"Well yes, but you have to admit it's a pretty funny joke."

"Not if you've already heard it."

They left the barn went back across the yard and found the back door locked.

"I don't think we locked it did we?"

They went up the lane between the hardware store and the hotel. The trolley of area mats had been put inside the door was locked.

"Joe," Libby said, "that man."

"You have a spare key?"

"I don't know. Maybe up at the house. Anyway, it doesn't matter. There's nothing to sell except for some paint somebody bought and paid for but never picked up and those scruffy area mats. I'm sorry about the boards."

"Looks like you have a day off."

Libby crossed her arms and looked down at her polished Blundstones.

"So, you might paint nudes," she said.

Bill was surprised at the question.

"I might, if I find the right model."

"What kind of nudes?"

"That's a good question Lib, how many kinds of nudes are there?"

"There could be disrespectful nudes?"

That was good, that was part of the problem, really, because to render someone poorly, not to reveal some essence, some truth was, if not disrespectful, then at the very least, not worth the attempt.

"Nothing disrespectful."

"And do you think you could find someone in a place like Mollybush?"

"Right, exactly. Everybody in your back pocket."

"Unless you were leaving or didn't care or were desperate."

"You have somebody in mind?"

"I might. I'll have to see."

Based on what he had just seen it sounded to Bill like she might consider applying for the job.

"Right, on to the next thing," he said.

"Did you know I found a patch of violets? They might still be in flower. It's up towards the old mine. I might go up and see. If you decided not to paint clouds or nudes, you could paint violets."

There were Marion's errands and chores but sparing an hour or two wasn't a problem and he had warmed to the woman who counted stars and teased him and who had listened so attentively to his childhood story. Good, then, no harm to follow.

"I could use a walk."

Libby looked at him sideways.

"Really?"

"When I get here I go up to the mine to pay my respects and then to the graveyard."

Libby put a hand on his arm.

"It's a nice thing to do. Sad, but nice."

They walked to the end of Main Street and then went up the path that led to a stand of birch and poplar trees. The path veered northwest across a flat pan of granite mottled pink with feldspar and then down into a wet grassy ravine with a narrow creek at its bottom. They jumped the creek and climbed up the other side of the ravine and found themselves in a stand of mixed conifers with some birch thrown in. The sharp scent of the conifers was everywhere.

"How are you?" Libby said.

"Fine, really."

"It's your knee, left or right?"

"Right knee and everything else at my age."

"Just how old are you?"

"Sixty-three."

"Oh."

"Not good?"

"This way, old man," Libby said.

She led and was careful not to let branches whiplash in his face. Bill appreciated that bit of bush craft.

"Here," she said and stopped suddenly.

The violets were in a small clearing near a large pine tree and they were still in flower, purple, light and pure set against a crust of snow under the bows of the pine. Bill sat himself on a rise of granite and massaged the back of his left knee.

He had an affinity for wildflowers. The subject of his series of paintings after Brown's Creek was the meadow, fields of wildflowers and grasses that he had discovered the previous year while hiking in the hills to the west of the slimes, or the mine tailing pond that had once been Moon Lake, the sister lake to Mollybush, that was Sun Lake until Lionel Hammond had it renamed after his wife.

Northern Meadows were delicate though he had used a rough, pointillist approach; bright yellow and orange flowers, orange and yellow hawkweed against a swath of dark green black spruce, interspersed with white rods of paper birch. One critic compared them to the work of Jackson Pollock, nonsense, but that's what you often got.

Libby joined him on the rock. There was nothing to say and he was content to sit and allow himself to be drawn by their beauty into a meditative sympathy with existence. Libby, too, seemed to content and he enjoyed the peace of the moment and gentle touch of Libby's shoulder against his.

"It's probably clouds then, no shortage of those," Libby said, so quietly that it didn't seem like an interruption, but more like the peeling back of an invisible membrane.

"Or these folks."

"They're beautiful."

That summed it up; the deadened, used-up word was resurrected in that intimate moment, just the two of them, quiet as pilgrims at a shrine.

"In case you're wondering, Joe and I are split up. I've got a room upstairs over the store. Your old room in fact."

"I'm sorry."

"If you did decide to paint nudes, I might be available?"

"I suppose," Bill said, and watched in amazement as the flowers nodded on their slight stems, a thread of air stirred somewhere to the west and tobogganed down the hill to seize the delicate flowers and slip away unnoticed.

"And would that be a paying job?"

"Yes, paying," he said, wishing he had his sketch book and then wondering if he could find this place again; borrow Marion's camera as the blooms would be gone in a few days.

"I'd have to stand still."

"Who would?"

"Me, if I was your model."

Bill blinked as a shadow passed over the violets. He looked up and a large raven had settled on a nearby branch. He watched as it folded its black wings black and then a pebble of sunlight ricocheted off one wing and landed at his feet. He looked down.

"Bill, are you sure you're alright?"

Bill breathed deeply and found himself suddenly unsettled, not physically, more like a psychic elastic band had snapped in front of his eyes. He felt the need to stand and stretch and he did so and turned directly into the sun and closed his eyes and relished the sun and the strength of the sinews that held his old bones together.

"I'd give you nine hours for say, a hundred and fifty dollars," Libby said.

"For what?" Bill said, as he continued to stretch.

"This nude modelling we've been discussing."

"Oh. You were going to start a business."

"I'd need some start-up money."

He looked at her and the vision of Libby on his couch with a dark green background, maybe draped in something, a scarf, say, and big leafy plants and decorative wallpaper and maybe vase of some sort with flowers spilling out of its mouth. Suddenly he was seeing a full-blown vision of a modern odalisque sans the hairy armpits and the soufflé paunch. He was channelling Matisse.

"We could walk up to the mine. It's not far if we get back on the path."

"You'll think about it, the modelling," Libby said.

"Yup, I will. But I like these violets. I might come back with a camera. Come on, then. The thing is, Libby, with your life in turmoil, maybe nude modelling isn't the way to go."

"My life isn't in turmoil, it's at a dead end," she said, and Bill thought he heard a little frustration in her voice.

"Just the same."

"Just the same what?"

"Come on," he said.

"I'm sorry if I was a little testy."

Bill stopped and faced her.

"Tough times."

"Right, I won't say it isn't."

"You need a loan, I can help."

Libby coloured right up and he thought he might have gotten that wrong, offering her money not realizing the obvious, that she was a proud woman who would model in the nude for him, risking the approbation of the village rather than take on the burden of a loan.

"No, thank you. I don't want to owe money I don't have."

"Fair enough."

Bill led the way back to the path that led over a stretch of pink granite and then through a stand of white and black spruce. They came out onto the old Mollybush Mine asphalt road in the place that overlooked Pigtown, a shantytown settlement on Crown land that had been there for as long as he could remember and had burnt down at least twice and then once had been dismantled by the Ministry of Natural Resources only to spring up again like an acre of noxious weed.

There were about twenty shacks arrayed along a single rutted road. There was water in the ruts that shone in the sun and pools and trenches of water everywhere. Some of the shacks were made of corrugated tin, others of corrugated fibreglass, some were just thrown together with bits of wood, railroad ties and scavenged two by fours and plywood sheets.

Several of the shacks had a blue tarp for a roof. In one shack an attempt had been made to build a wall out of cinder block, but it had been finished with some car doors held together with baling wire and then roofed over with some clear plastic sheeting. Not one of the shacks would have been more than twenty feet by twenty feet. Most were under a hundred square feet.

Around the shacks, there was a collection of junk: old cars, pickup trucks torn down to their frames, washing machines ripped apart, stoves, fridges with their doors torn off, chunks of cement with twisted rebar poking out, rusted bed springs, rotted mattresses, broken furniture, bent and broken bicycles. There was almost anything you could imagine that had once been whole and useful.

There was a pile of gravel at the far end of the road that seemed incongruous in that it had a smooth conical shape while everything else around it was torn and jagged. There were some mongrel dogs in the street and a few children, some without shoes, others with running shoes that were worn and dirty. They played listlessly or threw stones at the dogs.

Behind the shacks were what appeared to be a few outhouses. There were some wire cages that held chickens or rabbits. A pallor of smoke hung over the little settlement, mostly from pipes that protruded out of the walls or roofs of the shacks, but in a couple of places there were smoldering fires. The smoke hung around and the ashes fell on the shacks and children and dogs.

After a few minutes some of the children became curious and some adults came out and looked up as well. They were mostly women and their clothes were filthy and their hair clung to their foreheads. A couple of the women were far gone in pregnancy. Bill saw a man emerge from a shack at the far end of the street carrying a shotgun. He stood in the street and cradled the shotgun in his arm and looked up at them.

"Marion comes out here with food baskets. I don't know if it does any good."

"I didn't know she did that."

"You see the pregnant woman standing under the blue tarp?"

"Yes."

"Awful thing. It was the same place when I was a kid," Bill said.

"Me too."

Bill waved at the man with the shotgun and got no response.

"The church came out here once and Pastor Kirby set up to preach while we handed out blankets and canned food. Some people came out and listened and some didn't but they all took our gifts. The next Sunday a woman came to church with her two children and Pastor Kirby brought her in front of us and when she saw the altar, she knelt and crossed herself and Pastor Kirby called her out on that and shamed her in front of us. She left and never came back. I've always wondered what happened to those children. Are you religious, Bill?"

"No, not much," he said and turned away from Pigtown. They walked on.

"Did your church ever go back to Pigtown?"

"Once a year, during Lent, to hand out hand-me-down clothing. They took what we brought but I think they hated it, the charity. Anyway, all these years later it's still here."

"It's here everywhere."

"I guess that is one sorry story."

"Come on, there's another one down the road."

They came up to the chain link gate and looked upon a bleak landscape. The entire site, forty acres give or take, was surrounded by a rusted barb wire topped chain link fence and there were rusted-out NO TRESPASSING and TRESPASSERS WILL BE PROSECUTED signs hanging askew or fallen on the ground. The fence was broken down in places and in one place vandals had thrown down boards to make a bridge over the fallen barbed wire.

When the mine was operating there were two big head frames towering over the other buildings like great prehistoric monsters. The other one and two-storey building, offices, workshops, warehouses, were somehow alive and seemed to vibrate with an intensity the he found slightly unsettling.

Trucks came and went along the access road setting up rooster tails of dust and there was always the presence of the railroad cars and an old black engine huffing and puffing up a head of steam that drifted over the site like a grey, translucent veil.

The buildings, including the big head frames, had been torn down purposely, or scavenged. There were the remains of concrete and stone foundations, rubble scattered around, basements where spindly poplar grew. What had been a lively place of human activity was now given over to the mice and crows and various small predators.

Beyond the mine site, there was Moon Lake. The lake had been destroyed by mine tailings pumped relentlessly out of the tunnels. Bill remembered a vast yellow surface that spread to the horizon. It was a kind of desert, where nothing grew, and no wildlife flourished except for tadpoles and frogs in the small pools that existed on the fringes of the dead lake. Locally they called it The Slimes.

Bill pointed southward towards the far side of the site. "Shaft two is that pile of rubble. My father and two other men are buried in one of the tunnels that veers off to the southeast and runs under the lake." he said.

"Towards Bad Bob," she said and turned south and faced the line of spruce that cropped the high granite ridge between the mine site and the lake.

"Maybe right under the island. I don't know. An investigation into the disaster determined that there was a methane build up and something set it off. Nobody's fault and no one paid the price except for the three men."

Bill picked up a small rock and tossed it across the chain link fence. The stone fell to the ground and rolled to a stop.

"I always do that when I first come up," he said.

Bill picked up another rock and then dropped it at his feet.

"It's just something I do," he said and felt Libby take his arm and realized he was on the verge of tears. He closed his eyes.

"I could say a prayer."

"I just did," Bill said, lifting his hand to the fallen rock. "The mine was at fault, not the great man himself, Lionel Hammond, but his son and management. They didn't give a fuck about safety. Sorry."

"No."

Libby folded her hands together and lowered her head.

"Love bears all things, believes all things, hopes all things, endures all things. Love never ends. Amen." Libby crossed herself and looked up at Bill, "I've always recited that when I was feeling down. I guess like you are now."

"Thank you," Bill said and found himself moved to talk and did not know why except that it had to do with the woman next to him, and her kindness in saying a prayer that he felt was directed towards himself and the emptiness that he felt in his heart as much as those who lay buried far under the lake.

Bill started back and Libby took his arm and matched his stride and he felt the softness of her breast against his arm, and warmth, some other thing that seemed as natural as it was uncommon to him, made him want to remember aloud, to tell her something about himself or try to.

Bill stopped and turned to her.

"I read about it in the newspaper or I must have because I don't remember my mother talking about it or anyone else and so I must have read about it, but it's more like a video loop in my head.

"There's my father Ben, who everybody called Big Ben, stumbling through this phosphorus light. I can see him right now as if I was there, close enough to touch, this tall, broad shouldered man going bare-headed, blood on the sleeve of his work shirt, blood and grime disfiguring his handsome face, a triangle of sweat and a random blood splatter on his chest, and then I'm reaching out to him except he becomes this ghostly being, a defiant creature, defying stone.

"My father, Big Ben Burnon, raises his arms to a mile of granite, muscles bulging, lifting the mile of stone up to the sky so that another man might pass and perhaps live. There's still two men further down the tunnel and my father steps over the collapsed timbers and into the darkness. I'm trying to follow but my legs won't work. I call out to him as the phosphorus light turns red and beats with a black heart.

"A black beating heart and I could hear the faint mewling of a terrified miner. In the newspaper report the other miners are scrambling back down the tunnel and they are the ones who will huddle for three desperate thirsty days before their rescue. But my father has gone back for the one man who was calling out and another who was unconscious and perhaps already dead. That's when the second blast happened, along the tunnel where my father had gone."

Bill's eyes were spilling tears and his cheeks were wet. He looked at Libby and saw that she was crying too. He took a bandana out of his pocket and dried her face and then dried his own.

"Sorry."

"It's all right."

"Usually it's just me comes up here."

Libby took his hand.

"It only hurts because it's real," she said, "even though it happened years ago or centuries ago it can still hurt if it's real."

Bill had never shared the vision of his father's death with anyone, not even Marion, though she knew the story, the bare bones of it, but never the way he had carried it inside himself for over fifty years and relived each time he came north. Along with everything else it was a pilgrimage; a sacrament of love inasmuch as he could make it so.

"You lose someone, I mean someone you love . . ." Bill said, unable to finish the thought.

There was one other part that he could not bear to utter aloud, not then anyway, so close to the beauty of frail violets and violent death beneath his feet. So with Libby's hand in his, he turned away and they walked together joined by something shared and yet mysterious. As they went back along the ruined asphalt road he found himself on the memory road.

Through the window there was a crescent moon riding low over the black forest. He slipped out of bed. It was not a car this time but a pickup truck. The truck went past his window and stopped outside the mudroom out of his vision.

He heard a door open and he heard male laughter and then the door slam shut as if in anger and then the truck backed up and swung around and he watched as it turned right onto Lakeshore Drive. He went to the door of his bedroom and pushed it open.

He was hidden in the darkness of the hallway and he saw his mother come into the kitchen. She was drunk. She fell, and she had to use the kitchen table to lever herself up. Her face was pale, her mouth slack. She sat at the kitchen table and took a package of cigarettes out of her purse. She lit up a cigarette and inhaled deeply. She held the heel of her hand against her forehead.

He should have gone to her, but he couldn't bring himself to pity her and in truth she had come to disgust him, so he went back to his bed and some time later heard his mother leave the house. He heard the side door to the garage door open and close. A few minutes later he heard the car fire up.

He lay there for a while listening to the engine of the car. It wasn't unusual for his mother to go out late, but he realized that she'd never before come home late and then gone out again. It was maybe ten minutes before he roused himself out of bed, thinking something was wrong, and he put his running shoes on and went through to the mudroom where he could see the garage. He saw that the big garage door was shut and there were exhaust fumes streaming out at the edges, but by then it was too late.

"Love bears all things, believes all things, hopes all things, endures all things. Love never ends," he said aloud and stopped.

"But you see it does, always and it never endures, there's fuck all to hope for and nothing to believe in and most of the time you can't bear the shit that goes on because there is fuck all you can do about it."

They had come to the path that led across the flat pan of granite.

"Sometime after father died my mother went into the garage and closed the doors and started up the car and then lay down on the seat. I was there, and I might have saved her, but I didn't."

Bill dropped Libby's hand, and burdened with the great weight of his guilt he groaned with the agony of it and went down on one knee.

"Do you have a prayer for that?" he said with more harshness than he had intended, hardly hearing his own voice.

Libby stepped back as if she had been slapped and let little out a little gasp and then abruptly walked off down the path towards the village.

Bill pressed the buzzer for the second-floor apartment but got no response. He looked again through the front window of the store. He went around back and tried the rear door. The door to the barn was unlocked and he went in there to look around. No Libby. He walked up Mollybush Ave to Watts Street. He wasn't sure which house it was but then he saw Joe's van, with Khrys Hardware and Lumber in the driveway of a two-storey wood frame house badly in need of a paint job, some patching for the sidewalk and probably a new roof.

He rang the doorbell and when no one answered he went around back and looked through the backdoor window but the house was dark. He gave up and went down the hill to Marion's and asked Hilda for a piece of paper and a pen. He sat down and wrote out the note and went around to Marion's bungalow and found some masking tape and her SLR digital camera. He went across the ramp and stuck the note to Libby's buzzer: *please forgive me for speaking so harshly, I was really speaking to myself. Thank you for showing me the violets. They were lovely, and I am just now going back to photograph them. Bill.*

Chapter 11

Libby went across the pan of pink granite and resisted the urge to run away from Bill Burnon, but she did not want to trip and fall and bring him down on her with his scorn or his ridicule and she did not want to him to see her weeping more tears and blowing indecorous snot balloons out of both nostrils.

When she made the stand of spruce she stopped and looked back. He hadn't followed so she wiped her leaky nose and dried the tears that had sheeted down her face and went on.

She ran up the stairs to her apartment over the hardware store and pulled her suitcase on wheels out of the closet, unzipped it, and was immediately overwhelmed by its emptiness and what that said about her prospects in life. In her whole life, she had never been out of the province except for the occasional trip to Ville Marie to watch the summer sledding races on open water. Once Joe took her to a bible conference in Kenora.

Libby went over to her chest of drawers: underwear, seven bras and seven pairs of underwear; sock drawer, white booties since it was summer; jeans drawer, three pairs of jeans; shirt drawer, two t-shirts and five pairs of denims. And that was it. Not a pencil skirt, nor a push-up bra, nor a pair of nylons nor any tight-fitting, low-cut blouses, not that she'd ever want to wear that sort of stuff but, she might, once just for fun, to find out whether it really was any fun. She opened her closet to the black leather biker jacket, with the Ray Ban sunglasses in the pocket, that she didn't have and didn't really want, except not having things like a black leather jacket, at that moment, with Bill Burnon's cruel rebuke in mind, was truly depressing.

She closed her clothes closet and sat on the narrow, single bed with the hard mattress and resisted the urge to cry. She cried anyway, leaking away until her nose was red and her eyes almost swollen shut. Were not the treasures of this world truly treasures of the heart, as she believed, and if so, where were hers?

All she had were absent treasures, distant as stars, though still bright, impossible, it seemed, to grasp and to hold them other than in a digital way, and that was truly depressing as well. What else, betrayed by her mother and father, by her husband, betrayed by her church, betrayed by her paint and wallpaper customers, and with a few hundred dollars in her bank account, what did it all add up to?

Nude modelling, apparently, and wasn't that enough to make her cringe inside. If there was a light at the end of the dark tunnel and it turned out to be nude modelling, what kind of tunnel was that except a tunnel to hell and right here on earth, contrary to what Pastor Kirby said and as Saint Matthew said, if then the light in you is darkness, how great is the darkness? Her eyes went to her bible, black and squat on the kitchen table, that, unlike the church was still a friend, though a difficult one.

"Alright then, bible, what do you have to say right now?"

She paused before she opened it, considering that it would be best to avoid Paul and the New Testament in general unless she could hit on the encounter with Jesus and the Samaritan woman at the well of Joseph and maybe hope for something of help from Ecclesiastes, which was more or less in the middle somewhere after the Psalms and before the Song of Solomon, which might be her best bet when considering affairs of the heart. Song of Solomon then, give it your best shot then, Lib.

Libby breathed slowly, once, twice, three times and scratched her armpit. She parted the good book; Ecclesiastes Three. To be honest, it could have been worse.

When her buzzer rang she ignored it in case it was her husband. She was packed up and ready to go in an hour: catch the bus to the big city, burn all her cash in a one night stay at a hotel room and hope to get a job with an advance the next day or she'd be sleeping on a park bench and then be forced to turn to a life of prostitution and drug addiction. Her flesh a slave to necessity, that had never been all that much of a necessity with her husband, three grunts and he's done.

The buzzer rang and if it was her husband there was no reason to answer it and if it was Bill Burnon there was no reason not to except she had, in view of her reading of Ecclesiastes Three, just gambled her life away and the bus was due at the corner of Mollybush and Main in fifteen minutes.

Was there, in a life of prostitution and drug addiction, a possibility of a glorious moment, such as the one moment, sitting on the seat of the old Massey-Ferguson, the vibrations of the engine tickling her bum and other parts, when the sky turned into a grey wall and out of that wall an angel appeared, clothed in glorious yellow with a crimson fire in his loins that reached out and penetrated her even as the wall broke asunder and gushed with a great flood.

Her one orgasm. In all her life. One orgasm. Well to be honest, not self induced, there had been a few of those, but it seemed that the middle finger and her clitoris were somewhat lacking in foreplay and intimate encounter and all the stuff that she imagined that preordained a big wallop of mind blowing pleasure, pleasure so great, so commanding and invasive, that it was leaking out of all your pores, no, blowing out, cascading, spouting out, so that in the morning you had to mop it up so that the paint didn't peel and the drywall didn't sag. And then, there was always the vision of the angel, who, if she was being totally honest, resembled Howard the Turtle and so even as she brought herself to that tickle of pleasure there was always the thought that in the real world she could do better than a prop or an angel when it came to ecstasy.

Down the stairs she went lugging her suitcase on wheels that she hadn't used for years, the last time for a convention down in the Bay attended by pastors from all over the north and she had come down with food poisoning and spent the entire weekend on the potty and read two steamy novels cover to cover that she had smuggled up to their room from the rack in the motel office. She remembered wondering if there really were that many women with large breasts in the world and those brief moments when her intestines allowed her to venture out to the motel pool she quickly convinced herself that the novels were exaggerating.

Libby saw the note pinned to the buzzer, read it and hauled her suitcase back up the stairs. She took out her toiletry and put on film of red lipstick she had owned for fifteen years. She had to run it under hot water to soften it up.

"There is a time for everything," she said to herself in the mirror. "Thank you, Ecclesiastes."

A few minutes later she came around the corner of the Mollybush Hotel just in time to see Bill in Marion's Toyota make a right out of the parking lot of Marion's and shoot off in the direction of the Eleven Highway. She waved and whistled but Bill kept on going. Back upstairs she went and ran a shower and shaved her legs and armpits before she went to call on Valentina at the Unisex and wondering if she could find a push-up bra in the Village of Mollybush.

Chapter 12

From THE BOOK ON BILL:

Bill collected from the donors on my list. We had several full baskets, about sixty pounds of canned goods and fresh vegetables, including two dozen eggs from Rick Adler. Pigtown is accessible by car if you come at it from the north off the Eleven. Bill wanted to park on the old Mollybush mine road and have the squatters come up for the provisions. He was being protective of me and I resisted the urge to remark that it was a convenient piece of chivalry as I come up here once and often twice a week year-round. I wanted to check on the pregnant woman, Clare, who was nearly due. We drove into the town and parked by Papa John's shack, the most serviceable of the dwellings. It is made from railroad ties and has a tin roof and a good wood stove and hard packed dirt floor. It is surrounded by a sort of moat or ditch about eight inches deep that channels the rain and snowmelt. Anyway, you know all about Papa John. I think if there had been a tree nearby, Bill would have gone over and pissed on it to mark his scent. Clare was fine, well . . . fine as could be under the circumstances.

And here is something else; early on in our relationship you could say I was pleased with Bill's hostile response to the attentions of other men. It continues to this day, witness today's baiting of three of my regular customers. It's embarrassing now and I hate it.

Bill ran my errands like a good boy and fixed the leak in my kitchen sink and the one under my floor. The diner was deserted at 4PM except for some school kids waiting for their parents to get home. When I came across Bill was in the shower. I put out a fresh pair of jeans and a tee shirt for him. We had a nice sit-down dinner on the porch and I decided against mac and cheese because it's his first day up and so I had him pick up a rib-eye at the Mennonite butcher for us to share. He got a little testy when I wouldn't let him near the barbecue, but the man drifts off, really, it's like he has his head in the clouds sometimes and you know I have to hold onto him sometimes or I swear he'd float away, which he does anyway every fall, but by then my arms are exhausted and I could care less.

He told me all about Lucy Carey taking over the gallery, she who is the vampire's granddaughter. I have written about Anna Carey extensively in earlier volumes re: Bill's ongoing infatuation with that villainous creature.

He seems sad, more than usual, and I attuned to that. I had the sense that something was wrong, not with me or with us, because us is so wrong anyway, by normal standards, though what is a normal standard in a world where everything is relative to something that is itself relative. Well, he is sad, but he always is and though sad, he was thankfully obviously horny and so fuelled by his un-poached, faithfully husbanded deep wells of testosterone and whatever other ones contribute in faith and anticipation to the climactic event, gracious enough over dinner to entertain me.

He went on extensively about things, events, people about what or whom I could care less, but it was nice just the same, comfortable as an old pair of running shoes. I don't feel so bad about myself and this arrangement that we seemed to have evolved into doesn't seem so bleak when he is within touching distance and I suppose that is another part of my brain talking, the part that goes dormant second or third week of September, after he has shipped his boards south and is anxious to be gone, from me, I might add, as well as the bad weather, back to the comforts of the City and whatever else he has down there for comfort. I can only imagine and I do imagine and imagine. I hate it.

Then we went to bed and I was determined not to let him know how I felt, not to appear too eager. But of course, I was, and so was he, and so another season with Bill Burnon has begun. And of course the entire village has their collective nose up against the bedroom window.

Oh, and about this nude painting; I don't know what that is all about. It's probably about nothing. Although, with Bill I've come learn that often the most important things are about nothing. He's upset about something. That's a given. More than usual. It's hard to say. About what? The usual. It's something to do with his Art. It always is when he comes up. He usually comes up depressed, and of course depending on my mood, we spar a little or a lot until we succumb to our mutual desire and attraction and make that quantum leap from table to bed. But, yes, it makes me angry that he doesn't confide in me. He'll be fine after a few days of 'sexual healing' and then he'll sail away into whatever it is this season, clouds, or these violets he photographed today, or the western hills and I'll hold onto him tightly with invisible arms because that's what I have to do and never seem to accomplish with any consistency as he is his own man, self sufficient, reclusive, jealous of his privacy and I am nothing against that.

Bill always seems to move in and out of shadows so that sometimes parts of him are invisible, even in broad daylight. I mean his chit-chat isn't about him and it is entertaining whatever I might say. I catch only glimpses of him, what's really going on. He likes to tell stories about the people he meets, the situations he encounters and he says very little about himself, he confides very little and it sometimes makes me angry considering the physical intimacy that we have shared, however absurd, that he would not just say what's wrong so that I might respond, so that our intimacies would be infused with the healing quality that they have always lacked, the spiritual element. Bill doesn't need that. He doesn't need the regenerative effects of love, just the 'lovin will do', thank you ma'am.

He wouldn't stay the night, but that's Bill, isn't it, and I should know that, but I don't and so day two and I'm already mad at him.

ps: regarding the collective nose, what was he doing wandering into the bush with Libby Khrys? According to the all-knowing nose, she's a bit slow and I can believe it, though I don't know her that well. A lapsed Pentecostal, I think, lapsed or otherwise to be avoided like the plague. Anyway, I was in the hardware store looking for a washer for the kitchen the other day and I'd say she was on some sort of medication. She's very plain and drab. I think she was caught shoplifting once or maybe twice, but I don't remember where. I do know she was stealing my salt shakers. Hilda saw her, and I saw her. I suggested she take her morning coffee somewhere else because I am not made of salt shakers. Joe's going out of business, no surprise there, but sad for the village just the same.

pps: it was always the salt shakers, never a pepper shaker, and I know that I am not going insane because one day I took all the salt shakers off the table. She came in for her coffee and sat down. Two minutes later she was out the door.

Chapter 13

Marion gave Bill a perfunctory wave and hurried along the counter and out the back door. He was pretty sure he caught a glint of light on her wrist, meaning that she had accepted the material token of appreciation.

Sacked Marion, always splendid, sacked her, and then it was a clean straight shot out to Bad Bob, the wind in his hair, existential problems in abeyance. Marion in the sack did that to him.

Lovely as the infinite possibilities of smooth sweaty skin imploding, exploding intimacy, fucking at its very best, choice. Of course, how would he really know, except for one harsh pounding with Anna Carey decades in the past, a vague remembrance, a prehistoric spice packet more dust than spice, some faint bohemian shrieks from Anna.

Bill took his usual seat at the counter. The diner was empty except for a couple of rough looking men in plaid shirts hunched over their Big Mans' in a booth towards the back. He didn't recognize them, but they would be partners belonging to the empty flat bed pulp truck parked outside. Hilda, who was as wide as she was tall and had a round doll face, came down the counter with his cup of coffee.

"Good morning, Bill," she said, brightly. "Toast?"

"Yes please, Hilda, thank you."

He replayed his harsh words to Libby Khrys. Then he moved on from worrying that he had upset Libby to worrying about this Mexico thing that had become some kind of a regular fly in his soup, morphing, if he wasn't careful, to the turd in the punchbowl.

He couldn't remember when it started, but she'd been going off to Mexico for at least ten years. It might have started the summer Anna Carey made an unannounced appearance, mid-July swooping in on a floatplane and insisting on an overnight in the cabin, to, as she put it, "better understand your creative process." His memory of the evening was hazy but to the best of his recollection, the only process that night was a bottle of scotch and a mean wallop of BC bud.

The next morning after Anna had lifted off, he had made the straight shot into the village to raid Marion's medicine cabinet for his hangover and she had gone right off the rails, not buying it for a second the nothing-happened scenario, although maybe he might have left off the 'to the best of my knowledge,' which in Marion's blinkered eyes was tantamount to a confession of guilt.

There was something of a rapprochement towards the end of the summer when a log he was splitting jumped up and split open his eyebrow and he had tracked blood into Marion's bungalow looking for something to patch himself up. She had come to his rescue and, sitting in the kitchen chair while she applied the bandage, he'd seen the travel brochure for the Yucatan. So that was ten or eleven years ago.

Hilda came back with his toast, sourdough with lots of butter.

"Can I ask you something?" Bill said, watching the back door. "What does Marion do in the winter?"

Hilda clucked her tongue, a habit Bill found annoying, but then it suited her if you saw her as a mother hen. He was sure she disapproved of the relationship he had with her boss, though maybe not with himself as a person.

"She works too hard, I can tell you that, except for one week. She went to Mexico and closed the diner. Good for my feet. Bad for business. I have bunions," she said and waddled back down the counter.

Bill reckoned Hilda was the wrong person to pump for information on Marion. If it was gossip he wanted, that would be Valentina's Unisex. Sit under a hair dryer for half an hour.

"You know you're not supposed to be in here, Libby," Hilda said.

Bill looked up from his coffee.

"I just need a word with Bill for a minute."

Hilda nodded towards Bill.

"Go ahead. She's just gone across the way. You're good for a couple of minutes."

Libby joined Bill at the counter.

"You're banned?"

Libby hung her head.

"I walked out with a salt shaker by mistake. Marion said I was stealing it. I wasn't. I just had it in my hand and forgot about it. She came right after me."

"It's a rare summer I don't get banned for one reason or another. Marion was probably a referee in a previous lifetime. Say I have a word with her ladyship . . . and now since you're here, I'm glad you're here. I don't know if you got my note. I owe you an apology," Bill said.

He realized that he had never seen her without the red smock. Bill took the opportunity to run his eyes over her upper half and judged the slim blue denim shirt did not do her justice. He liked her hair in a ponytail as it showed off her long, Botticelli or Parmigianino neck. Her hair, normally a platinum shade, was now entirely blonde and shiny as a light bulb. Add to that a frosty crimson lipstick and a little eye shadow, it was not, to Bill's eye, an unpleasing ensemble.

"I did Bill, and I'm sorry if there was any misunderstanding between us."

Libby put her hand on his wrist.

"It was so sad about your mother."

His mood began to lift again in the presence of Libby Khrys and he found that he was remembering the tenderness of the moment when she had said the prayer and afterwards his need to confide in her, convinced, for a moment anyway, that it was necessary.

"Yes. Thank you. It was nice, I mean to finally share all that with someone."

"Oh, I would have thought Marion."

Bill detected genuine surprise and thought maybe he'd best to move on to something else. Libby beat him to it.

"Can I ask you something?"

"Sure."

Hilda came along and lingered nearby to polish a serviette dispenser. Bill gave Libby a nudge with his elbow and nodded towards Hilda and they waited until she'd gone back to her kitchen.

"The serviette dispensers have ears," Bill said. "Safe now, ask away."

"I was wondering if you'd thought any more about the modelling thing. Joe's closed the store right down and I need to find some work, not that he was paying me anyway."

"Right."

"There's no rush and I was just wondering."

Bill felt a draft as wind and looked up as Marion came in the back door with a file folder in one hand and that ubiquitous dishrag in her other hand. In another age it might have been Zoro's whip or a Knight's mace, though in another age she would have been his chattel and dutiful, willing and plump as a pigeon.

"No."

"Well thank you anyway, Bill, and thank you for a nice afternoon yesterday."

She leaned sideways and gave Bill a chaste kiss on the cheek. Libby went down the counter and out the door.

"Morning, Marion. I thought we might . . ."

Marion flicked her dishrag at him.

"That woman was flirting with you."

"Libby? Come on?"

"She never finished high school."

"Half the population of Mollybush never finished high school, what's that got to do with anything?"

Marion flicked her dishrag. He hated that dishrag.

"Not only that, she's a little thief. Every time she comes in here a salt shaker goes missing. It's not just here. They watch her like a hawk when she goes into the Food City."

"You sure you just don't like her."

"No, I am positive I don't like her and what are you doing with her anyway?"

Here we go, Bill thought. The door opened, and some teenage kids came in and took a booth and they instantly huddled over their cell phones.

"You come here with me, mister."

Marion picked up Bill's coffee and went down the counter. She came around to the last booth next to the back door. Bill paused. He'd had enough, more than enough, of Marion and her paranoid suspicions over the years, and didn't he, just like a dog who had just been cuffed on the snout, tuck in his tail and follow her down the counter. He slid his ass into the booth across from her.

"So, what are you doing with Libby?" Marion said, coldly.

"Yesterday we went for a little hike and had a nice conversation. She heard that I might be looking for a model and offered to pose for me."

"Why do you want a model if you're going to paint clouds or violets this summer?"

"I might have changed my mind."

"You can change it back."

"You realize you are talking to an adult."

"I realize you have an exaggerated opinion of yourself."

Bill could sense her twisting that dishrag under the table.

"You're telling me I can't paint a nude."

"Yes."

Marion sat back and crossed her arms. Right, Bill thought, here we go, straight to DEFCON.

"You're sure."

"I am positive."

Bill blew on his coffee.

"Stop that. I only nuked your coffee once and that was ten years ago after you, I can't remember what, but it pissed me off royally."

"Yes, you remember and don't say you don't. Anna Carey came for a visit in a float plane and stayed the night out on Bad Bob. We drank a bottle of Scotch. Anna slept on the sofa and the next day I had a hangover. I came here and got a pill out of your medicine cabinet and then I came over here for a coffee. I took a sip and then somebody had to drive me to the hospital because I had second degree burns on my lips because you nuked the coffee before you served it to me, total pre-meditated vindictiveness for no good reason, and you know that. And you still don't have any shame or guilt over that or all the other bullshit I've had to put up with over the years."

Bill took a proper sip and glanced up at Marion in case she was planning to take a swipe at him with her dishrag. He wasn't sure what he was reading there and maybe, after all these years of batting recriminations back and forth it was best to let that one go.

"I might just paint clouds, or the bush violets. I like the violets."

Marion started to twist the dishrag again.

"But you keep coming back for more."

Bill had to put the cup down because his hand had started to shake.

"Fool that I am," he said, angrily.

Marion got up and went out the back door, flicking at the air with her dishrag. Bill looked over his shoulder, but the kids were still hunched over their cell phones. Hilda was chopping something in the kitchen, not that she hadn't heard it all before. He was about go after Marion because if he left her to herself she'd reduce herself to a little knot of meanness and he'd be a whole summer trying to untangle it.

"Fuck it," he said.

Chapter 14

Marion watched from her porch as the Doral went up on plane and sped across the lake. She flicked her smoke onto the scree and put her feet up on the balustrade. Maybe she had been a little hard on Bill but sometimes she couldn't help it. The man would do that to her. It was his sense of entitlement.

Though, maybe, just maybe, she encouraged that. Some years she'd last a whole week of watching that smug look on his face when he'd come into the diner for his coffee and then toss a bone, like a box of expensive lingerie, in her direction and then walk out without paying for his coffee. She hated that and there wasn't one person in the village of Mollybush who didn't know that Bill never paid for his coffee, or his toast.

It galled her. It really galled her.

"Alright then, Bill, one and done this year," she said to the shrinking boat.

Libby Khrys, the klepto, now there was a piece of work. Valentina was convinced she was a little slow. It was also no secret that she and Joe Khrys were pretty much split up and that the hardware store was kaput. Well, maybe she is a little simple, but Marion would bet her bottom dollar she wasn't so daft that she couldn't figure out that Bill Burnon had some money.

Marion reached for her Suite Française and then dropped it back on the rail next to her binoculars. She went into her office and found her Box Of Bill. Marion lifted volume one out of the cardboard legal box and flipped it open to a favourite memory (it was actually volume one and a half because Bill had pilfered some of her earlier notebooks) and went back to her seat on the veranda for some cheering up.

From: THE BOOK OF BILL:

I was watching from under the bleachers, sitting on a wooden box and nobody seemed to notice me. That was fine because I didn't want to be noticed except by a 'certain somebody' who probably wouldn't notice me if I stepped on his foot in the middle of a desert.

The boys were playing 'three-men-up' because they didn't have enough boys for teams and a 'certain somebody' had worked his way up to first base when two older kids I didn't recognize showed up. The bigger kid walked up to the plate and took the bat out of the batter's hand and gave him a shove.

"Throw me a pitch," he said to the pitcher.

"Throw him a pitch," a 'certain somebody' said.

The pitcher lobbed one at the big kid and he got all of it, a rocket over left field and into the swamp around the creek that runs down to the Lake.

"Throw me another pitch," the big kid said.

"We ain't got another ball," the pitcher said.

"Yeah ya do," the other big kid said, as he upended a canvas bag one of the boys had brought along.

He tossed the ball over to the pitcher.

"Now throw me a pitch," the big kid at bat said.

"That's our last ball, you hit a good one and it's lost in the swamp," the second baseman said.

The big kid stopped practice swinging and tapped the end of the barrel on the piece of wood they we're using for a plate.

*"Throw me a f****** pitch," he said.*

A 'certain somebody' smacked the pocket of his glove with his throwing hand.

"Hey, over here," he said to the pitcher and held out his glove.

The pitcher tossed him the ball.

"That's my ball, don't let him have it," the second baseman said.

This 'certain somebody' looked over his shoulder and saw the outfielders on the other side of the fence sweeping the bulrushes with their gloves.

"This is our last ball. You had your hit."

The big kid sneered at him.

"Well, maybe I want another one," he said.

"You ain't gonna get it," a 'certain somebody' said.

The big kid stopped swinging the bat.

"Say again," he said.

"You had your hit," a 'certain somebody' said, "that's all there is."

The big kid stared at I-know-who for a few seconds then he dropped the bat and put his hands on his hips and stared at him some more. I-know-who didn't move. Then the big kid walked up the first base line, slowly, staring him down the whole time. A 'certain so and so', didn't move except to drop his ball glove with the hard ball in it off to the side on ground. The big kid stopped an arms length from I-know-who and held out his right hand.

"Fair enough, no hard feelings, sorry about your ball," he said.

He nodded his head towards the creek without taking his eyes off a 'certain somebody.'

"See you later," a 'certain somebody', said.

"No hard feelings," the big kid said.

'Somebody' didn't answer.

"You gonna shake my hand," the big kid said.

"Nope," 'somebody' said, staring him down.

The big kid looked away, dropping his hand and then dipped his right shoulder as if to turn away. 'Somebody' never gave him the chance to come back around and step forward *with a punch. Instead, as soon as the big kid looked away, 'somebody' came off his back foot and kicked him sharply in the left knee. The big kid went over on his side grasping at his knee and howling.*

The kids all scattered. A 'certain somebody.' bent down and picked up his glove and the ball and then turned and went down towards the rink and then over to the grocery store. I followed him and waited outside the store. He came out with a bottle of pop already opened and drank it down in one swallow. His hand was shaking so badly he spilt some of it down the front of his t-shirt.

"I guess you just made yourself an enemy," I said.

"You saw that?"

"Yes, I did."

"You gonna tell anybody."

"I didn't see anything if you buy me a pop," I said.

"Sure. What kind?"

"Tahiti Treat."

He went inside and came back out with a bottle of Mountain Dew.

"They didn't have any Tahiti Treat. I hope this is okay."

"It's fine."

"Maybe I made a friend too," he said when I lifted the bottle to my lips, "what's your name kid?"

"Marion, what's yours?"

Like I didn't know.

From the BOOK OF BILL:

I snuck out of the house and it took me an hour to walk around the lake. It was pitch dark and all I could think about was I am going to get eaten by wolves. Now just what was I doing? I can't tell you even now because I am too ashamed to admit it to myself.

I stood on the road outside Mr. and Mrs. Connolly's house on Lakeshore. I had a fishing rod that was as old as Moses and a tackle box that Daddy had from before the war that I think was rusted shut but when I shook it some things rattled around.

The sun came up and Bill came around from the back of the house with his fishing rod. 'How you doing,' he said, as if he expected me. I hated that. Then he said, 'just passing by?' I hated that even more and I was fit to be tied when he said, 'Come on then, kid.' Well, I was a kid, wasn't I?

"What you fishing for?" he said.

"Pickerel and maybe a pike, same as you," I said.

"You got a spot picked out, then," he said, and I was pretty sure he was making fun of me.

"What's in the bag," I said, to keep him off balance, I guess, or to pretend to myself I wasn't totally embarrassed.

"A baloney sandwich with mustard, an apple, an Eat More chocolate bar, and a jar of live minnows."

"Minnows, my favourite," I said, and shrank to about the size of a toad.

"Come on then," he said and started down the road.

"Don't walk so fast, you might trip and never play goal again," I said.

He slowed down and we fell into step. The top of my head just came up to his shoulder. A few yards down the road he stopped at the last street light and waved at the house on the north side of the road. A curtain fluttered on the closed in veranda.

"Mrs. Kaminski, our neighbourhood snoop," he said.

I was all out of smartass but then we heard a rifle shot, then another. The shot echoed but he guessed it came from the hills to the west and north and close, maybe less than a mile distant.

"I hope they missed," I said.

"So do I," he said, "or a ranger gets them. I don't care for hunting out of season."

We started up the narrow path that took us through a stand of poplar and over a hump of pink granite. We walked in single file, Bill leading the way. Occasionally he looked over his shoulder to make sure I was keeping up. I was, pretty much, except I kept getting my rod caught on tree branches.

By now the light had spilled over the high rim of the eastern hills and came flooding across the village and the lake as we came to the pebble beach where he had left his fiberglass canoe the last time out instead of paddling into a stiff wind out of the east. He asked me if I'd ever paddled a canoe.

"Like a champ," I said, having never in my life been in a canoe but I guess I did all right, sitting up front just about killing myself before we were even halfway to Bad Bob.

"Can we slow down?" I said when my arms were ready to fall off.

"Sure thing, champ," he said.

Ha, ha. We drifted for awhile and I got my strength back and then we paddled some more. The lake was calm and he paddled slowly so that I could keep up. He steered the canoe east as we came up to the island and then rounding the high granite point his grandfather's cabin came into view. There was smoke curling from the tin chimney and the air smelt faintly of fish and he said his grandfather was smoking pickerel over an open fire at the back of the cabin.

Bill steered the canoe east and then south, about a mile until the canoe was positioned over a deep valley that ran for several miles east to west along the spine of the lake. He said he knew he was over the valley that is only about twenty yards wide by marking his position off the tallest spruce near the mouth of Brown's Creek to the south and a cleft in the western hills.

We fished towards Brown's Creek, he set his down rigs and pried open my tackle box with his filleting knife. I felt like a total idiot. Well, he got me set up with my pickerel rig and then he lay down in the middle of the canoe and went to sleep.

He said, "I am listening for the great leader of the pickerel, Chester." I said, "I wasn't born yesterday." He said, "day before." I sulked. He went to sleep. Chester never showed. Bill woke up and he shared a baloney sandwich with too much mustard.

He had that jar of live minnows in his knapsack and he said, do you want a drink and held the jar out to me. I went, 'ooo yuck.' So he opened the jar and took a drink. Right out of the jar with the live minnows. I couldn't believe it. You want a drink, he said again, so I did. I was right, ooo, yuck, ptewy.

"Your favourite," he said.

Then I saw the moose swimming towards Bad Bob. Bill turned the canoe around so we could watch it come ashore. It seemed to be having trouble and kept slipping on the granite, but finally it got up and we saw the most amazing thing, two legs sticking out of its rear end. Bill paddled closer and we saw that its side was covered in red, or blood.

"Paddle," Bill said.

When we got there the cow had dragged itself up on shore and the calf was about half way out and covered in slime. The cow looked like it was barely alive. Bill went up to the cabin and came back with his grandfather. Mr Connolly had a rifle and he put the muzzle behind the cow's ear and shot it. Then he and Bill got a hold of the calf's legs and pulled on it and it came out and they were slapped with some of the slime, but the calf was alive. Mr. Connolly slit the calf's throat and then we dragged the cow and calf up to higher ground. Mr. Connolly had brought some knives and he started to field dress the two animals. I arrived home with two big moose roasts and my mother said, "Marion where have you been?"

"Fishing, see," I said, and I showed her the two big roasts.

Chapter 15

Bill stepped out of Marion's just as the high bank of plush white clouds was frayed and shredded by a wind out of the north and the sun broke across the lake, like a dollop of spreading butter. He saw Libby sitting on the concrete municipal wharf.

"Change of plan," he said, as she turned to him coming along the wharf. "Feel like a boat ride and a little modelling?"

"Well, why not? I'm probably leaving town. I don't care and I sure am desperate."

"My kind of gal, come on."

They made the straight shot out to Bad Bob and Bill felt the heavy lids of Marion's binoculars on his back. A hundred lashes then and he felt his anger begin to peel away and, as always, he was down to the bone before he felt normal, half way across the lake and the other half relishing the peculiar freedom in the suffering that Marion gifted him from her intimate distance.

Libby hopped out of the Doral as soon as they sidled up to the dock and tied it off with nice bowline knot.

"Very nice."

"Joe, in our early days, was a fisherman and he had a little aluminum skiff until somebody stole it and the trailer. He still talks about it. Or used to, when we were talking."

Libby raised her hand.

"Sorry, I shouldn't be saying anything."

"I take you back, you can drive," he said.

Libby's eyes went wide.

"I'd need to practice docking."

"We can do that," Bill said, noting the potential there for a double entendre. "Say we go upstairs."

Libby hesitated.

"This is all pretty new for me."

"Why don't we sit and enjoy the sun for a minute?"

Libby took the old aluminum lawn chair with a vinyl tartan seat that was frayed in places. It had washed up mysteriously one day on the shore and he put it out on the dock in case some one came by to lay claim to it and then he had bolted it to the dock to keep it from blowing into the water when a wind came up. There it sat winter, spring, summer, and fall, for about twenty years. A voice in his head said, 'don't be mean, come clean.'

"The thing is, Libby, I don't know that I want to paint a nude. I'm a landscape artist, always have been. I don't know that I have the skill and I'm not sure I have the inclination."

He explained about Alice from The Chop and how the beauty of her hands had instilled in him the difficulty of making a quick segue into a more figurative style of work.

"Fair enough, then. I can't say that I was exactly thrilled about the idea. I'd do it though because I'd trust you that whatever you did would be respectful and that nobody around here would see the paintings once they were done. My plan B is to set myself up as a handyman somewhere."

"Or a handywoman."

"That works too."

Bill took a seat on the other delinquent chair, likewise bolted, older still, retrieved from the ditch by the northern exit to the Eleven Highway, another version of the aluminum lawn chair, a chaise lounge variety, faded yellow, the metal elbows covered in rust and the plastic armrests cracked.

The truth told, he relaxed, sun on his cheek and arm. A cheerful or so it seemed, companion of the non-contentious variety and towards whom he harboured no unchaste thoughts, but rather a gentlemanly, fraternal curiosity.

"I saw Marion on her veranda and she put a pair of binoculars on the railing."

Bill laughed, not with pleasure. It was a thin and bitter expression of resignation.

"Right."

"Is she watching us right now?"

"Possibly."

Libby leaned forward and whispered, "Marion is spying on us?"

Bill crossed his legs. Yes, Marion was probably spying on them.

"She occasionally glances this way."

"That is an invasion of privacy," Libby said, testily.

"It might be."

Libby sat back and crossed her arms. Bill was about to offer an apology and suggest he run her back to the village when Libby leaned forward and elbows on her knees, whispered "I know she's your girlfriend Bill, but she was quite rude to me the other day."

"I'm sorry."

"And she banned me from Marion's which I don't think is fair, because there's nowhere else to go for a coffee on foot."

Bill opened his hands in a gesture of 'no comment.'

"The other day she came into the store during my quiet time and it was clear that my current circumstances were not convenient to her liking. That's the feeling I got."

He could see Marion provoking that impression, if she was in a hurry, and she was mostly in a hurry.

"Again, I'm sorry."

"It's not your fault, but you know, and now she's spying on me and invading my privacy. Again, I must say."

"Well us. Possibly."

"Shocking, Bill, just shocking," she said and grinned.

Bill had no response. Marion had been training binoculars of one sort or another on Bad Bob as long as he could remember. In some ways it was comforting knowing that she was watching out for him, time permitting, of course, but he could see, or thought he could see, Libby's point.

"Maybe you just need to practice drawing a little," Libby said, whispering.

"Years ago I wasn't a bad draftsman. Maybe it would all come back. I'm dubious."

"Maybe we could un-dubious you. It's nice here on the dock in the sun."

"It is."

"Say we give Marion some serious privacy to invade."

"No, best not."

Libby started to unbutton her denim shirt. His left-side brain said no, but said it with so little conviction that the 'no,' the vocal communication, never made it out of that part of his brain.

The right side of his brain levered him into action and he went up the stairs and when he came down he carried a sketchpad and a soft lead pencil. Libby had cast off her shirt and had stepped out of her jeans and stood before him in just a white bra and panties. She did a pirouette and flounced her ponytail.

"What's the verdict, Bill?"

"Very nice."

Libby reached around to unhook her bra.

"Wait. Maybe I should limber up first. Do a few gesture drawings. Maybe just sit."

Libby was slender without being skinny and her arms and legs were muscled.

"You are bad," he said, laughing, genuine this time, a happy laugh, a fuck-you-Marion-in-Mexico hoot.

"Thank you, Bill, that is the nicest thing a man has ever said to me."

"No."

"I confess, I have been unhappy in love and most other things."

Libby crossed her legs, right over left and he noticed that the bottom of her foot was dirty and thought it was time to mop the dock.

"Sorry, can I cross my legs?"

"Of course. I'll practice my foreshortening."

He had just started on her legs when she sat forward again and whispered, "I am getting you in trouble."

Bill leaned forward and whispered back, "She can't hear us."

Libby whispered, "How do you know you're not wired for sound, too?"

It was too funny. Libby sat back.

"First rule of modelling Libby, don't move."

"Aye, aye, Captain. Can I talk?"

"Only if you have to."

"If I talk it'll take my mind off the fact that this is the wildest thing I have ever done in my life. I know that may sound strange."

In fact it did, but he was jaded from living in the city, from those occasional episodes of self analysis, pondering life, the meaning of things, what's it all about, stuff like that. If you saw a man riding a bike backwards, or a black plastic sheet with an alleged dead body under it on a sidewalk, blood on the pavement, threads of blood drawn towards a sewer drain stopped short by coagulation or the heat, or a woman in white robes standing on an overpass waving a white wand, or a man in a wheelchair with no legs living it rough under a cat walk, it was all part of the passing mural. You raised your hand to confess your complicity and voila, a taxi pulled to the curb, and you went wherever you had to go.

"Pretend you're at the beach."

"Is Marion still looking at us?"

A smooth rhythm and a rough figure emerged, and then another and another as Libby prattled on, and another, and each one became a little less vague. Then another and another and the gesture began to evolve into a form that slowed as he added additional detail, changing rhythm.

"I am one hundred and seventy-five centimetres tall and I am forty-one years old."

"Fascinating," Bill said.

"I grew up on a farm and my parents were strict Pentecostals. My older sister Mary ran away as soon as she turned sixteen and we never heard from her again. I didn't mind it so much. We had some livestock but mostly we farmed canola. This was west of New Liskeard.

"I went to school and the kids made fun of me because I wore long dresses and industrial strength brassieres and never any makeup. I didn't like school. I preferred driving a tractor and working on machinery. I did a lot of that because I was the son my father never had, and we couldn't afford to hire labour. I didn't get along with my father as he was sometimes a cruel man.

"That's about it. I finished high school and stayed on the farm. I never expected to be married until Joe came along, and even then I didn't want to, but then my father died and my mother wanted to sell the farm to go live with her sister. I married Joe, who was studying to be a pastor at the time, and we moved into his parents' basement and there were lots of silverfish. Next thing you know, here I am right into the nude modelling."

Bill worked on her upper body, the elegant long neck and the curve of her cheekbones, her close set, large eyes. He worked his way through to the end of the pad and put it aside. He was exhausted. Libby was rubbing her arms.

"You're cold. Put your clothes on, we're done for the day."

Libby dressed quickly and while Bill stared off towards the village and resisted the urge to smile and wave at his seasonal beloved.

"Can I see?"

Bill handed the sketchpad to Libby and she sat in the lawn chair and opened the book. Bill looked up at the sky that had clouded over again and guessed that it was getting late in the day; he was hungry and wanted a nap. He studied the clouds, noting the rough texture, the pallid colouring. More like torn and dirty sheets, these ones.

"Bill?" Libby said, sounding upset.

"I'm sorry," he said, ready to plead his case.

"I've never seen myself before except in a mirror and I never really knew what my husband saw in me. When I look in the mirror I just see myself; Libby, plain old Libby, Libby nobody would take a second look at, not even my husband, though he might have early on, once or twice, and so this is the first time I've seen myself from somebody else's eyes."

"I'm sorry," he said, still ready to launch his defence.

"I'm beautiful."

"Sorry?"

"Thank you."

Bill, understanding that an explanation of his lack of competence was not necessary, experienced a word deficit—not unusual, though often embarrassing. This time not. Libby went on.

"I don't mean I'm Scarlet Johansson beautiful, I mean I just never thought of myself as anything but plain, and I guess I still am, but seeing me plain as I am, it's beautiful. I don't know what I'm saying do I?"

Yes, she did, eloquently, right brain, intuitively, spot-on.

"Let me see."

Libby appeared reluctant to give up the book.

"I'll buy it from you."

"No."

"How much?"

"It's yours, and I'll write you out a check for a few hours of modelling and travel time."

"Thank you, Bill. That might get me started."

Libby hugged the book to her breast and smiled beatifically minus the halo.

"I have a question."

"Sure."

"Doesn't your painting make you happy?"

Simple question, easy to avoid answering or to dissemble but Libby, who had heard his most sacred confession, made him want to confess again, and in doing so, attempt to tell the truth. It was spooky. If she was, in her naïve way, trying to manipulate him, that was fine.

"Yes, Art makes me happy. Eventually. Lately though, no. Sometimes it seems superfluous, the art for art's sake stuff that maybe at some time made sense, I thought it did anyway, and then you see something and you say what can I do?

I joined with protest marches down in the city. I volunteered at the food bank. I got involved with an art program at the local Library branch and volunteered my time. I wrote letters to the various levels of government. I did what I could. Not much. No effect that I can see. Last time I checked, the world was worse off than when I began taking an interest."

Libby looked down at her hands, clasped and unclasped the book as if she were trying to make up her mind about something.

"Bill, what if I had wanted something to drink?"

"Well I've got some beer under the dock, a bottle of white wine in the ice box, a quart and a half of rum under the sink, and well water. I forgot to buy coke this morning."

She clasped her hands and rearranged the book on her lap.

"Say we went at it for another couple of hours and I got hungry."

It was a fair question.

"I have Irish Stew."

"Say I preferred a salad, being a vegetarian?"

"Well, right now you'd have to settle for the peanut butter or you could pick the vegetable bits out of the Irish Stew."

Hands back on the knees the book rotated a half turn.

"I could do you a favour before I'm modeling tomorrow, if that's what you want. I could do a little shopping, maybe even bring you out a steak from the Mennonite butcher in Liskeard, a baking potato, some coke, beer, ice—anything you might need, if I could use your truck."

Hands clasped around the book. Nervous but not so shy, up to something.

"I'm afraid the brakes lines are gone on old Belle-bleue."

"Fix your brakes too."

"You can do that?"

No, she was making that up. He was intrigued.

"Sure. Well probably. I've fixed brakes lines before. Not for awhile, though. If I couldn't I could run the truck up to the Jiffy Gas, work the gears and coast in."

Hands and sketchpad back on the knees.

"Tell me something, Bill, why couldn't I be like your assistant? It would make your life a lot easier and you wouldn't have to worry about the Marion factor, you know, once I painted over the lenses on her binoculars, not that I would ever do that. What do you think?"

"Are you saying that if you were my assistant, I'd have to worry about the Marion factor?"

That appeared to annoy her a little and a little colour appeared on her cheeks.

"I was just saying, but I don't really know about a Marion factor."

"Come on or we're going to get wet."

He pointed to the sky. Rain.

"Say you bring the beer," he said and pointed to a piece of rope that hung down into the lake from a dock cleat. Thunder to the north then and the wind came on.

Bill went up the stairs. He set and lit the fire in the wood stove and then settled at the table. Where the heck was Libby. He was just lifting himself out of the chair when he heard her on the stairs.

Libby was back in flash of lightening, and then in another flash he had an opened can of Fifty at his elbow and another five on the kitchen counter. Libby joined him at the table and put her hands beneath her knees.

"Geez Bill, granny knots and that is no way to treat fishing net."

Her shoulders lifted as she breathed deeply and then relaxed.

"Breathing relaxes me," Libby said.

"Mostly it just keeps me alive."

"The thing is, Bill, I'm just wondering if being an assistant pays as well as being a model, with or without the hank-panky, which we haven't discussed yet, although I'm guessing that comes with the territory of nude modelling, and if I could get an advance from right now?"

"What hanky-panky?"

Libby went bright red.

"I'm sorry. I didn't mean to say anything."

"No hanky-panky."

"Of course."

Bill sipped his beer and looked at Libby over the rim of the can. She was laughing at him.

"You are a bad girl," he said, and felt the heavy emotional malaise from the argument with Marion tumble off his shoulders.

Bill let the silence stretch out between them until it was taut as a string of cheese curd pulled from a mound of poutine. A drop of maple sap exploded in the wood stove, lightning struck through the rain and hit the lake and set it on fire. Thunder smacked the roof of the cabin, and the roof began to leak in front of the sink.

"Well, Libby," Bill said.

"I am staying the night."

"Yes. No hanky-panky."

Libby covered her face with her hands, laughing. Too funny. When had there last been any too-funny in his life?

The summer of love with Marion? Not a lot and what there was of it was serious, an under current of sadness woven into the experience of life. The consciousness of a warm breeze, the taste of salt on sweaty skin, the chittering of chipmunks in a nearby spruce, the smell of lilac in her thick hair, all of that, the experience of Marion was part of his life consciousness, itself stitched up with sadness and so, ergo, not a lot of too-funny.

Now with Libby, after his confessions there was this too-funny and it was effervescent, truly too-funny then, vaporous. Where had the sadness gone? Was it that easy? Fucking hell, with Libby, maybe it was.

The storm bullied its way onto the lake. The sky turned to black. Bill lit a kerosene lamp and put it on the counter so that if they chose to sit at the table they could look out across the lake: almost black, obscured by rain and low black clouds.

"You ever play cribbage," Libby said?

Chapter 16

She walloped him, totally and completely walloped him. Whatcha got there Bill? Nineteen. Just nineteen, Bill, gee? Whatcha got there Bill, fifteen-two, fifteen-four and there ain't no more? Ha. She was a fast horse and he was a donkey. Whatcha got there Bill? Six. Well Bill, fifteen-two, fifteen-four, fifteen-six and six is twelve. Ha. All night long.

The cabin creaking and swaying in the storm, pegging like she was the wind, skunked you, Bill. Skunked you, Bill. She was having so much fun and Bill was groaning and whining and hanging his head and wasn't he having fun, being walloped and finally he won a game.

Ha, he shouted and then strode about the room, ha! he shouted at top of his lungs and chug-a-lugged a beer. Ha, Bill Burnon rules, he shouted, and it was so funny, and he kicked over the can and they had water everywhere. She had never had so much fun. In all her life, never so much fun.

And drunk to boot, one jigger of rum and a sip of beer and she was flying. Fifteen-two, fifteen-six, a pair is eight and . . . unbeatable. And it was so much fun. Then Bill said, Libby sweetheart, I am done.

"Long day, time for bed."

Libby didn't know what to say. She wasn't tired. She really wasn't drunk, just pretending, but she could see he was tired.

"You're on the couch."

She didn't want to be on the couch. She didn't want the evening to end. She had never had so much fun in her life.

"One more game," she said, trying not to sound as if she was pleading.

"Nope, I am bagged, young lady."

Young lady. Oh my. Bill went into the bedroom and came out with a sleeping bag and a pillow.

"These are clean. Pretty much."

He dropped them on the fold-out couch, then stoked up the fire and put another split log into the burn box.

"If it gets too hot you can open the front or back door, depending on which way the rain is blowing. The screens need replacing, by the way."

He emptied the pail of water into the sink.

"I can't do anything about the drip," he said and placed the pail under the leak in the roof.

They did a blackfly and mosquito sweep. Libby with the dishcloth, Bill with the fly swatter. Great fun. Bill over there. Where. Over there. Bastards. Death to blackflies.

Libby and Bill folded down the fold-out and Libby laid out the sleeping bag.

"I usually need to take a leak the middle of the night," he said, "so it's not the ghost of Bad Bob."

"Wouldn't that be something?"

"This storm clears off, you might see something. If not, I'll show you where Robert Smiley and Millicent Hammond set up house and probably where he killed her and the child."

Libby felt an unpleasant shiver down her back.

"Sometimes you'll see a light through the spruce trees, on the hump of granite in the middle of the island. It's faint, could be a swarm of fireflies, but the colour's wrong. It's a white light, almost fluorescent, there's a tinge of blue to it that makes it so white. I don't know that it's a ghost of anybody, but it might be Robert Smiley."

"You are kidding me, right?"

"Maybe."

Bill went to the cupboard next to the sink and took down a candle in a glass. He lit it with a match from the burn box and brought it over to Libby.

"This will burn for several hours."

"Thank you," she said and felt odd. She was alone with a man who was not her husband or father or the school bus driver.

Bill turned down the kerosene lamp until it was just a dribble of light.

"'scuse me," he said and went out the back door.

Libby looked around and wasn't sure what she should do next. Usually she got into her comfy jammies and slippers. Should she sleep in her clothes? What if the ghost of Robert Smiley decided to ravish her? Would he prefer clothes on or off? It seemed to Libby that for ravishing, it would be better to have her clothes on.

What if Robert Smiley just wanted to come in from the rain and cold and snuggle up to a warm body? She guessed clothes off would be best. What if Robert Smiley was lonely and just wanted to talk? What would they have to talk about? Oh, Mr. Smiley, what about flocked wallpaper for your room in hell, or might I suggest an egg shell white for the walls, a light mauve for the baseboards and trim?

Bill came through the door and stopped, and Libby realized she was talking out loud.

"Everything okay?" Bill said, as he shook off the rain and dried his face with the dishrag.

"I don't know."

Bill came and sat next to her.

"How did you find the modelling?"

"It was strange."

"Like now?"

"I was thinking about ghosts."

"I think you'll make a good model."

"Not a handyman."

"Handywoman."

"'Course."

"I don't see why not. All the things you said need doing and if you can do them, then you can do them and you can still be my model. I need to practice some basic drawing skills that I had once but have neglected, and then we'll see. How does that sound?"

It sounded too good to be true, and it probably wasn't, but it was something to be hopeful about, one or two things anyway, and maybe the rest would follow. Bill put his arm around her shoulders and gave her a little squeeze. Libby wanted to throw her arms around him and say, please don't go. Please sit here with me. I'm afraid of ghosts. I'm afraid of being alone. She wasn't really, but she wanted to be so that Bill would stay and keep the ghosts and the loneliness and even the bogeyman away.

"I don't have a way to get out here," she said, thinking that could be a deal breaker right from the get-go.

"I can put you up in my studio. You'll have some privacy. I have a spare cot and there are some shelves for your clothes. I don't start working up the boards usually until later in the summer. You can get started on the repairs I need, and we'll see about the nude modelling."

Libby thought she should get right to the heart of the matter and so she said, "What about the Marion factor."

"I don't see how she could object. I offered her the nude modelling job first and she turned it down. She can chop wood, but she doesn't know any carpentry."

"What about appearances?"

"It appears you are my handywoman-slash-model."

Well, she wasn't about to talk herself out of two jobs and a place to stay away from her husband.

"What about the Joe factor?" Bill said.

The question surprised her. She didn't see her husband as anything close to a factor. He was barely a man to start with, unless being a bully counted for something.

"I can't say there is one. We have been estranged for years, paying lip service to the marriage and then not even that when the hardware store went in the tank."

"Good," Bill said and got up.

Libby stood up and wished he wouldn't go. But there was something else, a sense, right from the beginning or near the beginning of the two of them sitting by the violets, that something was wrong with Bill Burnon. A long-time wound, confirmed with his reliving the death of his father for her and what could only be termed a confession of guilt in the suicide of his mother, and she wanted to ask, not out of any selfish interest, but simply by asking it might help bring things to a resolution in some good way.

"Bill, can I ask you something personal?"

"I guess. I don't have to answer, do I?"

"What's wrong?"

The question seemed to take him by surprise.

"Sit for a minute," she said.

Bill sat on the sofa and leaned forward elbows on his knees. Libby had an urge to put her arm around him.

"Always, most always after I finish something, a series of paintings that I've worked hard on for a year, there's a transition period. And often, but not always, it's difficult. It's a hard time because I'm creatively, emotionally, and physically drained, and it's just like that until a new idea presents itself and then off I go, everything in equilibrium. How's that?"

"I didn't mean to pry."

"I'm still leaning towards clouds."

"Let's hope so."

Bill went off to bed. Libby sat there for a minute wondering if she had any thoughts to collect and decided that there were about a million and there wasn't room in her brain just then for more than one or two. She went to the counter and blew out the kerosene lamp and the cabin was pitch dark except for a small cylinder of light around the candle. She looked out the window over the sink for the ghost of Robert Smiley, but couldn't see a thing through the rain. She listened and there was just the rain prattling on the tin roof, the cabin creaking and the wind whistling and the drip from the leak in the roof.

Libby sat on the edge of the fold out couch with her back to Bill's room and put her hands between her knees and squeezed as hard as she could. That was better.

"Libby," Bill said, from the door to his bedroom.

Libby shrieked and jumped up.

"Sorry," Bill said, holding up a yellow lumberjack shirt.

Libby felt her heart slow down to normal and breathed in deeply. Bill handed her the shirt

"This is brand new, never been worn, cotton, size large. I thought since you didn't come prepared you might want to wear this to bed. Also, there is a brand-new toothbrush in the cupboard under the sink. If you have to go in the night, don't bother with the outhouse. Just pee through the slats on the back stoop or the front porch, whichever is best. We'll go into town tomorrow, so you can pack a bag."

Bill came through in the middle of the night waking her from a dream that was warm and erotic, but she lost the thread of it right away as Bill walked quietly past her and the candle, still burning, fluttered and distorted his figure as he went out onto the back stoop. A minute later he came back and knelt by her head. Libby's heart rate began to climb even more as he whispered to her face.

"Libby, Libby, wake up. There's something for you to see."

She opened her eyes and saw his lips and had a strong urge to lean forward and kiss them, and maybe stroke his face, but the face was gone and Bill was tugging on her hand.

"Come on."

Libby slid out of the sleeping bag and followed Bill. The floor was freezing on her bare feet.

"What is it?" she said.

Bill pulled her along and then they were on the back stoop. The rain had stopped but the spruce trees were dripping and there was a wind blowing around in the canopy of the birch tree behind the studio. She was shivering mightily and holding onto Bill's arm as the only source of warmth.

"Look," he said and pointed.

Libby gasped as she saw the light in the spruce trees. It was faint and appeared far off and it was hard to tell if it had a shape other than it was oblong and perhaps the height of a tall man, if Robert Smiley was tall. The light was stopped dead and Libby wondered if it was aware that it was being watched. She was transfixed and the light simply disappeared as a cloud passed in front of the moon, leaving a slight afterburn in her retina that quickly faded.

"Gone."

Bill ushered her back inside and sat her on the edge of the fold out bed. He went to the window and looked out.

"Gone."

Bill took a split log from the burn bin and lifted off the iron plate and slid the log into the burn box and poked it until sparks flew up about his face. He set the plate back, came over and sat next to Libby.

"Scary?" he said.

"No, cold," she said and pulled the sleeping bag around her.

Bill patted her on the shoulder.

"Busy day tomorrow. If you're up before me, stoke the fire and put water on for coffee."

"Yes, sir," Libby said and gave him a sideways nudge.

Bill went back to bed and Libby stretched out on her side in the sleeping bag and blew out the candle. The roof was still dripping though not as much. The wood spat and crackled in the stove and she could feel the new strands of heat that had reached her.

Chapter 17

Bill passed Libby the keys to Belle-bleue and went across the scree to Marion's for a cup of coffee and maybe some toast. He planned to spend a peaceful hour or so in reflection; a walk up to the Anglican graveyard to pay his respects to his mother, an hour or two, maybe to think things through regarding Libby…

As far as Bill could tell she was planning to pick his pocket with this assistant and handywoman ploy, and in the larger scheme of things he did need a new outhouse, roof, rooves, etc., etc. What did that really matter anyway, the large scheme being this annual angst thing that came with being William Henry Burnon.

Marion's and Marion to cheer him up, then, if that were at all possible. He knew it wasn't. It wasn't that hope springs eternal, rather it's an eternal spring, long gone dry, an absurd wadi, a dry gulch full of the bleached bones of pilgrims clutching horsehair brushes like crucifixes. Jesus, Bill. Enough, old man.

Marion's, the habitual first stop of the day that might be his last of the home stand, a to-hell-with-it kind of day. Whatever way the wind blows, a cheque for Libby for hearing his confessions and forgiving his rudeness, for entertaining him for an evening, for seeing the ghost in the reflection of moonlight off the mirror just beyond the stand of spruce.

High tail it out of there, Bill. That kind of day. Gut it out with Marion; been there, although, maybe this time, he might end up at has-been-there. After fifty years, had that time now arrived? Why the fuck not? When was the last time he had any fun? 'Too funny, Bill,' all over the place. 'Death to blackflies,' Libby had shouted.

He stepped into the diner. It was filled with light, the booths full, the counter full except for a seat at the end, dishes clattering, the buzz of conversation, air heavy with the aroma of bacon and toast. Marion at a booth dropping off four plates of Big Man's to a construction crew, Hilda pouring out coffee along the counter.

Bill's took the seat at the end, annoyed already that his preferred seat was occupied by the construction boys, as Marion whisked by him without so much as a word or a glance. A minute later she came back with plates of Home On The Range Westerns and two more Big Man's.

"Morning, sweetheart," he said.

Marion declined to acknowledge him. Well, all right, that was annoying too. He waved at Hilda who looked away and set about cracking eggs over the grill. He sat there for a minute, unsure of what to do, and felt riled that his presence, even during the morning rush, was being ignored. He felt the dishrag flick at his heart. Christ, he hated that dishrag.

"What is going on with you and Miss Klepto?"

"You mean Libby?"

"I was expecting you last night."

"No you weren't."

Marion snapped her dishrag and went down the counter to the kitchen were Hilda had two plates ready to go.

"Coffee when you get a minute, sweetheart," Bill said as she came by with an order for one of the booths.

She ignored him

Hilda came out of the kitchen to tend the cash as a booth in the middle of the diner cleared out. Marion went down the aisle to clean the table. Bill waved at Hilda who looked away as she cashed out the customers and went back into the kitchen. A section of stools opened up next to Bill and were filled by another construction crew, all in orange, *X*'s on their backs, hard hat and tool belts on their hips, MTO road crew or maybe Hydro, young guys.

Marion cleared the table and set the dishes on the counter and came back his way. He went for her waist, but she twisted away and snapped at him with the dishrag. That brought some snickers from the construction crew boys. Bill ignored them and made another grab for Marion as she went down the counter.

"Yes, I was," she said and slapped his wrist with the dishrag.

Fucking dishrag. There was some sideway looks and snickering from the construction boys. Marion taking it out on some old guy, some washed up old fart. Marion picked up the dirty dishes from the counter and placed them in the dishwasher. She went to the cash register as another booth cleared out, followed by three seats from the counter. The diner was beginning to empty. He wanted his coffee.

A man edged by the exiting customers and took an empty seat at the counter. Hilda was right there with a cup and the pot of coffee. Bill considered his options: shout, throw something, leave, or all the above, all of which would draw more attention to himself and the public shaming that he was currently undergoing, as it appeared the remaining seats and booths had grown quieter, attuned to the unfolding drama between the diner Queen and her lowly drone. Fuck it. No 'too funny'. No 'death to blackflies.'

Bill regarded the aluminum serviette dispenser in front of him. It was attended by a salt and pepper shaker and a red plastic bottle of ketchup. Bill looked down the counter. Marion was busy at the cash register and Hilda was scraping grease from the grill.

He slid his right hand forward, slowly and edged the serviette dispenser closer to the back edge of the counter. He checked on Marion and Hilda and had a quick look around the diner. Nobody was paying him any direct attention. With his index finger, he pushed the serviette dispenser back a little further until it toppled onto the floor behind the counter with a clatter.

He withdrew his hand and placed both hands palms down on his thighs below the counter. He stared straight ahead at the decorous Art Nouveau Mucha Job cigarette paper poster, one of several that Marion had in the diner and was part of a shallow genuflection to that design style. Bill thought of the décor at Marion's as art nouveau-tacky.

Marion came down the counter. She stopped in front of him, stopped to simper and to pick up the serviette dispenser. She replaced the serviettes that had spilled out and put the dispenser back in place next to the salt and pepper and ketchup.

She came around the counter and went down the aisle to clean a table near the cash. Bill pushed the serviette dispenser off the counter again and this time folded his hands neatly in front of him. Marion cleared the table, and on her way back around the counter picked up the dispenser, replaced the serviettes that had spilled and place it back on the counter between the salt, pepper and ketchup.

"I can do this all day," she said and went down the counter and gathered up the dishes and went about putting them in the dishwasher. Bill pushed the serviette dispenser off the counter.

By now he was beginning to attract some attention, particularly from the recent construction gang arrivals a few seats down the counter to the right. The construction guy nearest to Bill leaned in his direction and said, "Don't do that."

Bill turned to the man, "Don't do what?"

"You pushed that thing on to the floor."

"No I didn't."

"You did, man, I saw you."

"You're lying."

"What'd you say?" the construction guy said jumping up from his stool, work belt tools clinking against the hard hat hanging from his waist.

"I said you're lying."

The construction guy, broad of shoulder, narrow of waist, sneered at Bill, "You have a death wish?"

A light went off in the middle of the blob or clot of his failing fail-safe mechanism, the old Bill caught in the headlights of the absurd truth that had often insinuated itself into his journey, like a drunken guide manoeuvring along a precipice. Yes, some days he sure did have a death wish.

"Yeah, only it's not passive. I mean, I'll take somebody with me, or at least inflict enough damage the poor fucker will wish he'd never got out of bed."

The construction guy seemed confused.

"Yeah, well, just fuck off, old man," he said and sat down.

"How about a kiss?" Bill said.

The construction guy jumped up again and his compadres were leaning forward to get a clear look.

"How about a kiss?" Bill said and winked at the construction guy.

Marion was right there with his coffee. She splashed it down in front of him, grabbed his ears and pulled him across the counter and kissed him on the lips and then confronted the construction guys.

"My apologies, boys. He was talking to me. Bill here's myopic. That means he doesn't see that well, and also, he's in the early stages of dementia. Sorry for the misunderstanding. Tell you what, you relax and let Bill here buy you breakfast."

The construction guy mollified, Marion dragged Bill out back and pushed him up against the propane tank.

"You stay put."

Bill walked down to the end of the lane between Marion's and Marion's bungalow, hands in his pockets, head hung between his shoulders, wishing that at the end of this ten yard trek he would look up and see Marion in all her glory. Marion who had taken his breath away, who had impaled him with her eyes outside the grocery store chugging a pop all those years ago and whose glory was simple and direct, this beauty, this courage, a liveliness that over the years may have faltered, but in the GPS of his heart was never gone, could never be gone, because it was her, or so he had believed.

Libby was just backing Belle-bleue out the parking lot. She turned her around and went off in the direction of the south ramp to the Eleven. He stepped out a little further and watched as old Belle disappeared around the corner.

"Totally brakeless," he said to the disappeared pickup.

"Bill."

He turned to witness Marion hanging off the end of one of her Putters.

"Where is Miss Klepto going with Belle? You might never see it again."

"The Jiffy Gas, I expect."

"Without brakes?"

"She's a farm girl."

Bill came back down the lane.

"This farm girl is leading you down the cow path."

"Thank you for the advice. Would you like to come out to Bad Bob sometime and inspect the sheets?"

Marion took a deep inhale on her smoke and then flicked it onto the scree.

"How do I know you're not doing it in the pine straw. You have a nice summer, Bill, and I would appreciate it if you stayed out of my diner," she said.

Banned again. Bill watched her go up the steps and through the back door. It wasn't the first time she had barred him from Marion's, but maybe it was the last. Bill blinked and that was it. He did not feel himself going down and when he woke up he was lying on his side on the scree looking at the wrinkled butt of one of Marion's cigarettes.

He had a headache and a sore shoulder when he pushed himself up onto his hands and knees. He stood up and felt wobbly and staggered over to the bungalow and put both hands against the wall to hold himself up. He took a few deep breaths that helped clear his head. He was thirsty, and he had to pee. He went inside, sliding along the wall of the bungalow until he got to the mudroom door.

He went inside. He peed, and foraged in Marion's medicine cabinet for, as it turned out, two extra strength ibuprofen that he took with a tall glass of water. By now he was in the kitchen and felt the need to lie down. He stretched out on Marion's living room sofa and a few minutes later was sound asleep.

Chapter 18

Bill walked into the marina parking lot just as Libby came out of the boat barn. His headache was gone and his head was clear, but he was a little shaky and his shoulder still felt sore. He waved at Libby.

"Good to go, Bill" she said. She dropped the rag she'd been drying her hands with in the oil drum by the side door. "You all right? You look pale."

"I fainted, apparently, just fell over. Never happened before. I had a nap. I'm fine."

"Oh, oh."

"How is Belle?"

"I took Belle up to the Jiffy Gas and they rented me a bay with a lift and their tools, and they had brake lines on hand that fit her, so it wasn't a big deal. I said you'd come by later and settle up."

"What do I owe you?"

"I could run you up to the hospital."

"Let's see how it goes. How do you feel about chauffeuring?

"My pleasure.

Libby got motherly on him and drove straight down the Eleven to the hospital in Cobalt, bullied him into the emergency room and sat him next to a stack of Miss Chatelaines, then went off to do his errands; the Rona, the Mennonite Butcher, Loblaw's, and when she got back to the emergency room Bill was sitting outside on a bench talking to a nurse.

"Stress, anxiety, that sort of thing," he said as he stepped into the cab of old Belle.

"I've only been gone two hours, you sure you saw a doctor?"

Bill looked over his shoulder at the boards settled comfortably into the truck bed. No, he hadn't seen a doctor, but that wasn't anybody's business.

"You got my boards."

"I can't believe I am going to end up on one of those," Libby said.

"We'll see."

"What'll I look like?"

"Yourself."

"And who is that?"

"Remains to be seen," Bill said and had to laugh because that was really the truth of it.

They stopped at the Jiffy Gas, gassed up the truck and Bill paid for the bay, the materials, the tool rental, the gas can, and bought a litre of two-stroke engine oil. That done, they were done. Bill was impressed with how smoothly Libby handled the three on a tree.

He liked having a chauffeur and Libby wasn't a big talker, which was nice too, and when she did talk tended to stick to a practical conversation, such as the need for an engine tune up and that his tires were down to the wear bars and the sorry state of the town roads, the amount of road kill suggesting that food was scarce in the bush and so on, and that with the lack of snow during the winter it might be not be a plague of blackflies for a change.

"So, I am modelling today," she said when she shut off the engine back in the marina parking lot.

"Not today."

"Oh. Well."

She didn't sound too disappointed.

"You need to dig a new latrine. I could do that."

"I don't know if there's anywhere to dig one."

"Why don't we have a look?"

She looked at him quickly.

"I promised to show you Bad Bob and Millicent's cabin."

"Am I staying the night?"

"Up to you."

"I saw you have Monopoly."

"Where did you see that?"

"Under your bed."

Too funny.

"What were you doing under my bed?"

"I was testing your floorboards."

"For what?"

Too funny.

"You need new linoleum."

Too, too funny.

"To be honest Bill, what about Marion and her factor?"

"Marion is quite territorial, which means she can be particularly annoying at times, and I said to her, at least I think I said to her, why don't you come out and inspect the sheets, and she said how do I know you're not doing it in the pine straw? That is Marion's sense of humour."

"Oh," Libby said.

"I hate Monopoly."

"Back in ten," she said and went off to pack a bag.

Bill went into the marina office and arranged with Rory for the boards to be unloaded from the back of Belle-bleue. Bill wasn't sure about a delivery. No hurry was good for Rory as the pontoon boat was hauling some lumber to the south side of the lake where the road in was still washed out from the spring run-off. They made a straight shot out to Bad Bob and again Libby did the driving. She got the docking on the third try and hopped out of the boat and tied it off. They went up the steps to the cabin and dropped off Libby's overnighter.

"How are you feeling?"

"I'm fine."

"Alright then."

"Come on, I need to stretch my legs. Let's go see Bad Bob's cabin. What's left of it."

Bill led her through the spruce trees.

"What is that mirror doing there?" she said.

"It was an experiment," Bill said, having forgotten all about the mirror.

"Why would you have a mirror leaning up against a tree?"

"An experiment, a few years ago.

"That mirror was in the outhouse yesterday."

"You sure."

"Are you playing games with me?" she said and slapped him playfully on the arm.

"Come on."

They went across the hump of pink granite that split the island and then through more spruce and fern.

"That mirror was the ghost I saw. The reflection of the moon. I can't believe you did that," Libby said, as they entered into a clearing that opened onto the western shore of the island.

She sounded angry, though it wasn't a Marion type angry; a sharp sting from a wet dishrag.

Bill pointed to the middle of the clearing on the edge of the pebble beach. About a half mile in the distance the western shore of the lake was a wall of dark green spruce mixed with ribbons of birch.

"That's all that's left. About five hundred square feet, total."

The foundation was overgrown with grass and moss, barely visible. There was a square of rectangular rough-hewn stone that was about twenty feet in diameter.

"This was Robert Smiley's cabin. It was his base of operations. He ran trap lines to the west and the north beyond those hills and traded his furs in the village. He did some prospecting without any luck. He had better luck with moose and it was said he was a good hunter. He sold the meat and hides in the village. This is where he brought Millicent Hammond, and, if you believe the story, killed her here. That's the legend, anyway. He went to some trouble to haul this stone. I'm guessing he stole it from the mine. It looks familiar."

Libby stood in the middle of the cabin.

"There is no ghost of Robert Smiley."

"Probably not."

"You are not a trustworthy person and I don't think I can work for you."

Libby started back.

"Wait. Do you want to hear what happened?"

Libby stopped and turned back to Bill.

"Not if it's not the truth."

"Well let's see."

Bill stepped out of the cabin and settled on a boulder a few yards away. Libby crossed her arms and stayed put.

"Millicent Hammond kept a journal and pieces of it survive and are in my grandmother's papers. My grandmother, Ruth Connolly, was the village head librarian up until the beginning of the war when they closed it down. These fragments tell a story. About 1923, in the spring, Millicent Hammond met Robert Smiley. They fell in love and she came out to the island to live with him, a scandal at the time. Lionel Hammond was in England on business. By the end of the spring Millicent was pregnant and she gave birth to a baby girl sometime in February, who they named Ellen."

Libby sat on the broken-down foundation and crossed her legs. He should not have tricked her with the reflection, but why not, no harm meant, and if there was harm then he had the sense that she'd forgive him a little prank meaning no harm.

"What happened after that?" Libby said, sounding cranky.

"We don't know from the journal. We know that Bad Bob got into a gunfight and was killed."

"Why would he do that?"

Still cranky.

"My guess is that after the baby was born, Robert Smiley changed. He became distant, emotionally, and he spent more time away from here, the base camp. As the second winter approached, Millicent became fearful that Smiley was going to abandon her. She feared for the child. Also, some of the heady romance, or really a lot of it, had worn off and she began to reflect on what a hard life she had chosen for herself and her child."

"But what happened?"

"What do you think?"

"I thought I saw a ghost."

"You did."

"A trick ghost."

"Yes, but for a moment, very real."

"Is this about Robert Smiley and Millicent Hammond or you and Marion Barkley."

"Good question. I don't know."

"He didn't kill her," Libby said.

"He was a violent man."

"You think he killed her."

"Yes, because Smiley believed Millicent's father, who had returned from Europe, had turned her against him and he was possessive. He fought in the trenches during World War I, according to my grandmother, and so he was probably psychotic, suffering from shell shock. When Millicent confronted him with her plans to move off the island, he lost his temper and, unable to control himself, shot her and the child. He disposed of the bodies and then went after Lionel Hammond, knowing that he'd be killed."

"Where does it say that?"

"It doesn't."

Libby stood up.

"I have to go," she said.

"Before you leave, let me show you something."

Bill stood up and went past her, crossing the island through the spruce trees and over the hump of granite and through the ferns, trailing his hands through them until he came to the outhouse. Libby followed him, staying back. Bill opened the door.

"Look."

Libby looked inside and saw the cheap stand-up mirror tacked to the inside right wall of the outhouse.

"I never moved the mirror. That mirror in the spruce has been there for a long time. Some years ago, I had an idea, an *Art Pour l'art* idea and mirrors were part of it."

"Why did you have to trick me? I thought I was seeing a ghost. It makes me wonder what kind of person you really are."

"To be honest, I was pulling your leg."

Bill held up his hands palms outward.

"Would you like to see my rhinoceros?"

Libby narrowed her eyes.

"A rhinoceros?" she said.

"Right this way."

Libby hung back. Her world, for all its unhappiness, was always a sure thing. She woke up in the morning and she pretty much knew how it was going to play out, never for the better, some days not as bad as the day before. The idea that you could just make up the truth was, just then, astonishing. It was like saying you really could change the world and who could do that, outside of a comic book or the Bible?

Well, what about herself, right into the world of nude modelling and halfway to becoming a handywoman. That might not be changing The World, but it was sure changing her world. That is, if she believed it, if it was true, the facts would back her up. They sure better.

Bill led her to the hump of granite and they turned north and followed the pink granite until it fell away into the lake like a giant toe testing the water. There was a small cove.

"A cow moose that was wounded by a hunter out of season came ashore here and it was giving birth. Marion and I were canoeing near the island when we saw it and we found my grandfather who came and butchered the cow and its calf."

Bill slid down the rock where an over grown trail led back towards the camp. Libby followed and then, a few yards in, she saw it, nestled in a swath of ferns: a rhinoceros. Bill wasn't kidding.

"It's made out of two by four and chicken wire for the frame, then branches and twine. I call it a rhinoceros, but maybe it's not."

Libby was transfixed by the massive creature, tucked away in the dimness beneath the canopy of a tall maple tree.

"Come on."

Bill led her back towards the centre of the island, parallel with the dividing hump of granite. Every few steps a creature of some sort, a dream thing, she thought, or strange visage, faces that appeared to be hacked apart and put back together peered out at her from a crevice or a low branch or group of shrubs, and they were crouched or erect or lying down. Eventually they emerged by the side of the wood shed and stepped into the light of the clearing behind the cabin. Libby didn't know what to say.

"I made them all about twenty years ago one summer. I couldn't paint, couldn't get started on anything, and so I remembered the moose and her calf, and I started with that, only it turned into a rhino. I enjoyed being away from my boards and so I made other creatures and it was great fun.

"There's Virginia creeper on the island and some wild raspberry and I used those to weave the shapes. I worked my way along the hump of granite. Another summer, I placed twenty mirrors around the island. I got the idea from a Japanese haiku that I had come across, probably in Marion's bookshelf.

"I was intrigued by the image of the moon reflected in a clear pool, so I started to play with the idea of reflection. What does it mean, the objective physical truth of light glancing off a reflective surface, or something more mystical, the essence of a consciousness, clear and unsullied."

"Or a ghost," Libby said.

It was then late in the day and with the sun sliding down the western sky, there was a chill in the air. Bill appeared worn out from the hike and his face was as pale as it had been when she had seen him on the scree.

"You never saw that doctor."

"I did."

"Liar."

"Nap, maybe."

Bill went inside and left Libby to amuse herself. She poked around for a place to dig a new outhouse. She found a likely spot and got a shovel out of the wood shed. She was just a foot down into the soft loam that had accumulated since the last ice age between two soft ridges of granite and darkness was beginning to drift in between the feathery branches of the pine trees and the air had continued to cool. Time to wash up and call it a day.

She went inside and used the hand pump at the sink and washed herself off with cold lake water. What she really wanted was to stretch out in a hot bath. That would mean a trip across the lake. Unfortunately, the room above the store only came with a dinky shower with hardly any pressure. A hot bath would mean a trip up to the house and a possible encounter with her husband.

Libby regarded her reflection in the window above the sink and thought, I guess I am sort of pretty. She had trouble matching what she saw in the window above the sink and the portraits Bill had done of her towards the end of their modelling session. Surely the mirror of the window was the more accurate reflection of who she was. But then a mirror had also been a ghost and the forest was full of magical creatures made, like the ghost, by Bill Burnon. Maybe she wasn't prettier than she really was, but in Bill's eye she was and so which would you choose, or more importantly which was more reliable? She laughed and flicked some water at her reflection.

"Elizabeth Haller, you dummy, you don't ever have to be pretty."

She rolled her shoulders and relaxed and thought that if she had three or four wealthy seniors like Bill, she could do alright. She'd need a heated garage and a truck. A second-hand truck, something small like a Ranger. Surely, she could find a garage in Mollybush to rent cheaply. She just needed more Bills. Libby continued to visualize herself as a kind of independent handywoman extraordinaire with a tool belt around her waist and a power drill on her hip.

The vision was so pleasing, she went with it and then she was standing in front of the sink naked with her jeans, underwear and shirt pooled at her feet, giving herself a vigorous cold scrub with the wash cloth and a squirt of Dawn. She realized she was naked when she heard Bill on the front porch and realized he had probably napped on one of the cane chairs on the porch. Libby dried herself off and felt foolish as she quickly put on her clothes.

"In for a dime, in for a dollar," she said and opened the ice box. She took out two beers, opened them and went out onto the porch.

"Were you spying on me, Bill?"

Bill had his blackfly gear on, long sleeves and mosquito netting over his head.

"I was reflecting on the nature of the human form," he said, kidding her, Libby thought.

"What's the verdict, Bill?" she said, amazed at her forthrightness.

"Just fine."

"I have an idea about that. Why don't you take some pictures? You could pose me any way you want and then I wouldn't have to keep taking my clothes off and I could build you a new outhouse and run some more errands. To be honest, Bill, I need to keep myself busy and I don't think I'm really up for all the sitting around that comes with modelling. You also need a new roof on your woodshed and that other building, which I'm guessing is your outdoor studio, needs a new door."

"We'll see. Right now, it's sixty-forty I paint clouds or violets, and a hundred percent this old place needs some work."

Bill tapped her on the knee in a friendly way.

"Come on then."

She followed him around the side of cabin and across to his small wood-frame cedar shingle studio. Behind the studio there was a white, sloped-back bathtub about five feet in length set up on cinder blocks. The air had cooled and the blackfly population had gone wherever the little fuckers go when it's cold. A breeze out of the north helped and so it was all right, but she'd need to get some blackfly gear if she was going to survive.

"I lined it with cedar on the sides with some raised planks on the floor. I saw a fellow with it in the back of his truck and he said he was going take it over to an elderly woman who might want him to paint it blue on the inside stand it up in her front yard with a statue of the Virgin Mary on the inside. He said I could have it for twenty bucks. So I bought it then and there and brought it out here. I keep it over here so I don't burn down the cabin by mistake. We run a hose from the kitchen. You pump while I get a fire going underneath, then we take turns pumping. Fills up in about half an hour, heats up in about an hour. What do you think?"

Libby had her bath in the dark. Bill came out a couple of times to feed a few sticks to the fire and, as far as she could tell, kept his eyes averted. When she was done with her bath, she put on one of Bill's long-sleeved lumberjack shirts that smelt a little musty but was clean. She slipped into a pair of clean wool socks and a pair of moccasins, that were a few sizes too big for her, and she was good to go.

She came around the studio Bill had a kerosene lamp on the stoop to light her way. He had the barbecue next to the back stoop fired up. A big foil-wrapped potato nestled in the grey coals had turned grey. She came into the kitchen there was another kerosene lamp, salad in a bowl on the counter and some bread.

"I set up a cot for you in the studio with a pillow, a sleeping bag and a blanket. I laid some wood in the potbelly. You just have to light it. Should keep you warm. Flyswatter for the mosquitoes and blackflies."

Bill demolished his potato and even ate a little salad. He couldn't eat all his steak and wrapped it up in wax paper and put it back into the icebox. They ate without hurrying, by the light of the kerosene lamp, dimmed down so that they could look out the picture window at the moon and the distant lights of the village.

Libby found Bill easy to talk to. That was probably because he wasn't always interrupting with some sort of a biblical reference or moral admonition.

"You know a lot of stuff," he said, finally stopping her towards the end of the meal.

"Growing up on a farm you have to learn a lot of things, particularly if it's a poor farm, as ours was. Being self sufficient became a way of life."

"You need a truck," he said.

"I don't know if a truck is much help if I don't have customers," she said.

"You've got me, for a start. This place needs some work, like you said."

Libby finished her salad and broke off a piece of the crusty bread and spread a big wad of butter over its surface. Bill went around to his side of the table and poured out the last of the wine, stoked the wood stove and came back to the table.

"I might go out on the porch and have a cigar. Tomorrow I've got to figure out what I'm going to do about this nude business. To be honest, I don't think I can do it. I'm not confident with hands and feet and if I can't draw them, I can't paint them."

Libby washed her clothes at the sink and put them out on the back stoop to dry. She went out onto the front porch where Bill was halfway down a big cigar.

"There's something else, Bill," Libby said. "I haven't slept with a man for over eleven years and that is God's honest truth. Joe and I had separate bedrooms and when I couldn't stand him anymore, I took your old room above the store. Just the same, I'm not really in the market for a boyfriend just now."

"Very good, and to be honest, Libby, you are as refreshing as rain on a hot and sunny day and you have cheered me up. I am grateful, and I hope we can get to know each other as friends, particularly as it makes sense for you to stay out here while you get on with the outhouse and other stuff."

"Quite right, Bill."

"Good."

"You'll need some gear, the plague of blackflies is upon us, I think."

Chapter 19

Bill slept, woke up, slept, woke up and went for a pee off the back stoop. He dreamt of Libby's long graceful neck and how it fell away into the gentle swale of her shoulder. It had been that part, along with her round eyes, that he had enjoyed drawing, somehow the elegance of that next to the shoulder continuum had freed him of any awkwardness brought about by his self doubt.

He peed off the front porch and went back to bed and again revelled in that graceful line. He slept, woke up, slept and woke up, finally realizing that Libby Haller was real in a way that Marion wasn't, and while that didn't really make any sense, it had the swagger of truth and so he slept, if not soundly, then with less trepidation, less of the less-ness that clung to him. Towards the break of day, with the sun spilling over the eastern hills, felt some of the heavy scab of anxiety that he had hauled up the Eleven highway begin to flake off. The day dawned, clear sky, bright, sweet, coniferous air. He awoke to the sound of the kettle.

"Orders of the day, next," he said, taking a seat at the table by the window.

"Aye, aye, Captain," Libby said, smiling beatifically with maybe the beginnings of a halo, as she poured steaming water into his French press.

Libby joined him at the table with the French press and a bowl of five percent cream.

"And what is an order of the day," she said?

"Battle plans."

"Are we in a battle?"

"On several fronts. Blackflies. You need some gear."

Libby poured their coffee and mixed in the cream.

"We need food," Libby said.

"Eleven years, of no hanky panky," he said, and he felt giddy, a real juvenile sensation. This new 'too funny', but like his earlier recognition of Libby's presence in his universe, it had that swagger, incendiary, a comet of ice and fire. If she was surprised by his directness, she didn't show it.

"It's probably not like I knew what I was really missing."

Bill grinned and began to think geometrically, even as he recognized that the necessary enclosing points of reference were vacant.

"We need to go shopping: tools, lumber, whatever else you might need, blackfly gear. The pontoon boat is coming today with my boards, so we'll go and talk to the marina and maybe hold off the delivery for one day."

They made a list as they ate the last of the bread toasted on the wood stove on a coat hanger Bill had folded in half some thirty years previously. They used the hand pump for dishes and to fill the kettle for a personal scrub, Libby first while Bill split wood, death to the blackflies that rose to meet him like a black cloud, and by mid-morning they were good to go.

It was lovely, just lovely, to sit there, the aroma of dark roasted coffee in their nostrils with the gift of warmth streaming through the picture window. To banter with a lovely woman, banter made sugary with a coating of the erotic, and to know that he had sussed out her real agenda so that the banter was uncomplicated and he was relieved that he knew for sure where he stood.

If it wasn't on a hump of granite breaching in a field it was at least in a field, and with the best of intentions could hold out a hand with some certainty, friendship, a partnership, an outhouse, a roof, other repairs and the delight in her ongoing presence and living stone or forage for the assault on this new direction in his Art, whatever it might be, clouds or violets, the default projects and Marion, the grand fault of his life. And 'too funny'.

Bill and Libby made the straight shot mid-morning under a great blue sky. They churned through loose strands of the honey coloured sun that lay upon the surface of the lake and nosed Belle-bleue quietly through the tangle of boats tied to the white buoys that lay at peace on the still surface. The air was warm and dry and still.

Libby guided the boat into the concrete municipal wharf and then stepped up and Bill tied her to a cleat. They went along the scree, right out in the open and past the veranda of Marion's bungalow and all was quiet on that front. They passed the barn, now empty of boats, and approached the two-story, wood frame building painted a bright marine blue that served as office and domicile for Rory and Donna, who owned the marina.

Joe Khrys marched across the ramp, shoulders hunched and head bowed under a dirty ball cap. Bill stood his ground.

"Morning, Joe," Bill said, "you remember Libby."

Was it unfair to ridicule Joe to his face? Bill never liked the man because of his unfriendly manner. Now that he had gotten to know Libby a little and had begun read between some of her lines, his dislike had some distaste added to it.

He had the sense that Joe Khrys was a natural born bully, maybe not a physical bully, though he wouldn't put it past the skinny rodent, but definitely an emotional and psychological bully and that made him a coward, in Bill's mind. He felt Libby draw close to him and take his arm, proof enough that she despised the man.

Joe was, apparently, taken by surprise. He looked up from under the bill of his cap, at Libby clinging to Bill's arm and then at Bill. Big time angry.

"How's the business there, Joe?"

Joe Khrys grunted something unintelligible and tried to step around the pair. Bill pushed him back.

"Libby here is starting her own business as a handywoman. She has already fixed my truck and now she's going to do some work out on Bad Bob. You should be proud of her, or maybe inspired."

Joe Khrys sneered at Bill.

"She's a whore."

Bill gave Joe another shove and drove him backwards and felt Libby pulling on his arm.

"She's my friend and you're not, Joe. You're a little man, aren't you? Cruel, stingy bastard, a grasping little shit. You stay out of my way."

Bill stepped aside and hoped that Joe Khrys would take a swipe at him on the way by just so he'd have an excuse to put him down. Joe hurried off across the scree. Bill turned to watch him go and saw Marion observing him from her veranda. He waved, but she turned her back and went inside.

"Geez, Bill, that was a little over the top," Libby said.

"I never liked Joe."

"I'll admit, he's not easy to like, and I'm an expert."

They went inside to arrange the pontoon boat for the next day. They were just in the door and Rory coming out of the office when Bill heard a sharp crack. He went right back outside and saw Joe Khrys, elbows flying, fast walking across the ramp and around the corner on Main Street. Libby followed him out the door.

"Bill, look."

She was pointing at Bill's truck and there was a red brick sitting on the hood under a smashed windshield.

"Son of a gun," Bill said, "look what your husband did."

Libby grabbed his arm.

"You don't know it was him."

"I saw him running off a second ago."

"Let it go, Bill, he is not worth the trouble."

"He's worth the cost of a new windshield."

"I don't expect Joe has two nickels. I'll pay for the damage."

"Never mind that. Son-of-a-gun, we'll have to take Marion's truck."

Chapter 20

*From: **THE BOOK ON BILL:***

The MTO is doing a substantial amount of road work up on the Eleven Highway, re-paving and culvert work and this has meant a spike in business as some days there are over twenty men and women at work and they tell me it will go on until the fall. So that is good and some of the men have taken a liking to my Big Man's breakfast, but they prefer to have it served for lunch due to time constraints and I am happy to oblige.

This morning a vital piece of equipment broke down and the men were idle and several of them came over to Marion's and ordered Big Man's. I noticed that we were running out of eggs and would not have enough for the lunch crowd and so, not a problem, I'll just run over to the Avery farm. Not so fast. Where was my truck?

It didn't take me long to piece that mystery together once I saw the broken window on Belle-bleue and the empty peg where I kept my spare keys. Bill's sense of entitlement strikes again, only this time he had a confederate, a partner in his nefarious schemes to undermine my standing in the village and, worse, in my own mind. I am determined not to succumb to his rapacious approach to our ridiculous relationship; resistance is not futile, but it is a real pain in the ass.

He brought the truck back late in the afternoon, loaded with lumber and other things, I don't know what, and yes, I ran out of eggs at lunch, embarrassing, but not fatal when you have the Great Northern Fat Burger or the Power Poutine, as your go-to option, but I still needed eggs and yes, I got to the top of exit ramp to the Eleven and clunk, I'm out of gas and had to walk a mile to the Jiffy Gas and of course there's just Owen in charge and if brains were a volcanic eruption, Owen couldn't light a match on fire and so I gave him the ten dollar deposit on the gas can and bought two litres of gas and started off back to my trunk and saw some of the road crew boys streaming in the other direction and then, thankfully one of them, Tim, it turns outs, pulled off and asked if he can be of any help.

I explained my problem and Tim did a U-turn and I hopped into his truck, more like waded into, as the passenger floor was strewn with coffee cups and chocolate bar wrappers and all sorts of detritus. I barely noticed. Tim is very handsome, mid-twenties with bulging muscles and very polite and I was a mess, sweaty from walking, smelling of sweat and cooking oil, my hair plastered to my scalp and I am old enough to be his mother, why am I suddenly as nervous as a teenage girl on a first date. The word pathetic comes to mind.

Five minutes later, I am mobile again and Tim was just a dwindling memory of when I was a nervous teenage girl with my skirt in a knot as I stood barefoot in the soft mud of Brown's Creek tossing Bill Burnon's fly rod line with a woolly bugger tied at its end at a riffle in the slow stream. I was on the verge of tears and my knuckles were white as I gripped the steering wheel and pulled into the Jiffy Gas, and yes, they were now out of gas, after several of the road crew had stopped to fill their tanks before heading home at the end of the day, so lots of diesel but no gas and so now I had to call Rory at the marina and ask him if he had any gas and if he did, would he mind if I borrowed some, so I limped back home and put five litres of gas in the tank. Off I went and eventually arrived at Avery Farm, about ten minutes later and yes, they were all out of eggs. Bill Burnon is a monster, cleverly disguised, like one of those lizards on television that have taken over the world, in this case my world, thankfully only for the summer.

From: **THE BOOK ON BILL:**

According to Valentina, Libby Khrys now goes by the name Haller, her maiden name. She is a vegetarian which causes me to wonder just what they are eating out there on that island. Bill, on his own, prefers Irish Stew, or Habitant Pea soup out of a can, or Corned Beef Hash with tinned corned beef and tinned potatoes and for desert canned pears.

Of course he is always mooching off me, his chef du cuisine, boeuf bourguignon with a Caesar salad, fettucine alfredo with sautéed carrots, cedar plank salmon and to think that this has and does, up until his latest betrayal, anyway, given me pleasure, after an exhausting day slinging short order muck in the swampy confines of Marion's to walk across the scree on aching feet, to scan my Joy of Cooking for something to please my man.

God almighty knows I don't need my head examined, I need a brain transplant from a woman who, in life, had the courage and determination to pursue a full life of independence and integrity, as I have clearly not, June to September. So deep is my shame right now I'd need a backhoe to find my self-respect.

Bill is now happily entrenched on his island with his new, low-rent doxy and I am bereft. If I were to write my memoires I would have to entitle them: Marion, Made of Polymer.

Chapter 21

The temperature dropped early in the morning and in Bill's experience that meant they were in for some weather. Bill split enough logs to make sure he and Libby had a good supply against whatever the weather had in store for Bad Bob.

He settled in the cabin and after lighting the stove he sat at the table and looked out across the lake. A wind cut across the island and ribbed the surface of the lake and turned it a grey metal colour. Black storm clouds fell from high above and compressed the sky. The temperature dropped further.

Then, darn if he wasn't feeling his nose itch. He gave it a little rub and went down to the dock and stared across the lake towards Mollybush. The lake was empty of boats. He went up the steps. Rain began to patter on the roof. Libby was at the stove, stirring the pot and the cabin smelt of rosemary and cheese. The rain splashed on the window, obscuring his view of the lake.

Bill went down to the dock. At first, he saw nothing, then he thought he saw a boat light moving across the lake from the direction of the marina. He crouched in the rain. The boat seemed to be coming straight for the island, then it veered off towards the southern shore and Browns Creek. A minute went by and the boat abruptly changed course back towards the island. It was moving slowly, ploughing through the water. The sky opened up.

As the skiff neared the island the rain was sheeting down. The boat came on, but it was labouring, underpowered, wallowing in the heavy rain. About twenty yards from the dock the boat was on a course to collide with the swimming platform. Abruptly the engine cut out. Momentum carried the skiff a little way, but not far and she began to drift. Bill went back down the dock and began to work his way along the edge of the shore. The shoreline was sloping granite made slick by the rain. As he came abreast of the boat he shouted for Marion.

"Marion!"

He looked back along past the boat, worried that maybe she'd fallen overboard. He could see nothing but a streaked darkness through the hard-falling rain.

"Marion!"

He saw that the rain had begun to slant a little to the south. He was sure that left to its own wandering, the skiff would be pushed off the island and end up on the south shore of the lake out of his reach. Bill slid down a tongue of granite and plunged into the water. The icy coldness of the water took the breath out of his lungs. He swam for the boat and, after some hard stroking, caught up to it as its nose turned lazily towards the south shore. He hauled himself up

over the transom. Marion was sprawled on the floor of the
boat.

He ignored her and fired up the outboard. He brought
her in behind the Belle. The rain was sheeting down.

"Marion, chrissakes."

He caught her around the middle and slung her over the
shoulder and got her off the boat. She woke up and began
pounding his back with her fists and kicked at him.

"Marion!"

Finally, he upended her by the ankles and dunked her
head in the water. One steamboat . . . Two steamboats . . .
three . . . He pulled her up and handed her off to Libby while
he secured the aluminum skiff.

She was in rough shape when they got her up the stairs,
mumbling, drunk, smelling of rum and vomit. He laid her
down on the kitchen floor, stripped off her clothes and
washed her down.

"There's your Mollybush nude, Bill," Libby said, during
the ministrations.

"Not likely," he said, "but thank you for the suggestion."

"Do you think Marion's mad?"

"Definitely."

Bill picked her up and Libby helped him to get her into
one of his lumberjack shirts. They frog-marched her to the
sofa and laid her out.

"Do you need me for anything more?"

"No, thank you," he said, distracted by the sight of Marion.

Libby gave him a half hug and left to stoke her own fire.

He stirred the burn box of the wood stove, emptied the pail that caught the drip in the kitchen. He closed the back door when the wind changed and blew rain in through the screen door. He opened the window in the kitchen and the front door so there would be a breeze and the cabin would not overheat.

The storm intensified as the night went on. By midnight the rain was horizontal. The cabin shuddered and leaked. Sometimes there would be a lull and then a great howl of wind and rain would arise and come crashing into the cabin. It was as if the one-eyed god were hurling bowling balls down a tilted alley. The cabin held.

Towards the middle of the morning, the wind began to die down, the rain quieted to a light patter on the roof. By dawn the storm had passed over. The sky was a clear blue and the warmth of early summer had returned. Bill awoke in his bedroom, got into his shorts, and went to see about Marion. She wasn't on the sofa. He saw her out in the wood pile sitting on the splitting stump. He went out the back door.

"Morning there, sweetheart."

Marion looked away.

"You tried to drown me."

"Just for your own good."

"I guess I should say thank you."

Her face was pale. There were dark smudges under her eyes.

"Thank you. Where's your new girlfriend?"

"She's not my girlfriend."

"I'm ashamed."

"It's all right, sweetheart, little bump in the road that's all."

"Is she here?"

"Somewhere? She sleeps on a camp cot in my studio."

Bill shoved his hands into his pockets.

"I've been pretty good. A few shots at the end of the day. Maybe a couple of glasses of wine, you know."

"A smoke now and again."

"End of the day that's all."

"I know."

Marion folded herself into Bill arms. She sniffled a little.

"C'mon."

They went inside. Bill saw there was a sketch pad and pencils laid out on the table.

"I have the most gawd-awful headache."

"Couple of ibuprofens."

"I already took some. Maybe I'll go for a swim."

"Hypothermia this time of year."

Marion gave Bill a long hug. They sat in silence on the sofa for a few minutes. A house fly bumped against the picture window and buzzed madly until it dropped to the floor and lay still. Bill put the kettle on the stove.

"You were drawing Libby."

"How do you know that?"

"Nevermind. I want you to stop."

"Why?"

"Because I do that's why."

"I need a model if I'm going to paint a nude."

"All right I'll do it," she said and pulled the shirt over her head.

Bill looked away from her upper body nakedness. He stirred the fire and placed the kettle over the firebox.

"Coffee, then, before I take you home."

"I said I'll do it."

"I can see that."

"Well."

"All right."

Bill sat at the table and opened the sketchpad. Marion, stiff as a mannequin, sat on the edge of the sofa. The woollen work socks with the red stripe were incongruous but somehow appropriate. Ten minutes until the kettle boils. Coffee and that's it.

He wasn't in the mood to draw Marion, but neither was he in the mood for the protracted argument that would result from denying her this little moment of contrition, if that's what it was, unanimity, no, just the hangover stitched up with Marion's natural inclination to self-abuse.

He drew quickly and went onto another page. He felt less awkward than with Libby. Was it because of the years of intimacy, right brain doing what the right hand had done for fifty years?

Marion was compact, less angular than Libby and the lines that he drew were elegant, curved, and softer, and he found that as he drew he relaxed into what might be described, counter-intuitively, as focused stupor. He didn't hear the kettle sing and awoke only when Marion set his cup of steaming coffee on the table and he realized that he had not seen her move. She was there before time intervened.

"I want you to get rid of Libby," Marion said as she settled back onto the couch, tucking her legs under her, angled away from him.

"Why?"

"Because I'm asking you to."

"Sit."

Bill was startled to realize that he was a quarter of the way through the sketchpad and that the quick gesture drawings were of a quality that easily surpassed what he had done with Libby.

"Tell me about Mexico."

"I've told you about Mexico. Get rid of Libby."

"She is a friend."

"She's a leech."

"She's doing work for me."

"No, Bill, she's working you."

He centred the drawing on the bridge of her nose and found that her face emerged easily and naturally with the movement of his hand and this was a surprise and it was a revelation, not that it should have been, as the principles of accurately drawing a gnarled root and a face were, at root, the same.

It was natural in him when he drew a root or a limb or a great expanse of landscape to imbue it with something of himself and so he found himself, working the face, letting his rising annoyance with Marion's line of demands harden the line, unsoftening the natural softness of her face.

"Tell me about Mexico."

"I go every year. I wander around, fend off the men and the boys until I find somebody I like, and then I fantasize about it, and then I say no."

Bill kept his head down and drew.

"No."

"Yes, but I'm not done. I should tell you why I never came south after our third affair. Third or fourth, I can never remember, but before it became a routine. It's 1987, and Daddy was ill, and both my brothers were out west, and you said, 'come with me to Italy' and, well, I couldn't that time, and off you went."

Bill's hand fell from her face as it had become unrecognizable. He flipped the page and started again and drew quickly, the neck and shoulder, the gentle curve of her breasts as he was unable to face her face.

"Yes."

"I was pregnant."

Bill continued to draw, though the lines became harsher.

"I said I was pregnant."

"Is that what you came out here to tell me."

"I came out here to tell you to cut it out with Libby Khrys."

"It's Haller now."

"I don't care if its Anne of fucking Green Gables, stop it."

Bill looked up and her eyes were dead, just like Alice of The Chop with the fish on her breast and the beautiful hands. It pierced his heart.

"That time we were together I knew I was pregnant with somebody's baby. Not anybody from around here. Just somebody I met casually. I never saw him again. I didn't tell him, and I didn't tell you. I told Jack Ramsay, finally."

"You like the casual thing."

Marion stepped off the sofa and came over and looked at the drawing.

"Is that how you see me? Am I a saint or an angel?"

Bill turned the page.

"Anyway, I had a miscarriage before I began to show, a few days after you left. If I hadn't had the miscarriage I'd have kept it. Some days I wonder what would have happened if I'd had the baby, sometimes I wonder why I didn't just come down south and tell you everything. Throw myself on your mercy, so to speak. Bake bread in a brick oven in the Tuscan Hills, romantic."

Bill closed the sketchpad. He put his arm around Marion and gave her a little hug. She leaned her head on his shoulder and sniffled a little.

"It's just this place. It's how this place gets to you, like nothing good can ever come out of Mollybush. Isn't that something out of the Bible? Seems to me it is. Nothing ever has since the death of your father and those other men in the mine, and that's a fact.

"Somebody took a hell of a lot of gold out of this place, but you'd never know it by what they left behind," Bill said.

"I guess that includes me," Marion said.

Bill, shaken by Marion's confession, had nothing to say.

"If you don't mind taking me home, it would be most appreciated. I don't think I could eat anything just now. I knew I shouldn't have come out here."

Bill came around behind her and put his hand on her shoulders. He leaned down and gave her a little kiss on the earlobe. He rubbed her shoulders.

"You had sex with Libby."

"I did not."

"Liar."

"Darn, I forgot, yes I did. Libby and I fornicated. I must have been insane."

"Liar, but you wanted to."

"Never crossed my mind."

"Liar."

"Say I take you home."

Bill made the straight shot and took her back into town, silence the whole way, locked up as he was with anger, jealousy and the truth. If it was the truth, yes or no, but if so or if not, the intent was clear. They docked.

"You can come in; mac and cheese."

"No."

"Are you dumping me, Bill?"

"I am."

"I told you the truth."

"I guess you did."

"So, fuck you then," Marion said and levered herself up onto the municipal wharf. Bill watched her go. She didn't look back as she walked up the wharf and across the scree

and went up onto her veranda and through the door into her
bungalow.

"Fuck you too, there, Marion."

Bill pushed Belle off and backed water.

Chapter 22

Marion propped the butt of the .22 calibre rifle against the railing and steadied it with her feet. The barrel was tucked nicely up under her chin and she could reach the trigger with the bamboo back scratcher she had bought for a quarter in Chinatown in Toronto the year she drove south nonstop through a province-wide snow storm to surprise Bill Burnon at the opening of his first ever art show only to arrive and find a skinny woman with a man's haircut draped all over him.

She remembered his exact words: 'Well hello, Marion, glad you could make it. This is my dealer, Anna Carey.' The woman looked like she'd just come from a taxidermy repair shop and Marion hated her on sight, still hated her, though she probably wouldn't recognize her in a police line-up.

Marion was pretty sure that if she got the angle just right the single .22 calibre bullet in the chamber would kill her instantly. If it didn't, she might bleed out. That would be painful and so she had taken four double strength ibuprofens just to be on the safe side.

The one thing she was absolutely sure of was that she couldn't miss. She went through her death checklist. She'd made her bed and cleaned the bathroom. She'd put the gotta-eat-ems in plastic containers in the freezer. She'd left her will on the kitchen table. The will stipulated that all her worldly goods, including bank accounts and RRSP's were to be liquidated and the money transferred in equal portions to the hospital in Cobalt, her two brothers, and Bill Burnon. Let him chew on that for all eternity.

That was about it. To hell with the rest of it. She'd thought about a suicide note, but the best she could do was; fuck you Bill Burnon for murdering all my dreams.

That didn't seem entirely accurate and was more of a general complaint towards the man with whom she'd associated her emotional well-being for nearly fifty odd years.

She thought of another suicide note: chastity and fidelity was my middle name except for once, you fucking piece of shit. That one went right into the mental fire. She settled the barrel of the gun on her shoulder as she recalled her last chance at freedom; Rory and Donna of the Mollybush Marina and the hotel in the Islands. That had been a pipe dream, but it had been fun to imagine.

Sayonara Bill. Freedom, freedom. Donna started it coming into the diner one morning with a sheath of papers in a legal folder. She remembered that it was so funny, Donna sliding into a back booth at the diner with a stack of papers in that bright blue legal folder. Donna had spread a map of the Bahamas in front of Marion and traced down the spine of the island with the tip of a pencil.

"There," she said and drew a little circle around a dot on the map, "16 acres, a main house with six fully functional apartments and six cabins and two more under construction. There's docking for 5 boats under 45' in the lagoon and room for about ten boats of varying sizes in the little harbour."

Donna spread some photographs in front of Marion.

"How much?"

"That's a view of the Sea of Abaco, and the island of course is part of the Abacos."

"How much," Marion said, and she remembered thinking, Donna I am going give you the Abacos of my hand in a second. Ha, ha.

"Just a minute, now, there's more."

"I know there's more, Donna, but Hilda's down in the Bay looking after her sick sister, and I have bacon to par boil and burger patties to make and I don't have any bacon or ground beef, so honestly, just tell me how much and let's take it from there."

Donna, as far as Marion was concerned, was just about the happiest person on Planet Earth if you thought of Planet Earth as an enclosure with lots of little coloured plastic balls.

"The great thing is, you won't be alone. As a consortium we'll be sharing the risk, and that means minimizing the risk, and I think that is just terrific."

Marion was beginning to get impatient.

"What if there's a hurricane?"

Donna waved a hand airily.

"Hurricane smuricane, those buildings, you see right there?"

Donna pulled one of the photographs.

"Those buildings are hurricane proof."

"What about tsunamis?"

"Marion, they don't have tsunamis in the Bahamas."

"Supposing they have a revolution and nationalize everything."

Donna thought she was kidding.

"Marion, really, don't be such a silly."

Donna patted her on the hand.

"Honey, we're just looking for an expression of interest, that's all."

Marion looked at her friend's bitten down fingernails. For all her planetary happiness there was still the marina and balancing the books every month when all around her the village was falling apart. Marion had to admit that maybe Donna's happiness was a symptom of insanity.

"How much?"

Donna beamed at Marion.

"Five thousand dollars."

"No way. For a whole island?"

"For an expression of interest in a whole island, plus the estate buildings."

"How much for the island and buildings?"

Donna's smile faded a little and she hung her head.

"Eleven million US dollars, but I think if we move quickly with can get it for nine five."

Bite your tongue, Marion said to herself.

"Um, Donna, just who's in this consortium?"

Donna's smile faded a little more.

"Well it's early days."

"But we need to move quickly."

Donna upped the wattage a tad.

"We do need to move quickly."

"So who?"

"Bill Burnon."

Marion, bite your tongue girl.

"Bill Burnon is going to give you five thousand dollars?"

Donna's smile faded again.

"Not necessarily."

Marion shifted the barrel of the rifle to her other shoulder. Such a light load to bear and went back to the island memory, in the last moments of her life.

There sure wasn't going to be a Bill Burnon sighting in the Bahamas, otherwise why take the risk, spend the time, overcome all the obstacles just to throw down a welcome mat for the monster you were attempting to rid yourself of in the first place.

That night Marion got on Google and spent several hours sipping rum and coke, Cuban Libres, hasta la vista, and then she found the place. Eleuthera, a million nine, twenty rooms, nine cottages, near the airport, bargain destination, but do-able.

It had been fun to imagine, but it never went anywhere for reasons that had nothing to do with money. It really wasn't do-able, because it would mean leaving Bill in the lurch or bringing him along, equally as bad. Sad, but true.

Marion adjusted the rifle so that she could have one last drink before she killed herself. She heard a noise under her railing and then Skip, Rory and Donna's Heinz 57, jumped up and startled her and she almost shot off her ear but dropped the bamboo back scratcher.

"Skip, what are you doing," she said, totally annoyed that her segue into death had been interrupted.

Skip whimpered, sounding like a wounded animal. He came around the back door of Marion's after the diner closed, usually when Donna, whose job it was to feed the dog, had forgotten that specific chore for a few days. Marion kept scraps in tinfoil. Skip wouldn't eat out of a plate or out of a Styrofoam container. It had to be tinfoil. Marion put the rifle aside and got up out of her chair.

"Alright, just a minute. You stay down there. In case you're interested, I'm just about to kill myself."

Marion didn't like having Skip come up on the veranda in case he decided to sit on one of her cushions and leave behind a little critter, lice or whatever else might have found a home on his dogginess.

She went into the kitchen and dug around in the freezer for a leftover pork chop that she thought Skip might eat and went back out onto the porch. Skip had crept up to the steps and was sitting on the top step when she came out onto the veranda.

"Here, catch."

She tossed the tinfoil package onto the scree. Skip scooped it up and ran off immediately. Marion watched him as he went along the strand like some sort of apparition. She settled back into her chair and got back to the business of putting a bullet through the top of her head. She looked around for the back scratcher and didn't see it on the floor. She stood up and knelt down and looked under the chair. She looked over the edge of the railing but didn't see it in the shrubs. 'Skip must have taken it,' she thought to herself and then she realized that the rifle and its single bullet snuggled in the chamber was gone too.

She was half in the bag, and if it was a mystery, it could wait, and if that meant changing her travel plans to hell or purgatory or, if she got really lucky, a nice one-room apartment in heaven with a view, that could wait. What she really wanted was a smoke and another drink and to pour out her heart, kill herself tomorrow, softly. Fuck, Bill, get out of my head.

From THE BOOK ON BILL:

I know for a fact that Bill is worth some money. His house in the city, if what they say is true about housing prices, is worth a boat load of money and then there is the island, not to mention that a Henry Burnon will sell for about nine or ten thousand buckeroonies. He paints fifteen of them every year, so add it all up, and I am sure that woman has got him so completely bamboozled, I wouldn't be surprised if Bill doesn't have two nickels to rub together when she's done. And it would serve him right and I am not going to lift one finger to save him. She was running around there naked today like some sort of skinny bargain basement Amazon. The fucking blackflies are going to eat her alive.

All those years ago Bill went off to pursue his dream to play in the NHL and I was in that dream, he said so, and I believed him and then the dream failed. And then he had another dream and I wasn't in the dream except part-time. I went along with it because I was full-time and if I didn't go part-time I'd be out of a job. Pathetic Marion.

He hasn't been here a week and he's fucking Libby Khrys, the small time klepto, who is now Libby Haller, who like her namesake, is probably nuts. Right under my nose, really over my nose, the two-timing bastard. And now for whatever reason, he's gone public.

He's having some sort of life crisis. Maybe it's overdue, except Bill Burnon always seems to be in crisis. He wallows in it, comes up here, dripping in self pity, the poor artist, and I'm supposed to rinse him off, pat him down, the good mistress, the maid that he needs, cheer up Bill, you are the great man. And of course I fall for it every year, this year included, but this year I can only conclude that it's something more serious, since in all our pathetic years together he has never thrown another woman in my face, except that once with Anna Miss Taxidermy Carey on Bad Bob and, to be honest, I believed him when he said nothing happened.

Now with Miss Libby Vampirella Haller it's for all to see and smirk, and make snide comments and so I can only conclude that his intention is, was, to humiliate me and then flick, goodbye, like a piece of lint off a lapel. I deserve it. What else did I think was going to happen? And what was I doing, telling him about Mexico? Telling the truth for godsakes, and he didn't believe me. Or was I lying to myself by telling the truth, exposing the truth, that at the core of his being, Bill

Burnon hates me. It was just a matter of time and it's time, ladies and gentlemen, time.

Chapter 23

"Wake up, I think the village is on fire," Libby said kneeling at the side of the bed.

Bill, laying on his back under the warm duvet, was not asleep, though his eyes were closed. He heard, but what he heard initially had no meaning as he was buried deeply in the psychic blankets he had gathered to himself in an effort retain some sense of what had happened in the past few hours: the split with Marion, the split with the firm belief that over the years, notwithstanding one, count 'em, one, indiscretion on his part, he and Marion had created a mutual, self-sustaining . . . what? That was as far as he got. What? He had a hard-on and at the end of that hard-on was Libby Haller.

He had to skip over that part. It was too disturbing, more complicated than he could imagine and ultimately simple because it was so overwhelming and really, in consideration of his subsequent bold move, avoidable, at least for the time being.

When Libby informed him that the Village of Mollybush was on fire, he was observing a new trajectory, a shot out of a canon spun off the edge of the earth. The dream, a fantasy, the undeniable joy of a roll in the hay with Libby Haller, a law of carnal gravity in which two bodies, entwined in heart and mind, fall together in the same direction and whose parachutes open in unison, billowing congenial levity and stinking of sweat, Bad Bob redeemed in the ecstatic surge of bodily fluids. What a dream, not wet, but still, and then the truth, hard and cold; apologize to Marion for whatever, don't delay.

"Bill."

He opened his eyes.

"Too fun," he said.

"Bill."

"Geez Bill, look," Libby shouted as he opened up the throttle.

Bill and Libby were halfway across the lake before it was clear that it was the Mollybush Hotel that was on fire. That was fine by Bill. He'd have torn the monstrosity down and bulldozed it over years ago. It was an emotional relief all right, but the village was in mortal danger.

He was concerned about the fire spreading to the mostly wood frame buildings up and down Main Street or to the mostly clapboard houses that rose up above Main Street. Marion's was in jeopardy. Joe Khrys's hardware store was in trouble. It was the closest building, probably not much more than ten feet across the gravel lane between the two buildings.

The sun was still behind the eastern hills when he landed to the south of the marina and came across the strand and past Marion's. The hotel was an inferno with flames leaping out of every boarded-up window and the dancing on the roof like can-can dancers from hell.

They were coming along the concrete wharf when he heard a horrible staccato screech and then he saw a tiny fireball leap out of one of the ground floor windows. He reckoned it was the feisty old cat that had taken up residence in the hotel. The poor thing was lit up like a Roman Candle. Bill watched as it raced into the water. The water hissed and set up a little cloud of vapour.

Libby and Bill tied off Belle-verte and went up between the marina and Marion's to Main Street where they could survey the apocalyptic scene.

There were four pumpers arrayed in a semi-circle around the burning building. They were blasting water straight from the lake. Bill wasn't sure that was enough to put out the fire, but maybe it was enough to keep the fire from burning down the village.

There were two trucks to the north side of the hotel where the fire threatened to leap frog into the village, starting with the hardware store. One truck was stationed on Main Street and one between the hotel and Marion's. There was a command post set up in the parking lot of Marion's. Doc Ramsay was set up in a Temiskaming Shores Fire

Department SUV and was already treating one of the firemen for what looked like cut to the head.

There was another SUV from Kirkland Lake and several OPP cruisers, so it was a joint operation of full-time and volunteer fire fighters to save the village. There was a little breeze out of the southeast, so it appeared that, for now, everything to the south was safe, including Marion's.

As Bill and Libby came across to the command area he heard a great crash and stared in astonishment as the hotel caved in upon itself sending up flames and shooting embers high into the sky. The cave-in was like a bomb had gone off and the fiery embers began to drift over the village. Bill and Libby went across the street to sit in the shade of the flea market sheds with the rest of the village and enjoy the show.

The fire was still out of control, although to Bill's unpractised eye it seemed there was more smoke than fire, maybe a good sign but he couldn't say for sure. The pumpers on the north side of the hotel were hosing down the buildings on the west side of Main Street, and as long as the wind stayed out of the southeast, Valentina's, Food City and the small shops on the east side of the street were safe.

So far so good. Lots of damage done, no harm. The other pumpers concentrated on dousing the carnage caused by the fallen roof but again, to Bill, it seemed as if the building was in its death throes, collapsing upon itself in an agony of fire.

By noon the hotel was a smoking ruin, a pile of smouldering rubble except for part of the north and the east walls that remained standing. There was a backhoe on a float truck waiting for the order to collapse those two walls. The south wall had collapsed inwards while the west wall facing the lack had toppled almost entirely onto the strand.

Bill overheard one of the firemen say it was definitely arson and Bill followed the man's arm as he pointed to the north east corner of the building where he said there were clear signs of a flash point.

One by one the trucks pulled back into Marion's parking lot and the men were leaned up against the wheels their gear flung open chowing down on sandwiches and bottles of water provided by the villagers with Marion's outdoor tables as a staging point.

He saw Libby helping out. She was running water bottles and then trays of sandwiches. The fire fighters appeared exhausted but happy. After all, there had been no loss of human life, a few minor injuries, and the town was saved. Bill smiled in approval as Bert St. Cyr, one of the local volunteers, wiped the soot off his face and shouted out a toast.

"Tout le gang, hey boyce."

"Tout le gang!"

The police had blocked off Main Street and so cars were being routed up past the Anglican Church. Ken Rigby, the local OPP cop, was in uniform and took charge of the detour.

Another Constable was handling the caution tape detail. Everything seemed under control and the discussion around the flea market shed had turned to the origins of the fire. One of the volunteers came over to sit with his wife: he told the interested villagers that it was definitely arson, the flash point probably at the northeast corner where the boilers had been located.

"I'm not sorry to see the end of that old thing," Bill said to Libby as they went across Main Street towards the marina where they had docked the Belle-verte. They went between the overturned hulls of two dinghies, one red and the other yellow, and noticed that the hulls were peeling and that the oar locks were broken.

"Did you want to have a word with Marion?" Libby said when they reached the marina dock.

"Might as well. I'm not back in ten minutes, I'd like my ashes spread over Bad Bob."

"That's not funny," Libby said and gave him a shove in the direction of Marion's.

Bill went across the scree and stopped in the small lane between the restaurant and Marion's bungalow. He stepped into the mudroom of the bungalow. All was quiet. He went around to the front of the restaurant and found Marion tidying the outdoor tables where she had set up urns of coffee for the fire fighters, along with water and some donuts donated by the manager over at the Food City. She saw him but declined to acknowledge his presence, no doubt still harbouring her sullen anger from their argument of the day before and no doubt believing the worst.

"Good morning, Marion," he said, irritated by her continued and, as far as he was concerned, overdone approbation.

"Yes, Bill, how can I help you?"

"I am sorry," he said with all the penitential humility he could muster.

"You've got that right."

Not the response he was looking for.

"I apologize. I'm not the one who should be throwing any stones."

"No, you shouldn't."

"All right, then."

Marion pointed over towards the municipal wharf where Libby was just bringing in the boat after clearing the marina buoys.

"You're keeping your new girlfriend waiting."

"Will you stop that?"

"I will if you will."

It was like trying to untie a knot by pulling on it. Hotel up in flames, Marion on the slow burn, nothing to paint, the one bright side he supposed was his new best friend, his personal assistant and handywoman who, for better or worse, seemed to appreciate him and was a welcome antidote to the current venomous indifference of his eternal beloved.

"Right. Have a nice day there, Marion."

Chapter 24

Marion took a smoke break on the back stoop of Marion's and was treated to the sight of her long-time seasonal beau and dodgy King of her heart, in the light embrace of that bloodsucking interloper, Libby Haller. Miss Transylvania. She was surprised by her reaction. It was like a truth finally presenting itself, skinless and bloody on the cutting board, and you realize that all these years you've been making hamburger out of prime and what you should have done was pack it down your throat, à la tartar and suffer the consequences, whether fatal or merely life-altering.

She finished her smoke and observed the two vultures carefully. After a minute she decided that the truth was not to be fatal, but things were sure as hell about to get a little weird in Mollybush.

She saw Constable Rigby, the local OPP officer, hurry down the municipal wharf. She stepped back in the recess of the veranda as the Constable escorted Vampirella towards a cruiser that had come down and she observed Bill head in the direction of Mollybush Ave. and she guessed it was to pay his respects at the old graveyard behind the Anglican Church.

Marion went through the bungalow and into the diner by its rear door. Hilda was looking after the customers and there was really nothing for her to do except continue to tidy after the day's great and generally welcomed event. That could wait. She remembered the watch. Marion calmly unclasped the expensive watch and dropped it in the offal bin. That felt good. What else could she do that would make her feel good? She could burn Bill's clothes, a fair quantity of underwear, socks, t-shirts and coats that had accumulated over the years, including his first Mollybush Marauders jacket that she had wrapped up in plastic and hung at the back of her closet. Why not start with that?

Marion sat at the counter and took out her order pad and wrote at the top: **How to feel good about Bill Burnon, to do:**

Pitch expensive gift watch. Done.

Burn his beloved hockey jacket.

Burn his goal skates.

Stick a potato up the tail pipe of Belle-bleue.

~~Castration.~~

Sink Belle-verte.

Break his fly rod.

Stuff an oily rag in his stovepipe.

Put a dead animal in his icebox or under his bed, or
  both.

~~Burn down Bad Bob.~~

~~Shoot him in the back of his good knee.~~

With the fifth item and the last two items Marion thought she might be getting carried away. She wasn't about to go to jail for Bill Burnon and she certainly could not see how sitting in a jail cell would improve her frame of mind. She thought it best to start with the hockey jacket and skates in order get a handle on the measuring spoon of contentment that would sweeten the sour bowl of her life.

"Back in a minute, Hilda," she said as her long-time cook came along the counter.

A minute or two later, Marion had fetched the Marauders jacket and was walking across the ramp thinking she would torch the thing over the still warm coals of the destroyed hotel. She held the jacket in one hand and her butane lighter in the other ready to light the elastic waistband when a wave of remorse came over her. The jacket was, after all, a prize Bill heirloom, as was the hymen she had flung at him like a red cape. Kill the bull or the bull kills you. Spanish proverb, but she had read it in a book, unable to sleep, the smell of fish through the open window.

"Stop it," she said aloud and remembered that this was the jacket that Bill had given one of his idiotic girlfriends to wear in plain view of her, the Queen of his heart. Fucking guy.

Later, Bill had had offered the jacket to her. She was mortified that he would do so after that cow, Faith Cheevers, had contaminated it. She had refused. The jacket disappeared until one afternoon, twenty years later, she had gone out to Bad Bob determined to bring some order to the cabin, as in throw stuff out, when she had found it in the bottom of a duffel bag and rescued the jacket and had it dry-cleaned and mended.

Bill never noticed the loss of the coat, or at least never mentioned it, and then it was clear to Marion that burning it now was redundant. Well, item number two then and she was just trying to remember whether she had them or if they were out on the island when she saw Libby Khrys step out of the police cruiser and start across the street. Marion without even thinking about it slipped on the jacket and went to have a word Miss Vampenstein.

"You are nothing but a gold-digger," she said angrily, shaking a finger in her face. Marion was pleased to see her take a step back.

"I am not."

"You most certainly are and I'm onto you, so there."

"Excuse me but have you seen Bill?"

"I have not and even if I had I wouldn't tell you or I'd tell you he's gone to the moon."

"You are right, I am a gold-digger only not the kind of gold a shrew like you, according to just about everyone in the village, could ever see."

"You are so full of shit," Marion said.

"No I'm not, and I don't appreciate your profanity. And I don't know why you think you can speak to me like this, unless, of course, you're insane, which you probably are, even though you don't know it."

"You are after his money."

"I sure am, only you'd be surprised to know I plan to earn it."

"On your back."

"Sometimes, if I have a brake line to fix, and sometimes on my knees, if I'm doing a plumbing job, but mostly bent over or standing up."

Marion had expected the stupid woman to roll over and that she didn't, and was probably making fun of her right to her face, just made her angrier, not to mention the recent memory of her out on the municipal dock, practically on her own doorstep, rubbing up against Bill like a bitch in heat. Marion glared at Libby. Libby glared at Marion.

"Bill must have lost his mind to see anything in you," Marion said.

"No, it's because he has a mind that he can see good things in people, even if they're hidden. You'd know that if you were sane, but you're not. And something else, one of these days people are going to start dying from the food you serve in there. Maybe it's time you woke up in the twenty-first century and learned how to cook properly."

Marion was totally caught off guard by the sudden segue, but no way was anybody going to slag Marion's, a fixture in the village for nearly fifty years and because of her pathetic, soul-destroying relationship with Bill-the-fornicator-Burnon, her one and only source of pride.

"Listen you creature."

"Don't you dare call me a creature, you crazy old lady. When are you going to stop being such a mean person? I don't know how you can stand yourself. You probably can't, which is why you make life miserable for other people, especially Bill. I guess that comes with being insane."

Marion's eyes went wide and she slapped her thigh with the palm of her hand, thinking it was a dishrag.

"You are worse than a creature; you're a pariah, a parasite, a bloodsucking vampire, a leech, a mouldy sponge so far down the tree of evolutions even snails are walking all over you."

"Really."

"Yes, really."

Libby slapped her hard across the face. Marion wasn't even close to expecting it and didn't even feel the sting of it until the woman had pushed past her. Then it hurt and brought tears to her eyes.

Marion turned and screamed at Libby, "I'm going to have you arrested for assaulting a human being."

Libby didn't turn around. She lifted a middle finger and all Marion could do, such was the shock of being smacked around, was watch her stride to the end of the wharf and stand there with her hands on her hips.

Marion rubbed her face and hunched down in Bill's old jacket and not for the first time in her life felt small and alone.

Chapter 25

Bill came into the church from the side entrance and sat in a familiar pew under the bright stained-glass window depicting the two sisters, Martha and Mary. The church was quiet as a colourful quilt set upon a bed of darkness, tense in repose, in desire, for a supplicant in need of warmth and sleep and the hope that it all wasn't for nothing.

He let his eyes rest on the patchwork of light and dark and it was restful to sit wrapped in the blues and reds woven with golden sunlight and intricate threads of shadow. He opened the worn Book of Common Prayer that he had taken from rack on the back of the pew in front of him and opened it to the Order for The Burial of the Dead:

In the midst of life we are in death: of whom may we seek for succour, but of thee, O Lord, who for our sins art justly displeased?

Thou knowest, Lord, the secrets of our hearts; shut not thy merciful ears to our prayer; but spare us, Lord most holy, O God most mighty, O holy and merciful Saviour, thou most worthy judge eternal.

He went out the way he came in but turned left and went along the path to the graveyard where, in the shade from the canopy of the ancient maple tree, his mother was buried. The air was burnt and stiff from the fire. He noticed that there was ash on the grass and on the path. There was ash still falling, like grey snow. He could stick out his tongue and taste the ash, not in remembrance of his youth when he would throw back his head as the snowflakes big as pancakes fell from the huddled grey sky, but as a grown man familiar with loss, with bitterness, with loneliness, the trinity that had always transcended the success and happiness he had found in life, but he did not. And why?

It was just a thought. He was full of thoughts, weighted down and plunged into the deep waters of inaction and irrelevance.

Marion was sitting with her back to him on the little stone bench, supported by two caryatids that might not have been appropriate to a Christian burial ground, though Bill suspected those who noticed thought of them as cherubim, but they were caryatids, such as those Modigliani had loved.

Bill did not want to talk to Marion just then, not when he was composed from his encounter with the expansive silence at the root of his prayer, and not until he had sorted out his feelings for Libby Haller, and not before he had asked forgiveness of his mother as he had done for over half a century.

Marion looked over her shoulder.

"I want to talk to you," she said, standing. She brushed past him, a hand held to her face and went down the path.

Bill sat on the pagan stone bench.

"I've had enough of Marion Barkley," he said. And that she would intrude on his sacred moment, rudely and so full of whatever the fuck was up with her.

The ashes fell on his head. Bill spoke aloud to his mother: "We will meet again on the other side and you'll say to me, 'Billy how did you get to be so tall?"

Big Ben Burnon will pick me up and toss me as high as the moon and you'll spread out a blanket of roses to catch me. I'll say, 'how did you get to be so beautiful,' and you'll say, 'you're as bad as your father,' and then it will all be all right, forever and forever. I love you."

As always, he was a little while composing himself, and when he went through the gate he was dry-eyed. The sight of Marion hanging off a smoke annoyed him all to hell. She looked up and flicked her smoke onto the street. The left side of her face was red and a little swollen.

"What happened to your face?"

"That bitch slapped me."

"Libby?"

"Your new favourite."

Bill registered that she was wearing his old hockey jacket, the first one he'd ever had and that he'd paid for out of his own pocket, hauling cinder block for a summer, the one that he had thought was lost and gone. Seeing it again was a great and unexpected pleasure. He smiled.

"I hate you," Marion said.

"You're wearing my hockey jacket."

"It is not your jacket."

"It is."

"It is not because you gave it to one of your girlfriends to wear and then you forgot about it."

"I gave it to you."

"You gave it to somebody else first and then you tossed it at me like some kind of a hand-me-down, like I was only good for second-hand goods."

"But you're wearing it now. Number One."

Marion opened her mouth, but nothing came out.

"Is that why you hate me, the jacket?"

"You know why I hate you," she said.

"I don't hate you."

"I'm working on that."

There was a whoop-whoop and they turned towards the sound. There was a police cruiser blocking the intersection and a police constable was running police tape from one lamppost to its opposite across Mollybush Avenue.

"So what, Marion?"

Marion slapped Bill across the cheek.

"We are done, you and me, forever and a day. You are the alpha and omega of I-am-so-done-with-you."

Bill staggered back. It wasn't unusual for Marion to take a swing at him if she was in a mood, but usually it was more of a play tap, mostly with her dishrag, and after some tense and tactile negotiation usually ended up with a tumble, a hot wang-dang-doodle, but this had some bad oomph behind it.

"Ouch," he said.

"Fair play," Marion said and started off in the direction of the police cruiser. Bill went after her.

"That's my jacket," he said, catching up to her.

"That's neither here nor there. Stop following me."

"We happen to be going in the same direction."

"You are only going in one direction and that is out of my life."

There was police tape across Mollybush Ave. and an OPP constable leaning up against his cruiser. Neither Bill nor Marion recognized the man.

"Afternoon Constable," Bill said, amiably.

The police constable gave them a stern look.

"I'm afraid the downtown has been cordoned off and anyone west of here has been evacuated."

Bill looked past the OPP cruiser and saw that there was yellow police caution tape stretched across the intersection at Mollybush and Main.

"I didn't know Mollybush had a downtown," Bill said.

The cop ignored his lame attempt at humour.

"There's an information officer on duty in the arena," he said nodding in a southerly direction.

Bill looked around.

"Information on what? We just had a big fire. What's next?"

The cop took out his police note pad.

"Name," he said.

"What exactly's going on?" Marion said, and Bill recognized the tone of her voice, zero to postal in a nanosecond.

"There's an information officer at the arena," the constable said, "check with her. And you are who?"

Bill took a hold of Marion's arm and walked her back up Mollybush towards the Anglican Church.

"Whatever is going on is going on in my back pocket," she said and then pulled her arm away.

Bill put his arm around her shoulder and walked her a little further.

"Stop pawing me."

"What do you do to control your temper when I'm not around?"

"I don't seem to lose my temper much when you're not around."

"Good, very good," Bill said. "And they say you don't have a sense of humour."

"They also say I'm a shrew."

"Really and who is they?"

"Your new girlfriend, Miss Transylvania, for one."

"Look will you stop with that."

Marion picked up the pace as they turned onto Hammond Street and came in sight of the old arena. There were two more police cruisers parked outside. Bill stopped and looked up at the sky thinking that another fire might have started from a spark spun off the hotel fire, but the sky was a clear blue, with a few clouds piled up to the north. Rain later, if anything, he thought. Marion was through the door to the arena and Bill went after her. He was just through the door when Marion came back the other way.

"Wait."

Bill made a grab for her, missed and went back out the door and latched onto her before she could scoot away down Taylor Ave.

"There is a hostage situation. Joe Khrys has got a rifle and some people in the diner."

Bill could believe it; Joe Khrys had finally lost it all.

"I want to have a look."

"No, you don't."

Bill made a lunge for her, but she twisted away and ran off, this time up Taylor Ave. Bill went after her, but he was having trouble keeping up as his bad knee was starting to throb. Marion reached the top of Taylor Ave and then abruptly angled off behind the last house on the street. Bill lost sight of her, but he guessed she'd go along the berm and then along Taylor Creek where the bulrushes would keep her hidden until she got to the flea market sheds across from Marion's. After that? Goddamn it, woman.

Bill went past the house and through the yard that backed onto the large playing field behind the arena. Marion had halted her charge by the bulrushes on the edge of the creek. He was a few minutes limping across the field and he was surprised that she hadn't moved until he remembered she had a morbid fear of slimy things in general and leeches in particular.

"Just in case you're interested, the creek's full of water and leeches, so you'll have to carry me," she said when he reached the creek, sore and out of breath.

"No."

"Think of it as getting in shape to handle the demands of a younger woman."

"No, and you're a younger woman."

Marion stepped around Bill and climbed onto his back.

"Hurry up, Bill."

"No," he said and staggered in the direction of Taylor Ave until Marion pulled on his ear to make him stop.

"Turn around and do as you're told."

"No, this is stupid."

Marion pulled on his ear and Bill got angry.

"All right, leave my ears alone. You get yourself shot, it's none of my doing."

Bill slung Marion over his shoulder and stepped into the creek. He nearly buckled. His bad knee was screaming bloody hell, but he managed to stay upright. It was easily a hundred-yard slog along the creek to the conduit that ran beside the flea market and then under Main Street and emptied into the lake just on the other side of the marina.

"Fasten your seatbelt sweetheart and enjoy your ride on the Bill Burnon express."

"Get your hand off my ass," Marion said.

Bill gave her rear a little pat.

"May I say, this ass has remained in fine shape over the years, and I mean that sincerely. I'm sorry I've seen the last of it, but *c'est la vie, c'est la guerre*, right sweetheart?"

The creek fell away suddenly and he nearly pitched Marion who grabbed onto Bill's belt as he managed to right the shipwreck that was his old body.

"How much do you weigh?" he said.

"None of your business. Now hurry up, Bill, the blood's going to my head."

"Really Marion, I never pictured you as someone with blood in their veins."

Bill was pleased that he was able to handle Marion's one hundred and fifteen pounds or thereabouts and they made good progress and they were able to trade barbs non-stop all the way to the marshy area. Some of those barbs had been around for over forty years. He almost forgot about his aching knee.

"Sorry, Marion, I feel a toot coming on," Bill said as he stepped through the muckiness around the bulrushes.

"Don't you dare," Marion said and slapped him on the butt.

"Glad to see you still have the soft touch there, sweetheart."

Bill was up over his ankles in muck and the suction from the mud made it difficult going forward. He was breathing hard and just about done in when his feet found solid ground and he stepped out of the bulrushes into the long grass behind the flea market building and set Marion down as gently as he could. Not gently enough apparently.

"You did that on purpose."

"Did what?"

"Tossed me on the ground."

"I wanted to toss you I'd have tossed you back there," said and slung his thumb over his shoulder. "I ever do anything right by you?"

"Never."

Bill settled next to her and rubbed his sore knee.

"Roll up your pant legs."

Bill did as he was told while Marion got out her butane lighter. There were several little black leeches just above his ankles on both legs.

"You wore socks this wouldn't be a problem.'

Marion burnt off the leeches and only managed to set his hair on fire a couple of times.

"Now what?"

"You are good to go."

"What about you?"

"I am good to go, too."

"Where?"

"Wherever, Bill, okay," she said testily. "Just leave me alone forever."

Marion got up and Bill, remembering he was angry at her and feeling the pain in his knee start throbbing again, took a hold of her belt.

"You listen to me," he said and held on to her when she tried to squirm away.

"You let me go," she said and squirmed until the belt broke.

Bill caught her by the wrist as she was about to scamper off.

"Nineteen sixty-nine: you were swimming off the pebble beach and I was down the shoreline tossing a line and you came out of the water and called to me and when I got there you showed me a stone and said you were amazed, and that it was just there as you stepped out of the water, as if it had been placed just there for you to find."

Marion squirmed and yanked on his hand hold. Bill pulled her over onto his lap and applied a bear hug that in other circumstance might have had her purring.

"You are hurting me."

Bill let off on the hug but not so much that she would consider an escape before he gave her his what-for talking-to.

"Shut up and listen," he said, "the stone was small and thin, almost the shape of a coin. It was granite, worn smooth and it had specks of quartz that sparkled in the sunshine. But you were right, and the amazing thing was in the middle of the stone coin, just a little off centre, was a tiny blood red spot, about the size of a baby's fingernail. It was almost the shape of a heart, so much so that looking at it you couldn't help but say that it reminded you of anything other than a heart.

"You handed the stone to me and I held it in the palm of my hand and stared at it for a long time until you plucked it away and pretended to toss it into the lake. I was fooled and looked away and waited for the stone to fall and when it didn't I looked at you and saw that you were still holding the stone. And then you kissed the stone with the drop of blood red at its centre and said to me, this is my heart and pressed the stone back into my hand and curled my fingers around it and kissed my closed fist."

Marion had stopped squirming and Bill, entranced by his own story, let go of her.

"So then I put the stone in my pocket and kissed you on the forehead and then I whipped the stone out of my pocket and reared back and threw it as far as I could into the lake. You let out this big gasp and then shoved me away and I saw you follow the high arc of the stone and as it fell and hit the surface of the lake with tiniest of splashes.

"You freaked out and started punching and kicking me and then you went over to the blanket and started packing up our picnic things. I came after you and you had poured yourself a glass of water and I knew right then and there that you hated me and so I took the glass of water and then I took stone out of my pocket and dropped it in the glass and you couldn't believe it. I had some lead weights in that same pocket that I was fishing with and I threw one of those. The look on your face when I showed you the lead weights."

Marion sat up and rubbed her wrists, "I still hate you," she said.

"I'm sorry for that," he said and slipped off his left sneaker. The size thirteen was full of muck.

"Always the left foot. Sneaker, dress shoe, goal skate, it didn't matter, otherwise I wouldn't be able to take a step in the world. It was always part of me."

"You're beginning to annoy me. What are you talking about?"

Bill stripped the insole and retrieved the flat stone with the little red heart in its middle. He held it up to Marion.

"You remember this," he said.

Marion's eyes went wide. She teared up and then snatched the stone out of his fingers and slapped him so quickly he never saw it coming. Twice in one day. That was enough. To hell with Marion Barkley. Bill put his sneaker back on and levered himself up and limped across the field in the direction of the arena.

There were maybe twenty people standing around in the corridor next to the ice. The concession stand was open and Babs Delorme was serving coffee. There were hot dog wieners stewing in a pot. Two police constables were setting up a microphone on a desk at the end of the corridor. There was yellow police tape blocking off access to the desk. Bill went over to Babs for a coffee and to see what the fuss was all about.

"I don't see Joe Khrys as a hostage taker," he said, shocked at her intel update.

"That's what they're saying, and I also heard he set fire to the hotel," Babs said as she handed over Bill's coffee.

Just then the speakers under the table went live and after some testing, testing 1-2-3's, the OPP constable lifted the mike and introduced herself as Constable Brown. Somebody shouted out, "What's going on?"

"That's why I'm here, to keep you informed."

"So, inform us," somebody shouted.

"Currently we have a hostage situation in Marion's at the intersection of Main Street and Mollybush Avenue.

"We know where it is," somebody shouted.

"What's going on?" somebody else shouted.

"Currently that's all the information I have for you at this moment, except to say that we are confident of a satisfactory resolution to this unfortunate situation and that current restrictions on mobility will stay enforced until further notice."

There were boos and catcalls as the OPP constable made her way under the bank of seats. Bill was now worried that maybe he'd been a little hasty in abandoning Marion who would, if she thought her diner was in jeopardy or was being in some way disrespected, attempt to involve herself in some way. He sidled through the crowd to the caution tape where a big bruiser of an OPP cop was standing guard, thumbs stuck in his utility belt.

Bill stepped forward. The bruiser cop looked Bill over.

"That's far enough," the cop said, scowling at Bill.

"I have some information that needs your immediate attention," he said.

"You are who?"

"Bill Burnon."

The information cop stepped out from the corridor. The two cops exchanged glances.

"We'd like to have a word with you," the female constable said.

Bill was put in a cruiser and that roared off lights blazing but sirens off up Tremblay Avenue and took a left on Taylor Avenue and then a left on Mollybush Avenue and then a right on Hammond Street, past the church and then left on Blanchard Avenue down to Main Street. The cop car bumped onto the strand and raced parallel to the lake until it skidded to a stop behind another police cruiser at the back of the Khrys Hardware Store. Bill was led in the back door and along to the front of the store.

There was an open laptop on the counter next to the old-time cash register and a tall female cop with her regulation hat pushed back on her forehead tapping away on the key board. Next to the laptop were four two-way radios and a large blue three-ring binder. It looked pretty low key to Bill, as in, no big deal. He recognized Constable Rigby, the local cop, who was in police uniform.

"This gentleman says he is Mr. Burnon," the info cop from the arena said.

"I can vouch for that," Constable Rigby said and nodded towards the cop behind the counter. "Bill, this is Sergeant

Gower, officer in charge until the special unit gets here. As you probably know, we have a situation here."

Sergeant Gower adjusted her hat and nodded stiffly at Bill.

"So, what have we got?" Bill said.

"Please have a seat, Mr. Burnon," the sergeant said, pointing to the pocked bench opposite the counter.

Bill did as he was told. The sergeant crossed her arms and looked Bill in the eye. Bill reckoned this was probably standard police procedure and stared back at the police officer.

"What we have here is confidential, but I think it's fair to say we have a hostage incident. Joseph Khrys is in Marion's with three individuals. To our knowledge he is in possession of, at least, a .22 calibre rifle. He has with him his wife Elizabeth Khrys, Hilda Farmer, and Sally Smothers. Mr. Khrys is demanding that you join them. In doing so he agrees to release Mrs. Farmer and Ms. Smothers."

"Okay, I'll do it," Bill said.

The OPP sergeant held up her hand.

"That is not my decision to make. The use of Third Party Intermediaries is up to the Major Incident Command Triangle, that is to say the Level 2 Incident Commander, the Tactical Unit Commander and the Crisis Negotiations Team Leader."

Bill held up his hand.

"Yes, Mr. Burnon," the Sergeant said, showing her impatience.

"That's Joe Khrys in there. I know for a fact he's not a hunter and doesn't own any guns. He's pissed off because he thinks me and his wife are having an affair. He's probably got Marion's twenty-two because she leaves it out on her veranda. It's a single shot and its sight is bent a little to the left. I know that because I'm the one who bent it in case Marion ever tried to take a shot at me. Marion only has one bullet and she keeps it in her undies drawer in her bedroom. So either Joe brought his own bullets or the gun's not loaded. In any case, it's basically a pea-shooter."

"What is your point, Mr. Burnon?" the Sergeant said.

"So I'll go over there. Take the gun from Joe. Hit him over the head with it for scaring Libby and the other ladies and we can all go home."

The Sergeant sighed mightily.

"We appreciate both your candour and your offer of assistance, however the lead Crisis Negotiator has spoken to the individual, the L2 IC is currently en route with the Crisis Negotiator, as is the tactical unit. We have the area secured with the help of some ETRs, and so we'll just hold tight for the moment."

Bill stood up.

"Lemme talk to Joe. He's fucked up."

"I'm sorry, Mr. Burnon, that is not possible."

"Ask your boss?"

"The L2 IC is an hour out and he is apprised of our current situation."

Bill approached the desk so that he was looking down at the Sergeant.

"I've never known Joe to handle a gun and I've known him all my life. So he'll be clumsy with it. Even if the gun's loaded he's only got one shot. I go right at him, his hands'll be shaking so bad he won't shoot straight. So, let's go and get this done."

"Sit down, Mr. Burnon," the police sergeant said. The bruiser cop stepped into the scene. Bill gave him a sour look.

"Am I under arrest?"

"If necessary, Bill," Constable Rigby said, stepping between the two men. "Say we see where we are. Right now, as far as Joe Khrys is concerned, we're trying to find you."

Bill stood his ground.

"He can see my boat tied up to the dock and my truck from Marion's, so he knows I'm nearby. Aren't too many places I could be. You don't produce me in the next five minutes who knows what the crazy old fuck will do?"

"Have a seat, Bill," constable Rigby said, gently.

Bill sat and then remembered what he was worried about.

"If I were you, I'd go and corral Marion. She is probably watching from behind the flea market sheds trying to figure out what is going on. She sees that her diner is being disrespected she has a little switch in her like a heat-seeking missile. Maybe send somebody over to the shed and haul her out of there before she does something stupid," Bill said, angrily.

"Not a bad idea," Constable Rigby said.

"See it done," said the sergeant. She nodded at the spare constable, who immediately went down the aisle and out the back door.

"Now, Mr. Burnon, we appreciate your cooperation," the Sergeant said.

"Fuck you," Bill said angrily.

The Sergeant's cell phone chirped.

"Gower. Yes, sir," she said and turned to the good cop. "The L2 IC has been held up, pulp truck roll-over south of Cobalt."

Gower reached for her computer cord and there was a pop, like a small fire cracker, and then the colour went from her face. Bill went for the door and was blocked by the big bruiser cop who put him down on the floor.

Chapter 26

The air in the room felt soft, a warm, dreamy flannel cloth. She registered a dull, throbbing pain above her left eye where her husband, ex-husband-to-be, had cracked her on the head with the butt of the rifle after shooting out one of Marion's windows. That was the last thing.

No, she remembered glimpsing Marion with a metal serviette dispenser in her hand. She was horizontal, in mid air, flying like Superwoman. That was the last thing before she blacked out and then when she next woke she was on a fast-moving ship in rough seas and her stomach started to roil and she blacked out again.

Libby opened her eyes and there were narrow bars of light on the opposite wall and a ringing in her ears. "Would somebody please answer that," she said, not realizing that she was whispering aloud.

"You're awake," somebody said. Bill.

It hurt to turn her head towards the voice. Bill. He held her hand.

"Hello Bill."

"Hey Libby, how are you?"

"I don't know. I guess I'm all right. I have a headache. Joe hit me with the rifle butt."

"Yup."

"The police think he burnt down the hotel. Did you know?"

"No. Joe?"

"He lost it."

"I don't think he ever had it, to be honest."

"He thought the fire would burn down the hardware store. I don't know. Insurance. What a day, Bill. I guess we made the news. Are you going to tell me your French fry joke to try and cheer me up?"

"No."

Bill looked worn out.

"I thought you were dead," he said and squeezed her hand.

"Thank you for thinking of me."

Bill managed a weary smile.

"You should go and get some sleep," she said.

"In a minute."

Libby was finding it difficult to concentrate. She had been thinking about something before she opened her eyes, or she was dreaming something, and it was important, but when she saw Bill the thought evaporated.

"I was thinking something, but I forgot it."

"It's all right."

"Mad Marion crashed the party."

"She sure did."

"She saved our lives. Joe was losing it and so was Hilda because she had to use the washroom. Joe was shaking like a leaf in a wind storm."

Bill squeezed her hand, gently, and it was warm and lovely to feel his touch.

"I wish you and Marion were getting along. It's about me, isn't it? I should leave."

"It's not about you. It's about Marion, and you're right, she is nuts."

Bill squeezed her hand.

"Do you need anything?"

"I love chocolate," she said.

"I'll bring you some."

"Dark chocolate, bitter."

"Done."

"I'm glad you're here, Bill. I wanted to talk to you. I thought we'd have a chance to talk and then today happened. We never got the chance."

"You'll feel better tomorrow. We can talk then."

"I can go home tomorrow. Will you come and get me?"

"I will, promise."

"I don't know where home is."

"I do."

Libby remembered and she thought, what a dummy, how could she forget.

"I love you, Bill."

She wasn't sure he heard or that she had even said it.

"I love you," she said.

Bill nodded his head and just like that it seemed too real to be true. Libby squeezed his hand. Wasn't it just wonderful to have dodged a bullet? Wasn't it wonderful to have someone like Bill who would come and get her in the morning? Wasn't it just something to feel safe? Wasn't it just terrific to have a place to go to, maybe too early to call home, but a place like what a home should be, a place of safety and comfort and love, sure as heck not like any home she'd ever had.

Wasn't it just great to have a friend like Bill, a helper on her voyage to a new life, freedom from the cage that had been her life until it became unbearable and she learned the awful truth that the cage had always been unlocked and all she had to do was step out.

Wasn't it wonderful, stepping out and even in her little closet of a room and her little cot behind the paint and wallpaper shelf, just on the edge of her new beginning she had felt free as a kite that's lost its string, and then Bill came along and didn't she have big plans for him, and the kite suddenly self propelled with her at the controls, wonderful, and then, just like that, presto, I love you, Bill.

Did she really say that? Clank. The door closes. Wasn't that a step back into the cage? Clank. Oops, locked up by love. Free only in love. Was such a thing possible? Not me, but Bill in me. Oh, Libby blasphemer, listen to you, shame on you. She drifted off and then she was so thirsty, and the sun was warm on her face.

She was somewhere else. There was a dry wind that had come up and swirled the dust and sand around the well. Beyond the well there were some trees, perhaps palm trees, and under the palm trees there was a flock of sheep. There was no one around, except one man, a stranger, who sat on the edge of the well.

She wasn't sure that she should approach the well with the man there and no one else around, but she was thirsty and she needed water for the household and so she came a little closer, still unsure whether or not she should go all the way to the well. She decided to wait and hoped that the man went away or that someone she knew came along.

But then the stranger showed no signs of leaving and she was thirsty, and it was getting late in the day and she had things to do. She came a little closer and this time the man looked up.

"Good morning, lady. I am thirsty, would you be so kind as to draw me some water?"

She realized that the man had no rope or bucket and had been waiting all along for someone to come along.

"A cup of water is all I want," he said.

But she was still nervous and said to him, "Why are you talking to me?"

"I am thirsty."

"No sir, I can't help you."

"You have a pail on the end of a rope and I'm thirsty."

"You're very observant."

The man seemed to find that funny.

"Wait. We can make a bargain, you and I: a drink of water from this well in exchange for living water."

"What is this living water and where is your bucket?"

"Everyone who drinks of this well will be thirsty again, but those who drink of the water I have for them will never be thirsty."

Intrigued, she came a little closer. If the stranger posed any danger to her she was now well within his reach.

"Who are you?"

"A man who is thirsty."

"What is your name?"

"I am Bill Burnon."

"Well, Bill Burnon, my back is sore from drawing water every day, give me this water, so that I may never be thirsty or have to keep coming here to draw water."

"What is your name," he says.

"It's Libby."

The man helped her draw water from the well and she gave him a cup to quench his thirst.

"Now, sir, where is this living water? I am thirsty," she said.

The man laughed and puts his hand on his heart and looked into her eyes and in that moment she understood.

"A French fry walks into a bar . . ."

Libby opened her eyes.

"Hello, Marion, is that you?"

Marion stepped up to the bed.

"It's me."

"I was dreaming."

"I just stopped in to see how you were."

"Can you give me a sip of water? I think the painkillers made me thirsty."

Marion passed her a cup with a straw and held it as Libby drank and then set it back on the table.

"Bill was here and he was saying something and I fell asleep. I think he said he would bring me something, but I can't remember what it was. Thank you."

"I saw him drive off."

"Joe's a lousy shot. Did you hurt him?"

"They said he has a broken jaw from one of my metal serviette canisters."

"Stupid Joe. He burnt down the hotel."

"Yes, I just heard."

"Thank you for saving us."

"No, stupid me for rushing in. I could have gotten everybody killed. The police would have talked him out of there and everything would have been fine. I came to apologize."

Libby felt better after her rest and she was no longer thirsty. Some of the shock had worn off and her head was sore in a dull, medicated way, and of course she was happy to be alive and it was her opinion, muddled though it was by everything that had happened, that if Marion hadn't barged in the back door at that very moment, Joe was ready to shoot somebody.

"I'll be up in a day or so."

"Good."

"I'm sorry about your window. Somebody told me the bullet broke your window."

"It's all right."

"I can fix it when I get better. I'm planning to be a handyman."

"We'll see."

Libby closed her eyes. The pain from bashing her head was dulled by the medication, but her mind was fuzzy. She wanted to concentrate and she wanted to say something. She opened her eyes again.

"Marion, stay with me for a minute."

"Of course."

"I'm sorry I hit you."

"It's all right. I probably had it coming."

"You did. You're really an awful person, but it was wrong to hit you. I didn't mean to and I surprised myself and frightened myself, because with all that's happened I'm not sure who I am anymore or why I'm even telling you this, but I shouldn't have hit you. I'm sorry, it was wrong, but I've never been so angry in my life, or not that I can remember, but it was wrong and I'm sorry."

"I shouldn't have called you those names."

"Thank you, except you think I've poached your boyfriend, don't you?"

"No joy lost there, believe me. You're welcome to have him, but don't expect too much."

"I want to tell you something."

"Yes."

"Before you see Bill."

Libby reached out and found Marion's hand. Libby's mouth had gone dry and she stopped.

"A little more water please."

Marion held the straw up to her lips.

"Thank you. Just a minute longer."

"Of course."

"I'm going to dig him a new outhouse and fix the roof of his woodshed and make him a bigger studio. We've talked about it. As soon as I'm better I'm going to start on it. He might even take some photographs for his nude paintings so I don't have sit for him and he might still paint clouds, I don't know. I know you don't want to be here and listen to this, but since you are you might as well hear it."

Marion dropped her hand.

"You're right I don't want to be here and I don't want you in my diner."

"There's one more thing.

"What."

"I never poached your boyfriend and I love him because he is the nicest person I've ever met, and I wish the two of you would sort it out between you because I'm pretty sure he loves you, although it's hard to tell because right now he's mad at you."

Libby felt herself drifting off again and really why should she bother with the old shrew, why bother at all, except that it was the right thing to do, whatever came of it. Libby closed her eyes and drifted off. She was thirsty again and the sun was warm on her face. "I love you," she said to the man at the well with the living water.

Chapter 27

There was crime tape on the front door of Marion's, but the parking lot was empty and Marion's Toyota pickup was nowhere to be seen. He walked out the end of the wharf and looked out across the water for a while in the failing light. The loons had settled on the water just beyond the safety buoys, dark silhouettes in a crimson band that stretched north to south and bound the lake in the dying grandeur of the day; crimson bands, purple and blue, and there was the black band of the hills under a thin band of crimson and then a band of deep blue and above which the wings of the sun still shone.

"Ooo, ooo, ooo," the loons cried mournfully.

"I hear you," Bill said.

He was tempted by the Doral and the cold beers and the bottle of Captain Morgan under his dock.

"Ooo, ooo, ooo" cried the mournful loons and Bill once again went down the memory road.

That winter of 1970, in January, the Juvenile goaltender broke his leg in a skiing accident and Bill was promoted from the midget team. Those Juvenile Marauders were in last place in the league and the first game he played was a Saturday night at the Hammond Arena against Kirkland Lake Legion, the top team in the league.

Marion, fourteen years of age, was leaning against the wall in the corridor when Bill was making his way back to the locker room. She'd taken off her ski jacket and she was braless under a tight white t-shirt. She was wearing blood red lipstick. He stopped, dropped his hockey bag, stared, and then looked around for her father or mother or her brothers

"They're down in the Bay. Mom's having tests. I don't know where my brothers are," she said.

He had no idea what to say. The lipstick had stuck him to the rubber carpet. One of his teammates came along and gave him a thump on the back.

"Robbing the cradle, still, are we Billy? Shame on you," the guy said and disappeared into the dressing room.

Marion crossed her arms.

"Don't you wish," she said teasing him.

The outline of her small breasts and nipples were visible. He had to blink to make sure he was seeing what he was seeing.

Another team mate came along, "Hey Bill, this your kid sister?" he said, giving Bill a shove on his way into the dressing room.

"I'm sure not your kid sister," Marion said.

Bill had no idea what to say. Fortunately, Coach Joly stuck his head out the door.

"Get in here kid," he said, "and leave the wildlife alone."

The Marauders won four-three. Bill Burnon stopped sixty of sixty-three shots. The sports scribe covering the game for the *Northern Daily News* would write: *Legion threw everything they had at him, including the kitchen sink, the bathroom sink, and the slop sink in the basement . . . eventually they ran out of sinks.*

He was the last one out of the rink. The sweat had dried on his skin and he walked through the little clouds of frozen air his breath made. Marion was leaning against the fender of his old Studebaker when he came into the parking lot. She ran up to him and gave him a big kiss on the lips.

"Guess what?"

"What," he said dropping his bag.

He was wearing half of that big smear of lipstick.

"You're the best goalie the universe."

"I am?"

"You are."

"And that's all I get? The best goalie in the universe gets a sloppy kiss."

Marion pushed off him. Bill reached for her. She spun out of his grasp.

"I'm sorry. I didn't mean it that way."

"Yes you did."

Bill picked up his bag and dug his car keys out of his parka.

"I was thinking we could go up to the Lucky Star for a plate of fries and chow-mien. What do you say?"

Marion began to sniffle and took a woollen mitt out of her ski jacket and wiped her nose and eyes.

"I'm sorry for the lipstick and for not wearing a bra and you know, everything else . . ." she said.

Bill stepped forward and folded her into his arms.

"It's alright."

Marion began to sniffle again.

"No, it's not," she said.

He kissed her on the forehead and held her. He pressed his hard-on against her stomach.

"Sorry," he said.

"No," she said and then she began to rub up against him, gently, slowly at first and then harder and faster as he tightened his grip. It wasn't long until he orgasmed with a short, sharp cry.

There were more like that. Memories that were like postcards, or now Instagram posts, but all photos, snaps of time peeled back to its hard core, hundreds of them and all of them alike in that there was a toxic mixture of passion and anger held together in rough tension, like the convex roof of a glass of water, by the suspicion of love, the moisture of that grand emotion, the lingering odour of that glorious ideal.

That was how it had to be, not true love, but its promise, come on, we know it's there, we just have to find it, but never do, do we? Not us, Marion/Bill, Bill/Marion, not ever, never do, not by any chance, nope, not a chance and then, now ask yourself as a grown man, William Henry Burnon, how is it, half a century later that it is still that, the other less real, less complete thing, a thing of less-less-ness because it was deficient, less than whole, a piece of the truth?

Ask yourself how could this less-thing exist unless some perverse element of yours and Marion's psyches preferred it that way, always the promise, the hope, the anticipation because, because, because the real thing, the real deal, love in all its magnificent splendour or whatever the fuck it is, was all a sham, a great hoax, a lie.

Why fucking bother? Answer me that, Bill. Is it because we are not all cowards, but some of us are? Is it because we are not all hypocrites, but some of us are? Is it because we are not all these scarecrow men, but some of us are? Bill looked over the end of the wharf and saw his reflection in the murky water. "But some of us are," he said aloud.

Bill went back along the wharf and across the scree. He stepped up onto the porch and went through Marion's bungalow to the kitchen where he made himself a pitcher of rum and coke and ice. He found himself a cigar and a wooden match in a small humidor in the cupboard above the sink. He went out onto the back stoop and sat on the step, lit his Montecristo, and took a sip of his drink.

Now, above the roof of the diner, there was a sugary sky and a fat moon, lots of stars for all that Libby had stolen and hidden away, wherever you hide stars. The village was settled into the night and quiet, he could hear traffic up on the Eleven highway and then he heard Marion's pickup turn onto the scree. He was illuminated by the headlights and lost his vision until Marion shut off the engine. He blinked his eyes and heard the pickup door open and close, then Marion's footsteps on the scree.

"Hello Bill."

"Hello Marion. I went looking for you. Nobody knew where you were."

"After I finished with the police I visited Libby and they let me see her for a few minutes and then I went for a drive and listened to a radio evangelist tell me that I'm going to burn in hell and it sounded a lot like *The Portrait of the Artist as a Young Man*. That's a book by a famous author by the way, and I thought, what would this foolish preacher be doing reading a book like that and then I guessed that he hadn't, and it was a confluence. Do you know what a confluence is?"

"No."

"It's when things flow together, like two rivers that converge to form one river or when separate ideas collide and out of that collision a new idea arises, a dialectic and out of that you get the truth and that can really fuck you up."

"How are you?"

"I'm okay. A little shaky still. Libby's a doll, really Bill, what a sweet girl, not a selfish bone in her body, a real merciful cunt. I'm sure you'll be ever so happy."

"I thought you were dead."

Marion sat next to him on the stoop and took his drink and drank it down in one swallow.

"It's a little on the strong side."

"I was planning to get drunk."

Marion filled the glass and the pitcher was empty.

"I thought you were dead."

"No."

Bill dropped his head between his shoulders and felt the weight of the world; not *The World*, but his small world, the world that, for all its insignificance had at that moment defeated him, held him up for ridicule, exposed him for all to see or no one to see. It didn't matter. If a tree falls in the forest, you are still a piece of shit.

"Marion I am sorry, truly sorry for everything. I don't know how to say it except to say I'm sorry from the beginning of time and hope that you'll understand what I mean."

Marion leaned her shoulder against Bill's arm. "What are you going to do about Libby," she said?

"Look after her until she can get back up on her feet."

"No, you're not."

Marion went inside and a few minutes later came back out with a fresh drink and one of her Putters.

"What is it you don't like about Libby?"

"We've been over that. I went to see her. She said she was sorry for smacking me. She wants you and me to be friends again. I didn't tell her that I hated her and was amazed at my self restraint. She makes my skin crawl."

"Are you sorry for smacking me?"

"No. Why would I be sorry?"

Bill puffed on his cigar.

"Can I ask you something?" he said and took a long draw on his Montecristo.

Marion fired up her smoke.

"Shoot."

"When was the last time you said you loved me?"

Marion took another puff of her smoke.

"What kind of a question is that?" she said.

"I can't remember."

"Neither can I?"

Bill puffed his cigar and topped up his drink and took a sip. Marion had squeezed in some lime.

"I don't know that you ever did," he said.

"What does it matter now?"

"Well, do you?"

Marion shook her shoulders, a gesture that Bill over the years had learned to associate with annoyance.

"I could ask you the same question."

"Okay, ask it."

"The point being."

"For the record."

"How many of these have you had?" Marion said, holding up her glass and then taking a nice slug.

"You could say no, and it could be a lie. You could say yes, and that could be a lie too. The truth really is what happens in the next five minutes."

Marion set her drink aside and stood up and smoothed her hands down the front of her jeans.

"Not tonight, Bill,"

"No, some kind of day."

"Come on. I'll make something."

They went inside. Marion turned on the lights in the mudroom and they went through into the kitchen and Marion lit up the kitchen.

"I'm not hungry, but I'll make you something. Mac and cheese in the freezer? I can nuke it. Ready in a few minutes."

Marion took the container of mac and cheese out of the freezer and put it in the microwave to cook. They sat at the kitchen table, across from each other; Bill avoided Marion's eyes.

"Look at me for a minute Bill."

Bill raised his eyes.

"We're perfect."

"Perfect what?"

"For each other. The way we are. This way of being together. It is perfect. Why do you want to ruin things with this Libby?"

Marion reached in her jeans pocket and slipped out the flat stone about the size of a quarter with the blood red heart shaped stain in its centre. She put it on the table in front of her.

"I have something of yours, don't I?"

Bill looked at the flat stone and reached across the table and took Marion's hands that were rough, though the fingernails were evenly clipped and painted blood red. He held them tightly.

"I'm bringing Libby back to Bad Bob."

"No."

Chapter 28

From THE BOOK ON BILL:

Marion's Mighty Mac and Cheese is the greatest of all comfort foods and, next to The Big Man's Breakfast and the Great Northern Fat Burger and Power Poutine, one of the mainstays of Marion's. I stole it from my mother's recipe book, deleted the Worcestershire and mustard and added a couple of secret ingredients that I will take to the grave unless I'm cremated, in which case the English curry powder might prove a nice new fragrance in the neighbourhood. People come from as far away as Lakeshore Drive for a bowl of Marion's Mighty Mac and Cheese, ha, ha.

Bill was hungry after all, and so was I, after all. We ended up eating out of the same bowl, him with a fork, me with a wooden spoon and there was this immediate intimacy in that sharing of the simple dish that was truly comforting and helped me to settle myself down, come down from seeing Libby toppling backwards after Joe hit her with the butt of my rifle and then Joe Khrys reaching into his pockets for what apparently were extra bullets.

And then there was the ill-advised visit to see Miss Transylvania. I wanted to say to Bill, that woman is a total

*cunt. I didn't. I bit my tongue. I can't even begin to describe
what that cost me in self respect. Did he not see that I would
feel humiliated? Of course not.*

Bill said, I thought you were dead.

*He has said just about everything to me that someone in a
long relationship can say, good and bad, in gentleness and
anger, but he has never said that, or said anything in such a
way that in his own way says he loves me deeply and truly.*

*I should never have doubted that, and he should never
have doubted me, as I know he did, those boring weeks in the
Yucatan over the years, reading everything from Aeschylus to
Zola and other times when I fabricated suspicion-of-jealousy
because I wanted to hurt him, but not too much, and so there
was never the reason to and so we did this fine violence to
ourselves, sandpapering ourselves so finely that it was like
water on stone. And so this doubt over fifty years has shaped
me and us as surely as if it were once a blunt chisel on two
pieces of green wood, and yet there we were, hunched over a
bowl of cheese and pasta in the aftermath of that monstrous
day and here we are now, somehow at the end of it, finally
with that dull chisel put away, the sandpaper, the swift stream
all smooth as a baby's bottom, and I can't but help thinking
and believing that the result, however long in its making, was,
at its end, both strange and beautiful. A marvel, not love, but
a marvel of invention, nevertheless. But we're done with that.
For now, anyway. Some time apart will do us good.*

In the end he left, as he always does, but this time after the mac and cheese and the intimacy that was finally the truth, the lie firmly back in place where it belonged, the duplicity ensconced in its rightful place and it was fine. I imagine things, but it's not over between me and Bill, I'm not imagining that, but who can say what form it will now take. He's gone after Miss Transylvania, and will take her to his island, I suppose there, to nurture her back to health and to console himself with what gifts that phoney slut has to offer.

From THE BOOK ON BILL

Am I really stepping away from Marion's? Don't know. I have interviewed Hilda's granddaughter who has recently graduated from cooking school and is keen to start a career in the restaurant business. In her cover letter she mentioned that Marion's is excellently located for a four-season tourist business of mostly upscale clientele and would profit immensely from a more sophisticated menu featuring local ingredients. Ha. What is more sophisticated than a Fat Burger, if by sophistication you mean medium rare quality? McClean's Abattoir and Bed and Breakfast is a ten-minute drive. Hilda picks fiddleheads in the spring. We buy our vegetables at the flea market across the street. In winter we eat root veggies. Well, the girl was very assured, ambitious, and for some reason, perhaps that is because she puts slices of garlic in her socks, immune to the mosquitoes, as we did the interview on my front porch. I am trying to see the manipulations of Bill's quick hand in this. My magician. A hand and its manipulations that I know so well. I am a piano. Unhappily tuned now, but forever? I'll give him a week, maybe two, to figure out what Ms. Vampirella is up to.

From: **THE BOOK ON BILL**

Apparently, there are substantial renovations underway on Bad Bob. These renovations, from what I can tell, are designed to make the cabin more comfortable and liveable in the winter; improvements, according to Valentina, who heard it from Vampirella, are intended to include electricity from a solar panel, hot and cold running water, a full bath, a hot tub, a stainless steel kitchen, etc., etc., and so it seems everything a woman could want.

Chapter 29

Bill came and got her from the hospital and they drove up the Eleven Highway to the Village of Mollybush. She slept and when she awoke they had just passed the Jiffy Gas. Bill patted her on the knee and said something, but she wasn't paying attention. The sun was shining in the sky, not a cloud in sight, and the weather had turned warm. It was her lucky day, no doubt about it.

She rolled her window down and breathed in the northern air. There was wood smoke mixed with the freshness of the sap risen in the conifers and the birches and it felt wonderfully soothing; the virtue of white and black spruce, pine and fir, mingling with the promise of fire. Day one of her new life and it was off to a good start, never mind the dull headache and stiffness from lying in a bed for a day and a half.

"Do we need anything?" she said as they exited the highway and came down the ramp into the village.

"Just ourselves," he said.

Libby resisted the urged to look over at Marion's bungalow as they went along the concrete wharf to the Belle-verte. She had said her apologies, and if Marion wanted to sulk on her veranda, that was fine, no whispering in Bill's ear about that barefaced Libby Haller was just fine. They made a straight smooth shot out to Bad Bob. He helped her onto the dock and then up the steep stairs. She sat on the porch and looked out across the lake while he made tea. She took her medication with the tea.

"How are you feeling?" he said. So solicitous.

"I want to get started," she said.

"Give it a few days. Present for you."

He handed her a three-ring binder and a brand-new Bug Shirt. She was shaky getting it over her bandage and then it fit nicely.

"Is it a test?" she said, tapping the binder.

Bill put his hand on her shoulder and squeezed gently. The kind gesture buoyed her spirits.

"This belonged to Ruth Connolly, my grandmother. They're fragments of Millicent Hammond's journal. She must have had access to the original. This is my grandmother's handwriting, but the words are Millicent Hammond's. See what you think."

"Thank you for the shirt and hat."

"My pleasure. Three weeks, then it's just mosquitoes."

"Something to look forward to."

Bill tucked her pant legs into her socks and went inside. It was warm and comfortable in the sun and the specialized shirt with a hood and screen did the job. She tucked her hands into the jacket pockets and she was pretty well bug-proofed. She drifted off to sleep with the binder on her lap to the sound of Bill swatting blackflies and mosquitoes inside the cabin. When she woke an hour or so later, she was draped over with a comforter and the binder was on the side table next to her cup of tea. She picked up the binder and opened to the first page:

He wasn't prepared for the blood. I was. I knew what would happen from my younger sisters, who, of course, suffered the ordeal on their wedding nights. He knew about the blood, I think he did, but I'm not sure from who. Whores probably. He obviously never penetrated a virgin and I was certainly that, as in an old maid in training. I just mean he wasn't prepared for it. He just wasn't prepared for it from me. At my age. Well there wasn't a lot of blood but nevertheless, it upset him. In fact, there was very little. I had expected it to be painful, but it was more uncomfortable, not the precursor to childbirth I was expecting. I tried not to cry out, thinking I shouldn't and then I did, once, just as he entered me, more out of surprise than anything and I remember thinking, oh, this hurts, but it was more uncomfortable than anything. Well that only increased his ardour and so I determined to keep quiet through the rest of the ordeal that wasn't really an ordeal. As well, I kept thinking what should I do with my elbows? That may sound strange, but I was very concerned that my elbows were in the right place. Well, after it was over, he saw the blood. He got quite agitated and ran out the door after something, I don't know what, to staunch the flow. I caught my breath and thought well, that wasn't too bad, really. It hurt, but not that much and towards the end there was a little something that felt rather nice. He came in with a hand full of moss he'd scraped off a tree or a rock, I don't know. I burst out laughing. He looked at me and shrugged. Are you alright? he said. Yes, I am quite alright, I said. That seemed to make him quite happy. I think we have become rather good at it. I mean I have nothing to go on, but he seems to like doing it with me quite a lot and I don't know, to be honest, how often you are supposed to do it or what you are supposed to feel except that when we do IT, IT feels jolly good, jolly, jolly good. So much so that I realize that I must restrain myself and him or everything will fall into disrepair.

This is what I think; Robbie is my Prometheus.

Libby closed the binder and stared out across the smooth lake and then she was distracted when a chipmunk jumped up on the rail and stared at her through black liquid eyes.

"Hello," she said softly.

The chipmunk stared at her for the longest time and Libby became uncomfortable.

"Do you know me?" she said to the chipmunk.

The chipmunk flipped its tail as if to say, 'I know your dark heart.'

"It's not all dark," Libby said.

The chipmunk flicked its tail and ran along the rail and disappeared into the cedars.

Libby re-read the journal entry. Millicent Hammond did not make sense to her. Robert Smiley, her Prometheus, whoever that was, would turn out to be her killer? That was a puzzler.

She was unable to work the next day and the blackflies were out in force, so she retreated to the cabin. Bill mended the few tears in the screens and he went on a search and destroy with the flyswatter. Libby was unable to help, weak, dizzy, her head hurting. She watched from the sofa, listless and annoyed in convalescence. She spent the day cabin bound, re-reading the fragments, day-dreaming, staring off across the lake from the table.

We have taken a white tail deer. It is small, a young buck. Robbie and I are able to carry it on a maple sapling pole. He tells me we are close enough to our cabin that there is no need to field dress the creature. I am strangely unmoved by the killing. I admit there was some trepidation to begin with. Robbie was watching me. It is commonplace for him to kill things and I think he wondered how I would take to it. It was, I think to be the first test of our partnership. I should say second test. Ha, ha! Ooh la la! Of course, with winter approaching, it is only sensible to admit to oneself that we must have food to survive. A sizeable amount and of a certain variety, I might add. He is insistent that I learn to shoot. I know how to shoot. He means to shoot to kill an animal that in other circumstances I might admire for its grace and beauty. I know about that, too, but I don't say. I have shot pheasant and grouse in England. There are also bears and cougars to be wary of, particularly if food is scarce. He tells me this food scarcity happens every five years or so. Next year, he says, food will be scarce. But back to the present. We must skin and butcher the deer, then preserve it through smoking. We must preserve it long enough that it will last to the big freeze. We must kill more deer or a moose, we must catch a quantity of fish, although this is not so important as he says we can fish through the ice. This I know something about, having seen the men and their shacks out on my mother's lake as I call Lake Mollybush. We must gather and preserve certain berries and mushrooms. We must harvest carrots and potatoes from the garden that he started in the spring. We must fell and cut enough wood to keep the little cabin warm during the winter when we are not attending to his trap lines. I'm not quite sure about the trap lines, how long we'll be out there, or how we'll survive out there. Nevertheless, I am incredibly excited by the prospects. I mean Robbie has done it and so I know it can be done. Well, I've always known it, otherwise how do the

At some point during the day Libby realized that maybe
she knew Millicent Hammond. Millicent's experience of
captivity, sentenced to a life of another person's expectations,
with little ability to act out of her own choices, her own
necessities, wasn't that familiar? Then she met Richard
Smiley and she felt free for the first time in her life. Bill said
she became disenchanted, that the romance wore off, so did
Millicent escape one cage to land in another?

Libby was restless. She put the binder aside and went to
look for Bill. She found him sitting on a stool in his studio.
He was looking at a blank, bare board.

"Millicent was happy," she said.

"Yes, to begin with," he said.

Libby put her hand on his shoulder stared at the board.

"Anything happening?"

"Not that I can see."

Libby went back into the cabin, spent a few minutes with
the fly swatter and then slept on the sofa. When she woke,
Bill was making dinner. Libby, her head still sore, ate a little
and drank some water. She took another dose of pain
medication and went out onto the porch. The air was warm,
no swarm of blackflies, some mosquitoes humming in the

cedars. She sat and started to read Millicent Hammond's journal while Bill washed up.

He is nothing like my father. My father is an ogre, a beast. My father delights in wielding power over other men. My poor mother lives in constant fear of displeasing him.

Robbie has infinite patience, not only with the world, but with me. For that I am grateful. He does not criticize. He says simply try again. I do until I get it right. When I do get it right it seems to give him immense pleasure. I have said to him, what is there that I can teach you? His reply: in the bush, not much.

I have decided to teach him French.

. . . least bit upset that he has slept with the whores in the company town. After all, men are made that way. Now that we are together, I expect I shall have to remake him into a rather different man altogether.

He has taken to calling me Mills. I like it. I mean it is like to him to sense that I hate Millicent and Millie sounds so common. But Mills I like. Mills. I call him Robbie. Robert is too formal . . .

Robert Smiley did not kill Millicent Hammond. They were lovers in love. Because they were bound by love, they were free. Libby could not imagine what that would be like, Millicent waking up each morning, happy, yes and a heart burdened with the burdens of the day, next to a man who shared those burdens, who loved her and did not feel the heaviness of those burdens but rather the lightening presence of her love.

Libby yawned and stretched. The lake had turned crimson.

The next day she was better and she got out of bed and came into the cabin. She lit a fire in the stove and pumped water for the kettle. She went out to the studio and changed into her jeans and denim shirt and went to have another look at Bill's menagerie and to re-read parts Millicent Hammond's journal.

You cannot live in the bush without making a very important adjustment. It is full of life. It's just that it is not the sort of life you were accustomed to, even in such a filthy and dreary place as the boomtown village that Mollybush has become. There is no civilization in the bush. And yet there is a moral order here. It is this: the sun rises, the snow falls, the winter night will kill you. That in itself is beautiful. Here life jumps at you from the second you wake up until the moment you slip into sleep. Death jumps at you. They are inseparable.

Hello Mr. Spider, oh there is a centipede, there is a haze of I-don't-know-what-they-ares, there are the bats at night feeding on the I-don't- know-what-you-ares!

It is so magnificently different from civilization. In civilization everything is rendered in shades of grey and if there is colour it's painted on. Civilization is the odour of the sewer. Civilization is the feel of velvet. Civilization is muted. Even in its horrors, in its glories it is muted through some ideology or some sense of privilege or lack thereof. Oh well, they shot the Tsar of Russia. You know well he was an evil man. Was he? You know and maybe it's a good thing to shoot a few of these Tsars now and again. Well, but then there was the war. I think we should shoot a few of the other guys, too, just to keep it even. I would nominate my father.

Here everything is too vivid, too loud, too quiet, too quick, too still, too ominous, too bountiful and yet it is, for all its too-ness, its harshness and serenity, beyond morality. There is no point to even speak of it and I shall try not to.

This afternoon I butchered a white tail deer. My arms were stained with blood up to my elbows. I lit the fire and hung the strips of meat. Winter is coming. Robbie is off harvesting wood, not so far that I can't hear the thock-thock of his axe. The rhythm of the axe echoes the rhythm of our love making.

But still, it's as if Robbie and me and our little cabin on this little island almost within sight of the great monstrosity that my father has built that he calls the Mollybush Hotel after my mother, the irony of which is too bitter to comprehend as it is little more than a glorified brothel with my father as the chief cocksman, with his whore and this lake and that town that my father has built. We are interlopers, aliens, foreigners who speak enough of the language to get by, but not nearly enough to communicate or understand anything of substance. Strike that. That's not true. Robbie is different from me, less alien, less different against the backdrop. He seems able to talk to them. I don't mean them, or it. It is this thing of awe, fear, love. He is much more comfortable inside his skin than I am in this place.

Robbie has been here longer. He has had time to learn the ways of life here. I am catching up. It's not a race. Love is not a race. We will never be equal, nor will one ever be less or more than the other. It's a hard life we have chosen. This is home. This is our home. This is who we are. Mills, have you ever been happier? This is love, beautiful and forever.

Libby held the binder to her chest. Why had Bill gone to the trouble? Wasn't he nice to fetch it for her? A gift then, something he thought might be of help, just the good bits, before it all went wrong for Mills, though who could tell?

How can you tell it's all going to go wrong? What choice is there except to start with the best of intentions? Fear, maybe, but not ruled by fear. The chance to fail, but not ruled by chance and not cowed by the challenge. Bill had given her a gift, a little spark of something that, if she was careful, she might fan into something useful, reinvent herself, a handywoman extraordinaire.

Millicent Hammond was a courageous woman. She wasn't afraid to fail and when it all failed she wasn't afraid to try again. Millicent was a force and a shady character like Robert Smiley, once revealed, would be for all his cunning and physical strength, with his guns and axes, unable to kill her.

This Libby knew in her pores and bones, in her saliva, in her eyes and she saw Millicent rowing across the lake in the dark of night, Ellen beside her, swaddled in linen, the two intrepid women, escaping to an uncertain future, but free.

Libby felt the binder warm in her hands, charged with an electric current; she felt Millicent's courage reaching out to her from its pages. She felt her radical spirit reaching out to her, sweeping up her fears, her failures, her insignificance.

"Millicent, you are my hero, and Bill, you are my Prometheus," she said, and laughed and didn't it feel good to laugh.

Time to get moving, then, Elizabeth Haller. Better get at something, Libby. Get going, grow, fear not, cringe not, clean the slate, scrub and polish, the time-to-shine, go, Libby, go, go, Libby, go. Still feeling weakened, she decided that she was going to start with the neglected menagerie. Work herself into shape and then tackle the larger projects. She went back to the cabin and searched in the shed for some tools. Bill was up by then. He had made coffee and had opened up his studio doors and was rolling gesso onto one of his boards.

"Morning."

He turned and she revelled, not gloried in his broad smile, coming across to the shed with his arms wide open.

"How are you feeling?"

"Much better."

A big Bill hug, a fatherly kiss.

"Ok, kid, come on."

Calling her kid. She didn't mind. It was lovely, and then drawing her into the cabin, coffee, some toast, yup, fixing up those creatures, wonderful idea and he searched in kitchen cupboards and produced a pair of secateurs that he insisted on sharpening and oiling while she had her breakfast.

"Something else, Bill. Robert Smiley may or may not have murdered Millicent. You're right though, he must have changed, or maybe he couldn't change and Millicent knew she had to leave. I think something else happened."

Bill began to reassemble the Felco #2's.

"All right."

"But she couldn't go back to her father because he would just put her back in a cage like a bird that has escaped, so she left on her own with the child and made her way Montreal, and because she spoke French she was able to get a job in a French newspaper writing about the English. Later she emigrated to Paris where she wrote for another newspaper. Her daughter Ellen grew up and fought with the resistance during the war. After the war she became a news correspondent and travelled the world interviewing crazy despots."

"So Ellen could be alive now?"

"I don't think so, but her children would be in their sixties, about your age."

Bill finished with the secateurs and handed them to Libby.

"I'm just making it up, aren't I?"

"Well, it's a plausible story isn't it, so why can't it be true?"

"Because there's no proof. Nobody knows what happened to Millicent Hammond."

"Except you."

"And you and me don't agree."

"Right, but I like your story better. I like the idea that Millicent reinvents herself. Maybe because it's what we're both trying to do, me as a painter of nudes, you as a handywoman."

"How do you think we're doing?"

"Well, it's never a sure thing is it. I wake up thinking about clouds and violets and then I come out here and look at this board. I can't move a finger."

"I wake up thinking about cedar shingles."

A few minutes later wearing her bug gear and with a thermos of tea that Bill had made for her, she was back under the tall maples and amongst the ferns with the menagerie. Despite the lingering headache she felt good, happy, intent on her little project, content, Bill fussing over her, nobody had ever fussed over her, ever, but Bill fussing, as if she mattered and then preferring her story, the happy ending, the courageous woman reinventing herself. All right, Miz Haller, to work, to work, it's off to work you go and death to black flies.

Besides the rhino, who she named Bruno, there were, as far as she could tell, three categories of creatures; faeries or elves who were the most life-like and well formed, goblin- and troll-like things, who sneered and grimaced and whose shapes were knotted and twisted, and the rest she could not identify other than that they were pint-sized monsters.

The faeries were mostly near the shoreline and in sun; Bruno stood apart, shaded amongst the ferns, and the goblins and trolls were half hidden by the cedars while the monsters were set away in the darkest part, barely visible, so tangled were they in the elder bushes and vines. After Bruno, she liked the faeries best and then the goblin creatures. She found the monsters, the Unmentionables, as she decided to call them, unsettling, perhaps because they were so misshapen and nightmarish, she could only wonder what sort of experience could produce such a thing. But she knew that, didn't she?

Bruno, because of his size, had a two-by-two and chicken wire frame and it was a simple matter to cover him with cedar boughs that she cut from a nearby grouping.

The elves and others were made out of dried twigs and held together with a vine that she recognized as Virginia creeper and found several bunches covering a dead stump near the foundation of the ruined camp. There were raspberries as well that grew on the south side of the island and red dogwood in the small lagoon. She spent the afternoon gathering materials from around the island and placing them in separate piles.

She was four days repairing the menagerie, and during that time her headache disappeared and her strength returned. At the end of her last day she fetched Bill. He was delighted and his generous approval made her feel giddy.

"It's just some patchwork," she said, responding to a gentle hug.

"No, it's wonderful. You've brought them back to life."

What a strange thing to say.

"Is that how you see them, alive?" she said.

"Yes."

"I don't see how?"

"Creatures of the imagination," he said, putting a finger to his temple, "alive in here. What these are is their form or appearance. Their blood, their tissue, and their souls, exist in the imagination."

Bill gave her another hug and more praise for the work she had done, particularly on Bruno and on the monsters and went back to his boards. Praise, for heaven's sake. When had anybody ever praised her for anything? Yes, it was only a little patchwork and Bill had over done it with the kudos, hadn't he? But still, still, still . . . and it didn't make sense, form and imagination somehow being alive, how could that be, but it had the ring of truth about it and it made sense to Bill and maybe it was something else to discover, new meanings in her new life.

"What do you think, Bruno?" she said and then addressed the faeries, six of them, though she had just named the girls, Dixie, Trixie and Pixie, "What do you think?" and then she went along the path to the Unmentionables, whom she had no plans to name, "And what do you things think?"

They were all silent. That was just as well, she did not want dead sticks and boughs and chicken wire talking to her because that would mean she was insane. Not insane like Marion, a different kind of insane. There are all kinds of insanity and maybe it was like catching a cold, you just never knew. One day you're fine and the next your new best friend is a talking bundle of twigs. Please, God, not me.

She was hot from the bug jacket and ready for a bath and she was hungry. She gathered up her tools and put her spare materials in a pile behind Bruno when out of the corner of her eye one of the Unmentionables moved. She was startled and then it moved again and suddenly she was afraid that the bash on the head from Joe had really scrambled her brains.

She was just thinking about insanity and there it was, right in front of her, staring her right in the face. The little monster moved again and then a chipmunk shot out of its forehead and Libby let out a great sigh of relief and had to sit on a rock for several minutes while the trembling passed.

Just before she left her menagerie, several questions came into her mind based on something Bill had said. If the creatures were alive in his imagination they were also trapped in there. Why couldn't they be lured out of Bill's mind to exist within their own space? If it was possible how could she accomplish that and once that was done, what would they live on, what sort of food could you feed an imaginary creature?

She built the outhouse frame and she and Bill set it in place. She covered it with plywood, sides and roof, then layered on the cedar shingle. As the building came to life, so did her confidence. The next time they went to the lumber store she bought two books on basic carpentry and that became her night reading and afterwards her dreams, when she dreamt, were strange but filled with light and sometimes her menagerie, speaking in a language only she and they understood, but that sounded like water rushing over smooth rocks in a narrow stream.

A month passed on Bad Bob. Summer had moved in. It was hot, about as far from a winter blizzard as you could imagine. Libby and Bill were moving in newfound rhythm. It had begun to assert itself after a few days. Bill rising first, kettle on the portable propane stove and down to the dock for ablutions, the whistle on the kettle drawing her out of the studio, hand-grinding the beans, pouring the water, day firmly begun, Bill taking over the studio, at his boards, mirror propped against his work bench, Bill in his underwear painting his Mollybush Nude. Libby thought it was too funny.

The day moved forward as it cycled back to the cabin for lunch and then moved off again, running errands in the village and elsewhere, her carpentry projects, the outhouse done, repairs to the cabin including new roof shingles, done, discussions on how to proceed with the studio with Bill in it, the revitalization of the old portable schoolroom Bill had bought twenty years ago, care of her menagerie, break-time down on the dock, cold beers, the water still too cold to swim but not for long, chit-chat, Bill worried about his drawing, but happily worried, it seemed to Libby, and Libby explaining the benefits of a moisture barrier under the cedar shingle she planned for the studio, wondering if it made sense to insulate against a cold spring or an early winter.

That sort of thing and then moving forward again until dinner, returning to the cabin, the barbecue, the two of them prepping vegetables, elbow to elbow at the counter, to the peppy sounds of Pure Prairie League or the Flying Burrito Brothers on Bill's old battery powered cassette deck, or CBC 2 on the radio, hi it's me, Rich Terfry. Then the day spinning slowly to a close over dinner, and if mosquitoes weren't too bad, sometimes a little bonfire on the pan of granite behind the shed, Bill puffing on a Montecristo, the silent warmth of friendship, contentment, without a whole lot of howevers, nevertdelesses and despites.

However and nevertheless and despite; though she did not like Mad Marion, it bothered her that Bill had not gone to see her. They had some sort of argument, over her probably or maybe it was some long-standing dispute that had flared up. She gave it some thought and didn't see how she could intervene or if it would be proper to do so.

Honestly and despite the harshness that had passed between them, she hoped and trusted it would work itself out whatever it was and that it wouldn't bother Bill too much, who she had to admit was cheerful and most importantly kind towards her. She felt safe, with Joe locked up and now

with Millicent Mollybush Hammond like a patron saint, she
was content, happy, and surrounded and protected by
goodness.

The weather had turned hot, the plague of blackflies
long gone, the lake water just warm enough for swimming.
She had just started on the studio when an idea presented
itself, from where she had no idea, but one evening they had
gone over to the west side of the island, near sunset, because
Bill wanted to cast flies. She collected some driftwood and
gathered dried sticks and with a few strips of paper birch she
was able to get a small fire going.

She was content to sit on a boulder and watch the fire
and Bill and let her mind wander between the earth and the
sky, thinking all kinds of things, her mind full of lists and
plans. Wandering but not lost, more comfortable in her body
than she could ever remember, a sense of contentment, open,
free, not fenced in by fear and then the fire flared up and she
found herself reaching out to it and the fire entered her and
ran along her arm and down her belly and flared in her loins.
She knew how to bring life to the menagerie.

The next day they went into the village. They avoided
Marion's and went down to New Liskeard to shop. They had
breakfast in a café on the lake and bought groceries in the
Loblaw's. It was there, trolling the aisle behind Bill that she
picked up a bar of dark chocolate and dropped it into her

handbag. Nothing could have been simpler. She shivered with anticipation as they went through the cashier. In the truck, driving back up the Eleven, excitement turned to pleasure that lasted until they reach Bab Bob and she was safe. Olly olly oxen free.

Later, near sunset, Bill again casting flies, she took her candy bar and a trowel and went along the path to the menagerie. There was the stump of an old tree near the rhino and hidden by vines, using the trowel she hollowed out a portion of the trunk. She placed the chocolate bar in the centre of the little hollow and it was the beginning of her shrine. She was observed by her rhinoceros, Bruno, who said nothing, and though it was wrong, it seemed to Libby that Bruno did not really disapprove and perhaps was a little jealous, locked up as he was in Bill's imagination.

Libby knelt by the tree stump and said a prayer and in doing so called to her menagerie to 'come out, come out, wherever you are and meet the young lady who feeds them from a star.' She felt the air thicken and the scent of metal before a lightning storm.

Libby began to chant olly olly oxen free over and over and as she did, she felt a tingle on her skin and she looked up and saw that there was an aura clinging to the rhino and beyond the rhino, to Dixie, Trixie, Pixie and the other faeries. Even the Unmentionables were alight, though their light was fainter.

Libby stopped chanting and wondered if Bill had felt the loss of a part of his imagination. She would see. It came to her then that she had done it, freed them from Bill's imagination and now they were their own creatures, not possessions but free, comrades. She was in awe, watching them, glowing blue and green from a magical transformation and now, were they not truly her responsibility?

She did not understand how it worked, just that it worked, that the joy of stealing something somehow invigorated her menagerie, so that, after placing an item in the shrine, a pair of pliers from the tool section of the lumberyard for instance, their auras would flare up and she would sense their presence in her mind. The rhinoceros, Bruno, the boss, gruff, cranky always with an eye on the Unmentionables, who if he didn't keep a close watch might sneak up from behind and pull his tail. That really seemed to be what those creatures were all about, annoying Bruno with their antics while one snuck around and yanked on his tale. Bruno would roar and stomp his feet. That was more than enough to settle them down.

The faery girls were forever teasing the faery boys. (She really must discover the names of the boys.) Pixie was the worst. Dixie and Trixie would make a scene and the boys would crowd around and try and find out what was going on.

Just then Pixie would jump out at them and tug on one of their ears.

That would make them angry and the boys would respond by trying to tickle the girls' wings. The girls hated that and would complain to Bruno. Libby thought Bruno had a soft spot for the faery boys and girls. He would get very stern with the boys for tickling and very stern with the girls for pulling, but not at all frightening as he was when disciplining the Unmentionables.

The goblins were confused. The faery girls teased them, but they didn't understand. The faery boys were wary of the goblins and the goblins seemed to be wary of the faery boys. The goblins liked to hide in the cedars and jump out when one of the faery boys or girls came near, shouting boo and then collapsing in a paroxysm of laughter when the faery boys and girls shrieked and ran away.

The goblins, the faery boys and girls, were wary when it came to the Unmentionables and rarely ventured into their part of the forest. When they did it was often just before dusk. Usually one of the boys would creep forward and that would encourage the others. They always kept their distance and were content simply to look upon them. There was something strange going on there, but Libby couldn't figure out what it was. She supposed that if she watched quietly and carefully eventually they would reveal themselves to her. If she was responsible about maintaining their auras they would come to trust her and so she was diligent about providing for them.

Chapter 30

Marion said to him once, 'you know Bill, no man is an island.' He couldn't remember what he had said in response and it didn't matter because Marion hated the island, or more probably hated the place that it occupied in his soul, but that was Marion. She was a mystery when she wasn't irritated with him and he supposed that parts of him were a mystery to her as well, the parts that irritated her, no doubt. There was an emotional equation there somewhere, and in fifty years he had not been able to note it down, let alone solve the damn thing.

The island had been his since he was a boy, if not on paper, then written on his imagination. It was a material extension. At times it was impossible to know where his imagination left off and the island began. Bill was convinced that without Bad Bob he would not have found the way to reinvent himself as a landscape artist. It was his first subject and engaging the island gave him the confidence to draw and paint Brown's Creek and thus secure, tenuously at first, his future.

Having Marion on the island always felt like a foreign presence, an alien interloper, uncomfortable with the environment, the culture of white and black spruce, pine, fir, maple, elder, mosses and lichens, fiddlehead ferns, the various native tongues of wind, rain, lightening, bird song and lake water sucking on the teats of granite.

The island confused and intimidated Marion with its insistence on intimacy and perhaps it was a feature of jealousy, the island possessing so much of the being that she had claimed as her own. The island was just something that Bill wore, another skin, and his understanding of the island entered through the pores of that skin. He lived the island.

Libby Haller had, from the moment she stepped onto Bad Bob, threaded herself into the biological tapestry, magically indigenous. It seemed to Bill that she had been there before him, before Robert Smiley, before the stone age tribes, as far back as the ice age, a primal spirit, tossed in the great upheaval and compression of the earth's crust, a rock nymph gestating in the crystals, in the regurgitating humus, in pools of rain water, swimming in ice, slumbering amidst the profusion of roots, home before home was.

One night they had hiked over to the west side of the island to watch the sunset, Bill with his cigar, Libby with a chocolate bar. They sat on a boulder near the edge of the water and watched in silence as the sun burned along the anvil of the western hills, smithing the sky iron black and then the stars appearing as flying sparks from an invisible hammer.

"We should put out sugar water for the hummingbirds," he said, "I used to do that as a kid. There is a lilac on the far side of the cabin. I used to hang the sugar water on a branch and the hummingbirds would come. It's too late now. Next spring."

"Done."

He wanted to tell her something about himself, not a confession as such, but something he believed was at his core and that he believed was inexplicable.

"The island has a shape. A moving shape that flows across the ice and into the forest in the winter and then ebbs back into itself as spring comes on. Then the island is surrounded with shapes within shapes and a long crack appears above the valley where the lake is the deepest. As winter fades the crack widens and then moves like a black snake slithering through white grass. It coils around Bad Bob and then spreads all the way to the Brown's Creek and the curves turn halos that surrounded pans of silver ice."

Bill looked sideways at Libby. She was staring into the sunset, still, only her chest rising with each inhale of breath and falling on the exhale.

"If you know what I mean," he said, embarrassed by his lack of clarity.

"I know what you mean," she said, and he believed her.

One day the weather turned too hot. By noon it was too hot in the studio to work and he went to look for Libby, who, because he was shillyshallying on the repairs to his studio had busied herself tending to the 'menagerie'. He fetched a bottle of water from the icebox and went in search of his island companion. Bill found her as she emerged from behind the rhinoceros with a wicker basket of cedar clippings.

"Too hot," he said, regarding his old sculpture and the other smaller constructions that made up the 'menagerie'.

"Yup," she said and put down her basket.

He was impressed with how the creatures looked, come to life really, now that Libby was tending to them. She had added wildflowers to three of the elves and they had a distinctly feminine appearance. The big rhinoceros looked very ponderous and healthy with a new coat of cedar branches. As he looked around at the creature he saw a solution to a problem that had arisen.

Now that Libby had completed the outhouse the plan was to start on improvements to his studio, a new roof, some sort of siding and possibly insulation, repairs to the doors, new widows, all of which would interfere with his painting.

"Swim," he said.

"Wonderful."

"I have a question about this menagerie" he said and spread his arm out towards the rhinoceros. "Why don't you give them some company?"

Libby put her basket down and seemed surprised by the question.

"Make more creatures."

"Right."

"I wouldn't know where to start," she said.

"Let's start with a swim. West side, no pandering to decency, warmer in the shallows. Come on."

They went over the hump of granite and through the patch of ferns under the great maple trees and along the path that cut through the stand of black spruce and came out into the clearing that contained the remains of the stone foundation of Robert Smiley's and Millicent Hammond's crude log cabin.

They went down to the pebble beach and, with mutual poise, stripped off their clothes. Libby sat on the rock foundation of the cabin to strip off her running shoes and work socks and then drop her shorts, panties, t-shirt, no bra.

Bill stripped closer to the water's edge, flip-flops, shorts, no underwear. Libby preferred to wade in. Bill, knowing where the floor of the lake dropped off, took a few steps and then made a shallow dive and swam out until he could stand with the water up to his shoulders. The lake was cool after the too-hot air and refreshing. He shook the water from his face.

"Over here, Bill."

Libby had surfaced about ten yards beyond him and was treading water. Beyond Libby, a black bear had come down to the water. A few seconds later two cubs tumbled after her. It was a rare sight.

"Look," he said and pointed to the western shore of the lake.

The mother bear stood up facing them on her hind legs.

"Can she see us?" Libby said.

"Probably hears us. Sound carries on water."

"Smell you," Libby said and splashed him.

"Beautiful."

The bear, sensing her cubs were in no danger, dropped down. The cubs splashed into the lake while the mother drank. Libby dog paddled over to Bill where she could stand on the lake floor and they watched for a few minutes until the mother bear abruptly nosed her cubs out of the water and followed them into the bush.

"Do you get bears on Bad Bob?" Libby said, dog paddling away.

"Once, years ago, the black flies were so bad we had moose, bear, wolves, fox, coming out of the bush. Moose on Main Street in the village and I caught a glimpse of a bear one morning by the woodpile. I banged a few pots together and he took off."

"You know, Bill, this island of yours is just about the closest thing to paradise."

"Really."

"I'm serious."

It was a revealing thing to say, was it not? He had watched her closely, from an awareness of her graceful form that emerged from the intimate touch of a pencil, to more complex things, like the passing of the salt across the table, or the washing of dishes after a meal, to the determined look on her face as she sawed through a two by four. In every movement, gesture and utterance he saw the revelation of a grand happiness.

Now, to admit this evident joy was aligned intimately with the island seemed, to Bill, of extreme importance. Was he not in the privileged place of witnessing some sort of transformation, a blossoming, a profound attachment?

Standing in the cooling lake with the sun hot on his face there were still some practical matters to attend to, island paradise or not. Bill slipped under the water to cool his head and when he emerged Libby had done the same and was looking at him with her lovely honey-coloured eyes.

"What's up, Bill?"

"Come on, pal, we have to figure some things out."

They were unselfconscious in dressing. To Bill this was indicative of their new friendship, a fast-drying bond of some sort that allowed an easy rapport between them, with none of the passions that might beset a man in the intimate presence of an attractive woman.

As well, there was Marion who, though near, had, with the emergence of his friendship with Libby, seemed distant enough that his mind was often free of her for hours and sometimes longer; a blessing he thought. Though not to have Marion in mind often, particularly after lights out, seemed like a sensory depravation when inevitably she invaded his newfound equilibrium.

They went, single file, back across the island and settled down on the dock, Libby in the lawn chair, Bill on the chaise longue, beers in hand. Libby slipped off her work socks and running shoes exposing her labourer's tan, tan legs, white ankles and feet. Bill, who worked in flip-flops and bare topped whenever possible was brown all over, except for his porcelain butt.

"Should I wave at Marion," Libby said, laughing.

"I should go and see her. Apologize."

"For what?"

"For being Bill Burnon, what else?"

Libby raised her bottle to him, smiling easily.

"Here's to you," she said. "Now what's the deal?"

Bill settled back into the old chaise and took a sip of the cold beer. Refreshing. It was pretty simple.

"We need to put a hold on your repairs."

Libby's face went from happy to shocked so quickly that it was like she had slapped him in the face. He threw up his hands.

"Wait. Wait," he said and pushed himself forward until he was pitched forward on the edge of the chaise, in an attitude of contrition. The look of panic passed, but she was upset.

"You don't like my work."

It was as if he'd physically wounded her.

"Your work is fine, but it's disruptive. Back at it in the fall after I've gone south. I'm thinking until then why don't you add to the menagerie?"

She put her bottle of beer on the dock and crossed her arms, narrowed her eyes and regarded him with suspicion. That was unfair.

"It sounds like a make-work project."

It was.

"Well it is."

"I don't know what to say."

Bill saw that she had relaxed and guessed that, whatever her reservations, the idea appealed to her. It also meant her dream of paradise was still intact. It meant that he could keep

her around at least until he went south. That little transaction
was still to be weighed and measured.

Chapter 31

From: THE BOOK ON BILL:

I am in a reflective mood. The booze will do that to me. So who am I reflecting about you might ask, O Book? As if you didn't know. I shall make a statement and it's not one you're going to like. I am a bookophile. Jealous? Yes, sorry. I am a total slut when it comes to books. I have read two thousand books in my lifetime. This includes cookbooks, books on philosophy, political science, geography, classic books like Pride and Prejudice _and_ Madame Bovary, A Tale of Two Cities, _the whole fucking canon, a canyon of books, including the Russians. I have read everything by Margaret Atwood. I have read plays, Shakespeare, Goldsmith right up to_ Who's Afraid of Virginia Woolf _and David Hare and a whole lot of others. I have read_ The Communist Manifesto _and_ A Modest Proposal. _I have read the_ Story of O. _I have read the Bible. I have read_ Finnigan's Wake, _cover to cover and never skipped one fucking word._

And if I don't understand a word of what I'm reading, so what? The world doesn't make sense so why should a book? My point is, I have been reading books non-stop since I started menstruating. Is there a connection? Not that I am aware of, *but if you read a lot of books and I mean real serious books you can be excused for saying things like that or things like, I have always hated squirrels since I began to menstruate. Or, as you are up to your elbows in ground pork and beef, you might remind yourself that a syllogism is a test of validity, not truth. All men have three legs, Bill Burnon is a man, therefore Bill Burnon has three legs. This is valid, though it is not true, except in a profane way. Now, pay attention, Book. All men are handsome, Bill Burnon is a total fucking asshole, therefore Bill Burnon is handsome. This is not valid. However, expressed in these terms, the truth cannot be anything but valid. All men are total fucking assholes, Bill Burnon is a man, therefore Bill Burnon is a total fucking asshole. This is valid and this is true.*

Chapter 32

When Libby came up from her wash in the lake Bill was making a lot of noise in his studio. She went into the cabin and poured herself a cup of coffee. They were almost out of five percent cream and bread, and the bags of ice had melted. She took the yellow To-Do pad on the top of the ice box and sat at the table with her coffee and started on her list; vegetables. Bill came in the back door and let it slam.

"Sorry."

"What's up, old man?"

Bill poured himself a coffee, helped himself to the last of the cream.

"We're out of cream," he said.

"On the list. Grumpy today."

Bill sat. He looked over the rim of his cup at Libby.

"Are you laughing at me?"

"Says who?"

Bill set his mug on the table.

"I was rearranging the boards, the bastards are conspiring against me. I may have to have a couple of them arrested and locked up. We'll see."

"Now I'm laughing at you."

"Look, kid, sometimes it just doesn't work."

"Go fishing there, gramps."

"Fucking boards. Anyway, I'm calmed down now. You have any meat on that list?"

"Not yet."

Bill reached across the table and took her hand. It was the smallest gesture, a brief squeeze and release, his hand warm, calloused from chopping wood, a firm touch and quick and gentle as a breeze. She felt her heart swell, her whole being lift up. It was magical, this sense of belonging that she had found in the heart and mind of Bill Burnon and in the heart and mind of the island, if such a magical thing were possible.

Yes, it was. It wasn't a belonging in any sense that she had ever known and she was still trying to sort it out, the contradiction, this freedom she felt in belonging, the open door of belonging, loneliness gone, fear mostly gone and most of all this grand confidence, so underserved as she knew in that dark place in her heart of sin and shame. This morning, as he cupped his mug again, she was leaking tears out of her eyes.

"Sorry," she said.

"What for?"

"I don't know, Bill."

She wiped her face. Bill went over to the stove and returned with a paper towel. Libby wiped her eyes and blew her nose.

"Rib-eyes," Bill said, "to go with your rabbit food."

"Aye, aye, *mon Capitaine*," she said, embarrassed by her foolish display.

Libby had the grocery list; last stop. First stop, the Jiffy Gas for gas and an oil change on old Belle. The cocky kid behind the cash asked her out on a date. Wow, wasn't that another first? She had never been asked out on a date before. She said to him in her best Sophia, Yahweh's holy spirit of wisdom, voice, "Thank you, you are a handsome young man, but I can't because I'm needed somewhere else."

Wasn't that something? It was wonderful. It must be what flying was like. You just went anywhere you wanted and if it wasn't wings that got you there it was the sturdy old engine of Bill's 100, beautiful, Belle-bleue. She felt as free as a bird flying down the Eleven to Cobalt and then back up the Eleven, straight as the crow flies, Haileybury, live minnows for down-rigging pickerel. She shifted the old three-on-a-tree like she was born to it.

She spent an hour talking to a local supplier of solar panels. There was a stop at the Mennonite butcher in New Liskeard before her last call, the lumber yard for the chicken wire and some two by two for her additions to the menagerie plus a roll of moisture barrier that Bill had agreed to allow her to install prior to the fall work schedule.

Poor Bill labouring away. It was taking its toll. She could tell. It was hard for him. All day in front of a mirror. He said to her, "It's absurd to look for meaning in a mirror."

"Right, Bill, looking at yourself, totally absurd."

On her way out of the lumberyard, a hefty yellow Stanley measuring tape in her purse, a sales associate approached her after the truck had been loaded up.

"Miss Haller, can I speak to you a minute?"

He was tall, close to her age, maybe late thirties; fit looking, boyish good looks. Libby remembered seeing him in the tools and small equipment section. He had been staring at her from the end of an aisle when she had made her first pass at the measuring tape.

"Sure thing."

"Let me show you something."

He moved beside her and held a cellphone in front of her face. Libby felt herself go cold. The man tapped the advance button on the video app and rolled the shot of Libby making her second pass at the measuring tape, a clear shot of her slipping it into her shoulder bag.

"Oh for heaven's sake, I'm sorry, I wasn't thinking," Libby said.

She reached through the window of the truck and picked up her shoulder bag.

"I'm so sorry, I'm in a bit of a hurry, I just forgot," she said, and her hands were shaking.

The man looked at her and shook his head.

"You didn't forget. I have more. You come into this store once a week with Mr. Burnon or by yourself. I have you on video three times. This one, another time, I caught you lifting a screw driver and before that a laser measuring tool. I guess you're busted."

Libby stared at the man, unable to say a word. She was frightened, ashamed.

"No."

It came out in a whisper.

"I like your looks," the man said.

Libby stepped back, reflectively, her back up against the door of Belle-bleue.

"Let me pay for everything. I'll give you some money. I won't do it again."

It came out in a rush. She was short of breath.

"I don't want money."

"What do you want?" she said, near panic.

"My name's Derek, Miss Haller."

"Look Derek, let me give you some money."

"Elizabeth, may I call you that?"

"I'm sorry Derek, really let me give you some money.'

He had moved closer. She could smell after-shave. He had nicked his chin shaving. There were blonde chest hairs curling out the neck of his work shirt. His hand came forward quickly, squeezed her breast and then dropped back to his side. Libby let out an involuntary sob.

"I know you don't remember me. We were neighbours. My parent's land was next to yours. I used to spy on you sometimes when you were out in the field. In the summer, sometimes when it was hot you'd go swimming in the stream pond at the back of your land. You'd take your clothes off thinking no one was around. I used to climb up into the big maple just the other side of the ditch that ran between our two properties. I've always had a big crush on you, specially when you had your clothes off. I came back from killing rag heads and you had married Joe Khrys. I couldn't believe it. Broke my heart."

"Stop," she said and shrank away from him.

"My shift is over in half an hour. Meet me at the truck stop north of the junction."

"No."

"What choice do you have?"

"Please don't do this to me," Libby said, pleading.

Chapter 33

*From **THE BOOK ON BILL***

It went something like this. Libby was sitting on my front porch steps. I don't know how long it had been, but it was after dark and I'd been doing the books for hours. My eyes were like sandpaper. I was having a nightcap and then it was off to bed, too tired even to jot a line down for posterity. But it turned out to be an odd encounter so here it is, no need to abbreviate because it was brief.

"Hello, Marion, I'm sorry if I'm disturbing you."

I doubted that, but anyway.

"How can I help you?"

Voice neutral, rinsed of all disdain, etc.

"You can't."

Okay well then what was she doing on my doorstep?

"I'm sorry we couldn't be friends."

Well, she did sound sorry, but I couldn't see her very well and so she might have sounded sorry, but I have no idea whether or not she looked sorry. There is a connection. In my mind you have to be both. I couldn't be bothered. I was dead tired. The books added up and what they added up to wasn't much.

"Why did you think we could?"

Voice, a little less neutral.

"I don't know why. I didn't see why not. I'm sorry I hit you."

"That might be one reason. Should I make friends with a bully?"

"No."

"There, you see, that's why we can't be friends."

"You're right. I see. Thank you."

She got up off the steps and started towards the concrete wharf. Then she came back.

"Did you know Bill fainted?"

"I didn't."

Voice neutral, a little tremolo creeping in.

"I took him to the hospital and did some errands. When I came back he was waiting for me. He said he saw a doctor, but I don't think he did."

She went off again and instead of getting into Belle-verte tied up to the wharf she got into Belle-bleue and drove off. That was odd. Well none of my business. La, la, la.

Chapter 34

Bill sat out on the dock in the lawn chair until his cell phone ran down, just after the sun set and the lake was a polished pastiche of crimson, teal, deep blue, deep purple, that was familiar in that it was never the same, day to day, something he had discovered after his hockey days when he was wandering about the city looking for a new sense of self and had converted to Art and then made the pilgrimage north to woo Marion again, arriving one evening with the sun spread across the western hills and the lake just like this and then the discovery soon after that the only familiar thing about the sun setting on the lake is that it set differently each time, as if the dying sun pressed a celestial thumb to its surface; here this is unique in all the universe, remember me, and so it became something of a touchstone of his life, the impossibility, nothing real could ever be held, or captured, because to do so was just taxidermy, the mummification of life.

But where was the comfort in that for a landscape artist, except in an absurd way, knowing the harsh truth that his Art was ultimately a mere shade, lapping at the river, with nothing to add to a universe already saturated with beauty.

Those were some of his streaming thoughts as he waited on the dock. That Libby had departed for parts unknown he was sure. Had she taken the Belle-bleue? The keys were gone from the hook by the door. What would happen to the old truck? Should he have called it in and why didn't he think to when she hadn't come back last night? An accident on the highway? No. Yes. What did it matter, knowing she was gone south or to the other side, either way she was gone.

The sadness, her loss entangled with the memory of her long limbs and arms, her beautiful neck and shoulders had overwhelmed him, stayed with him and when he called to mind her gentleness, her gentle reverence for things, her dedication to an outhouse, the loveliness of her mere presence, the sadness of knowing it was gone, was too heavy to bear and he had come down to the dock for the vigil that, with the setting sun was over and now he wanted to slip into the water and let the water carry him for awhile.

He saw the boat light coming quickly, Belle-verte, on her way back then and the hope flared up that it was Libby with a perfectly reasonable explanation. Yes, oh, my, and fold her into his arms, take her hand, soothe her if she was in distress, if not share whatever discomforting or happy event had over come her. A romantic liaison? Of course, hmm, well, does he have a job, where, how long, what does his father do, where does he/they live, what make of car, truck, SUV, how old, what colour, what about the wear bars on the wheels, the third degree.

No. Marion then, with news and whatever else she wanted with him.

Marion unreadable, as she took his hand and stepped up to the dock, a bottle of booze in the other hand.

"I'd like a drink, please."

"Of course, Mademoiselle, coming right up."

"Belle-bleue is safe," she said when he came down with their drinks, no lime, a little bit of ice in each glass, a remnant from the bag of ice in the ice box.

They sat opposing each other on the reclaimed aluminum lawn chair, their faces partially hidden by the half-fallen night.

"Yes, thank you."

"The train station parking lot down in the Bay. Yesterday morning, when I saw her with your duffel bag over her shoulder, I made some assumptions. Honestly, Bill, I gave her plenty of time to make her getaway. Our Constable Rigby made a few calls. I can drive you down tomorrow."

"Thank you."

"She's gone for good."

"Probably."

"Did she steal anything?"

"Credit card, my cheque book."

"You've cancelled your card."

"I will."

"Call the bank."

"Yes."

"Bill."

"She'll need some money, won't she?

They sipped their drinks in silence. The loons made an appearance just beyond the swimming platform and were quiet. Off to his left in the shallow inlet, a bass leapt into the very last of the light that had slipped off the skirts of a spruce tree and Bill was suddenly overcome. He wept openly, not bothering to look away or wipe his face. Nor did Marion look away and neither did she appear to relish his sadness.

"It was always going to be that way, Bill," she said as he stood and went over to the side of the dock and evacuated his nostrils.

"Preordained."

"Yes. Her type."

Bill sat down. He was calm as calm could be when it was sixty-forty that he would tell Marion to fuck off.

"Can you please not hate her in my presence."

"You're wrong, I don't hate her. I resent her. I resent her presumption."

Bill controlled his tears and wiped his face with his hands. He drank and let the last bit of ice melt on his tongue.

"Did you faint?"

"No."

"Yes, you did. Did you see a doctor?"

"Yes."

"What did he say?"

"She."

"What did the fucking doctor say?"

"A little stress, something to do with my erratic love life."

"Are you lying to me?"

"You said we were perfect. You were wrong about that. You should have said we were unique, one of a kind, an unrepeatable event in the unfolding of the creation, fleeting and insignificant, here and gone, no trace of our passing, once we're gone. Irrelevant in the great fucked up scheme of things."

"Are you trying to make up to me?"

Bill laughed because it was funny, very funny coming from Marion, Mad Marion, Libby had called her. Too right.

"All right, sure."

The loons seemed to agree, ooo, ooo, ooo.

"I came out for a swim."

"I never would have guessed."

Marion quickly stepped out of her clothes and dove in. She swam to the swimming platform and held on.

"Come on Bill."

Bill followed, the water was a shock and he was gasping for breath as he came up. Marion scooped some water at him as he swam up to the swimming platform. She pushed off and she swam away, scattering the loons to an underwater escape.

"Catch me if you can, Bill," she shouted.

He couldn't. Marion was the better swimmer, but he would, because as he knew, he had always known, though sometimes it was a lot of trouble, often after heartache, anger, sorrow, the whole shebang of life's emotions, but the outcome was never ever in doubt.

He pushed off and went after her, and with each stroke felt the soft entanglement of all Libby's needs and beauty loosen, until, on the far side of the dock, under the skirts of the dark pines, with Marion on the dock laughing at him, the nymph rising once more from her element to taunt him with her beauty and, with her numinous presence, ridicule his mortality, the water held him and relieved him of this burden of unstable love, freed him so that he rejoiced in the sorrow of his loss and thus was able to let loose sorrow, sense it drifting away and then its absence as it dispersed with the loons into the deep water and he was free and he was Marion's captive once more.

Chapter 35

From: *THE NEW BOOK OF BILL*

Here is something to consider, Marion: Bill and you make love, sometimes not and those times you do not it is not less intimate, those times you do make love, the intimacy is more layered, denser, as if you are immersed in a warm river and you are swimming against the current, breathing deeply of the swift and deep element, intent on a destination just there and then one last leap in tandem to achieve it and to rest in the intimacy, now less dense, less layered and residual vapour lingering over our bodies.

It was no less so that night of our capitulation to our long perfection or passing uniqueness. We did not not, we sure did in his smelly bed. In the morning Bill gave me the tour. First we went down to the north side of the island to view his creatures and they were wonderful, delicate faery monsters and ponderous nightmare beings made out of twigs and all the more amazing in that it was unexpected, a facet of this man I know as well as I know myself, pause here Marion to check your credulity, that I had never even remotely suspected, playfulness. We went on.

Vampirella had been busy. A new outhouse, cedar shingle, painted bright yellow with cut out windows of stars, a two-seater, very romantic. The studio, not finished and Bill muttered something about waiting until the fall and so the moment had arrived to view the extent of my soon to be public humiliation, and prior to opening the doors I engaged in little emotional self flagellation and I imagined that he had me up against the wall, had me on rough slats of wood, lined up against rough wooden walls, fifteen of me all in a row, had me standing, had me sitting, had me reclined, had me as a Venus on a swimming platform, as a northern odalisque, as a Madonna with the Christ gumming on a nipple, had me in every way imaginable, ha, ha, stop it Marion.

Anyway I imagine he had me in whatever way he pleased but in every instance totally butt naked for all to see, and I can tell you, I will start to attract attention wherever I end up, on a museum wall somewhere, and no doubt on Pinterest and elsewhere available for one and all, and then, not a day will go by when someone doesn't pop into the diner, unable to resist seeing the real thing in her element, Marion Made of Sweat and Grease, Holding Meat Cleaver, and feel the need to comment, 'I thought it was a very well rendered likeness, Marion.'

I was nervous because there was no way I, as whatever I was, was going to see the light of anybody's day and of course, back at it with Bill, again. And so I ventured, suitably

346

apprehensive, with the subdued and suitably sated Bill, this glorious and unexpectedly numinous morning into the artist's studio and this is what I saw. I am not the Mollybush Nude. Imagine my relief (no lawyers' bills and no ornery Bill to deal with), imagine my disappointment (no notoriety). But no, it ain't me bébé, that acrylic honour belongs to, no, not Vampirella, as I might have thought, it was no one else on this planet but Bill Burnon himself. Bill Burnon is the Mollybush Nude and this stands somewhere between an incomprehensible fact and an incomprehensible revelation.

What? I was struck dumb, floundering with surprise. There were fifteen boards, twelve stacked against the far wall, three had been started and two were just outlines, but clearly nudes, a man seated flaccid penis, a man standing with his hands on his hips; akimbo, penis erect as a mighty bollard and one from the waist up, nearly finished and that I barely recognized so misshapen, so contorted with what or by what machination I can't imagine. Who was this creature?

Was this Bill, the man standing by my side, silent as a slab of granite, and I stood there and wondered who was this staring back at me, and where in that mess of a face could I find him? Transfixed I stood there, knowing it was him and yet unable to find him and then I couldn't bear to look at him if it was him and I wanted it not to be, and I thought oh, this is a grotesque mask, but if it was, it was pretty tight to the board, and how would I pry it off, and if I did what would I find, something more hideous, or an island of love and beauty, I couldn't and yet I could believe that this was Bill.

I couldn't turn away because if it was him, if it was then, it is him, and why is it him and why don't I know this man, or no, why only glimpse him and I know I can't ask because Mr. Burnangelo does not stoop to explain himself to the unwashed such as I and so I stood there mesmerized by this tortured visage and I was held in thrall by eyes gouged and weeping blood and yet beyond weeping, blood dark, coagulated, flakes of blood on his chest, crusty bloody eyes, eyes past seeing, eyes dead as road kill and a dollop of bird shit dropped from an overhanging branch at my feet, naturally I stepped back, looked down and when I looked up again I saw on the swollen lips of this face mutilated by who knows what torment and something appeared, the slightest, tiniest, nearly imperceptible smile and in that instant, those dead eyes looking at me, at me, at me, me, the face was transformed, the visage morphed and something began to emerge, a little, then a little more, some brightness coming in, a little more and then wham, bang, pow, it leapt out at me and it possessed me, and is, in this, is renewed in me, in the light of the early day, I am his life, as long as I last, twenty years, at least that's what I'm hoping for and fuck, another twenty years of Bill Burnon, if this summer of love is any indication, I won't make it.

Acknowledgments

Thank you to Peter Guravich and Hilary Read for their insightful contributions to the story's development.

Kudos to Nicole Brewer for her excellent editorial contribution.

Cheers and thank you to the folks at UP for their contributions: Summer Stewart, Sophia Noulas, Rubie Grayson.

About the Author

Jim Read lives in the Port of Saint John, not far from the statue of Samuel de Champlain.

www.jimread.ca

www.ingramcontent.com/pod-product-compliance
Lightning Source LLC
Chambersburg PA
CBHW070826190726
48292CB00006B/2126